What the critics are saying...

࿇

4.5 Stars "EAST OF EASY is a terrific contemporary romance that is sure to captivate you. Linda Bleser has created a story with an interesting plot, sympathetic characters, exciting twists, and explosive chemistry." ~ *Romance Junkies*

4 Stars "Linda Bleser has penned a tale worthy of being added to my keeper collection." ~ *Ecataromance*

4 Cups "I just loved this book. The characters are vivid and real with faults as well as virtues." ~ *Coffee Time Romance*

"Bleser combines great characters, real life believable situations and a touch of whimsy into a story that reaches out and grabbed me from the very first line." ~ *Best Reviews*

"A well-written story, EAST OF EASY will keep the reader's interest as they root for Kate and the handsome Max to find their way back to each other." ~ *Romance Reviews Today*

"From the first lines I was captivated and eagerly read on to see what would happen next, and I think that is one mark of a book worth recommending. The reader is made to empathize closely with Kate, at the same time marveling and laughing at the small town antics." ~ *Joyfully Reviewed*

Linda Bleser

East f Easy

Cerridwen Press

A Cerridwen Press Publication

www.cerridwenpress.com

East of Easy

ISBN 1419956051
ALL RIGHTS RESERVED.
East of Easy Copyright© 2006 Linda Bleser
Edited by Kelli Kwiatkowski
Cover art by Willo   ─────────────

Electronic book Publication March 2006
Trade paperback Publication November 2006

Excerpt from *Heaven and Lace* Copyright © Linda Bleser 2006

Cerridwen Press is an imprint of Ellora's Cave Publishing, Inc.®

Also by Linda Bleser

ঙ

Heaven and Lace

About the Author

ঙ

Linda began her writing career publishing short fiction for women's magazines. Since then, she's completed several award-winning novels in a variety of genres, from rib-tickling comedy to bone-chilling suspense. Reviewers have hailed her work as unique, original, and impossible to put down.

Linda is the proud recipient of the EPPIE Award, the Dream Realm Award, the Dorothy Parker Reviewers Choice Award, and several readers' choice awards. She resides in upstate New York with her husband of over thirty years, where she splits her time between writing, remodeling, and starting a new diet each and every Monday.

Linda welcomes comments from readers. You can find her website and email address on her author bio page at www.cerridwenpress.com.

EAST OF EASY

ॐ

Dedication

ಐ

To the Sisters of the Lake,
for sharing the laughter and the tears,
for giving advice when asked for and a shoulder to cry on
when needed.
Thank you for enriching my life and nourishing my soul.

Trademarks Acknowledgement

ಐ

The author acknowledges the trademarked status and trademark owners of the following wordmarks mentioned in this work of fiction:

Band-Aid: Johnson & Johnson Corporation

Formica: Formica Corporation

Jell-O: Kraft Foods Holdings, Inc.

Juan Valdez: National Federation of Coffee Growers of Colombia

Lego: Interlego A.G. Corporation

Levi: Levi Strauss & Co.

Mountain Dew: Pepsico, Inc.

Old Spice: The Procter & Gamble Company

Stetson: John B. Stetson Company

Starbucks: Starbucks U.S. Brands

Tylenol: McNeil Laboratories, Inc.

Chapter One

ഌ

With her usual dramatic flair, Lillian Feathers died on the morning of her own funeral.

"Leave it to your mother," Bertha Pitt said, dabbing her eyes. "If I'd known this was going to be a real funeral I'd have made my Southern Pecan Pie, but in this heat…"

"It's fine," Kate said, giving Bertha's hand a comforting pat. "Mom always loved your Jell-O mold."

Bertha seemed more upset about her choice of dessert than over Lillian's sudden passing. Kate pushed the uncharitable thought aside. Most likely Bertha was still in a state of shock, half expecting Lillian to pop out of some secret hiding place to enjoy the proceedings. It was understandable. Kate felt her own stomach churning with emotions — shock, denial.

But not grief. Not yet.

She was still too furious to allow herself a moment to mourn.

Kate had come back to Easy, Arizona, for one reason only — to stop Lillian from spoiling her brother Jeff's wedding day with this ridiculous farce of a funeral. Only it was no longer a farce. Lillian had died quietly in her sleep while Kate's plane was en route from New York's Kennedy Airport to Phoenix Sky Harbor, and all of Kate's arguments would forever go unspoken.

Even from the other side, Lillian Feathers managed to run the show.

Kate turned to inform some late arrivals that the mock funeral was now official. The assembled guests formed a surreal tableau — half of them dressed in muted funeral garb, the rest in glittering wedding finery. The two events, which had split the town in half, now drew them together. An air of hushed expectation filled the room, as if people still expected Lillian to flounce to the podium and give her own eulogy as originally planned. The only thing convincing the guests that this wasn't another legendary Lillian Feathers Production was Jeff's presence in the front row.

Jeff wasn't supposed to be here. Today should have been his wedding day, and the reason Lillian had arranged her mock funeral in the first place.

"He's killing me," Lillian had said. "Might as well stab me straight through the heart as marry that no-good white trash. I'd rather die than give my blessing to this marriage."

And she had. All in all, it was an effective protest.

Kate made her way through the hushed mourners, her eyes focused on a spot straight ahead to avoid the curious glances aimed her way. But she couldn't ignore the whispers that followed her as she made her way through the packed room.

"They said it was a heart attack, but if you ask me, Lillian died of a broken heart."

"First her husband leaves her for that Tate woman — "

"Then her daughter leaves town and no one sees hide or hair of her for ten years."

"And now her son threatens to run away with the Tate girl."

"It's a crying shame."

Kate tuned out the voices. She knew first-hand how vicious small-town gossip and rumors could be. It was the reason she'd left Easy in the first place.

Composing her face, Kate took a seat beside her brother. Jeff's lips were pressed into a tight, thin line. He kept a white-knuckled grip on the hand of his fiancée, Sally Tate, who should have been walking down the aisle in bridal white this afternoon. Sally was a sensitive kitten of a girl, whose only sin had been entering the world from the womb of Lillian Feathers' lifelong enemy, Ginny Tate.

The Feathers-Tate feud went back either thirty years or three hundred—no one really kept track. It had snowballed with time, fed daily by imagined slights and attacks, and coming to a head twenty years ago when Jebediah Feathers left his wife and family to take up with Ginny Tate.

That traitorous deceit had torn Kate's family apart and split the town into opposing factions. Long after Jebediah's death, the rivalry between Lillian Feathers and Ginny Tate continued. The impending wedding of Jeff Feathers to Sally Tate was only the latest skirmish in a long and bloody war. Both sworn enemies had taken a stand. Ginny Tate vowed never to speak to her daughter again if she walked down the aisle with "that demon-spawn Feathers boy." Not to be outdone, Lillian had declared herself officially dead, shot through the heart by her son's treachery. She'd planned her funeral to coincide with the wedding, making her mock death official.

But not as official as the actual death certificate tucked inside Kate's purse.

The simple ceremony went by in a haze. Kate seemed to be running on automatic. All she wanted was to get the funeral over with so she could go back to New York, far from the accusing whispers.

In need of fresh air, Kate stepped outside, away from the cloying scent of death and lilies. The funeral director rushed past, a harried expression on his face. It was no wonder. Normally he would have had a day or two to prepare, but Lillian's death was sudden and she'd already booked the funeral parlor. It would have been a shame to waste all the preparations Lillian had made for the faux funeral.

A voice from behind her interrupted Kate's thoughts.

"I'm sorry to hear about your mother."

Kate stiffened. Even without turning, she recognized the honey-smooth voice of Max Connors. She'd spent most of her life letting it pluck her emotions—from adolescent adoration to teenage love and then, finally, to a betrayal so deep it had left her heart scarred. She tried to pretend that same voice had no effect on her now — that her stomach didn't contract to the size of a hard, shriveled peach pit.

She took a slow, deep breath. Max Connors was only one of the painful memories she'd left behind.

But he was the most painful one.

She composed her face, hoping not to betray the emotions churning through her, before turning to face him.

"Max," she said. "Thank you for coming." She studied his face. It was leaner, more angular than she remembered. It was the face of a man, not the boy she'd left behind ten years ago.

Run from, she amended. At the age of eighteen she'd left town, heading as far east of Easy as she could, all the way to the big, bad apple — New York City. There she'd taken on a new life, a new name, a new identity. No longer was she Kitty "call-for-a-good-time" Feathers, but Kate Feathers, assistant copy editor at the advertising firm of Stoller, Crumb and Crumb.

She straightened and tried to ignore the jumble of bittersweet memories conjured by Max Connors' voice, but found herself captured. When had he taken her hand, engulfing it in that casually possessive way of his?

"You look great, Kitty," he said, giving her hand a reassuring squeeze.

Damn right! She'd worked hard to shed her past and fit in with the trendy, casual chic of New York City. One thing she'd learned at Stoller, Crumb and Crumb was that half the presentation was in the packaging. Although it took a large chunk of her salary to keep up the image, she'd learned how to make the most of her package.

Unlike some people, she thought, giving Max the once-over. At least his jeans were clean and his shirt ironed. In Easy that was considered the height of fashion — although most men had more sense than to wear their jeans so tight.

"Kitty?"

"Huh?" With a guilty flush, Kate jerked her gaze upward, pretending not to notice the slow, sexy smile that crossed his face. She had *not* been checking him out, no matter what he thought. Straightening her shoulders and drawing herself up to her full five and a half feet, she still had to tip her head to give him her haughtiest glare. "It's Kate," she corrected him. "No one calls me Kitty anymore." She brushed imaginary wrinkles from her silk skirt. "Now if you'll excuse me — "

He gripped her arm and turned her to face him again. "I realize this isn't a good time, but I need to talk to you. I was doing some work for your mother."

"Work?" What was he talking about? He was a small-town cowboy. As far as she could remember, the only skill he had was charming the cheerleaders out of their pom-poms. What in the world was he doing for her mother? She glanced at his hand wrapped firmly around her arm, then back at his face.

He released her and cleared his throat. "I was helping your mother remodel the shop."

The shop. How could she have forgotten Lillian's pet project? In a world full of cappuccino and latté lovers, Lillian had perversely opened a tea shop. No one had expected the business to succeed, let alone thrive the way it had over the years. Not only was the Tea and Crumpet Shop still in business but apparently doing well enough to need a handyman, if Max's claim was true.

"I'll see that you're paid for whatever work you've done," she assured him.

He chuckled and the sound flowed over her senses like silk. "I've been paid in full," he said. "Your mother's business was doing very well."

He ran a hand through his hair, causing a tumble of glossy dark waves to fall over his forehead. He still had that same James Dean attitude she remembered from high school — a cocky confidence that used to turn her legs to jelly.

A familiar wave of resentment washed over her. "We can discuss business some other time. This isn't the time or place."

"I'm sorry," he said. "I just wanted you to know that I'll be at the shop first thing Monday morning. I always finish what I start."

She wondered why that sounded so ominous. He'd started plenty ten years ago, but she'd be damned if she'd let him treat her like some kind of unfinished business.

He ran his hand through his hair again in another quick swipe. She used to find the mannerism endearing. The truth was, she still did — but that didn't change anything.

She watched Max stride off and climb into a red pick-up truck that had seen better days. Well, whatever unfinished business he had with her mother didn't give him a claim on her. That was in the past and she intended to keep it that way.

She'd have to decide what to do about her mother's business — and Max. But she'd worry about that Monday.

* * * * *

Back inside the funeral parlor, Kate realized she wouldn't have that luxury. It didn't take long before the questions started. The first person to pull her aside was Nellie Granger, a plump, white-haired woman who smelled of cinnamon and vanilla.

"What are we going to do next week?" Nellie asked. "It's blueberry week."

It took Kate a moment to realize that Nellie was talking about the Tea and Crumpet Shop.

Nellie's hands fluttered nervously. "I've got a kitchen full of blueberries that'll spoil if I don't put them to use."

"I haven't decided what to do about the shop," Kate admitted. She was stopped from explaining further by the panic in the older woman's eyes.

"We have to open, of course. It's blueberry week! I've got scones and muffins and crumpets to bake. And we have a shipment of blueberry tea arriving first thing in the morning. Your mother wouldn't want to let people down."

Kate thought it would be insensitive to point out that her mother's concerns were no longer a consideration. Besides, how hard would it be to keep the shop open a few days until she and Jeff decided what to do about it?

Nellie looked relieved when Kate told her to go ahead with her plans for blueberry week. Kate got the same reaction from a ponytailed teenager who wanted to be sure she still had a waitress job, and again when she was confronted by Arthur Zimmerman, who handled the counter and cash register.

Apparently her mother had half the town on the payroll. Not bad for what Kate thought of as a little tea shop. Well, the fact that it was a successful business was reassuring. It meant they wouldn't have any problem selling it and moving on with their own lives. She'd talk to Jeff about the business later.

But it was hours before the last of the mourners trickled out and she had some time alone with her brother. They moved to a quiet sitting area away from the viewing room. Jeff and Sally huddled together on a plump floral couch while Kate sank into an overstuffed wingback chair.

"What are we going to do about Mom's little tea shop?" Kate asked, kicking her shoes off with a sigh of relief.

Jeff glanced at Sally then back to his sister. "Well," he said, clearing his throat. "That's what we wanted to talk to you about."

Sally looked at her with a hopeful expression. Why was everyone looking at her like their very lives depended on her all of a sudden?

"Sally and I," Jeff began, taking his fiancée's hand and giving it a reassuring squeeze. "Well, we've decided to go ahead with the wedding."

At Kate's startled expression Jeff barreled ahead, as if afraid he'd lose his nerve if he didn't get it out all at once. "Not a big wedding, just a private service with the justice of the peace tomorrow afternoon. I mean, we have the license and everything. And we've already paid for the honeymoon cruise."

Kate jerked to attention. A cruise? "You're going away? But what about the shop and the house and everything that has to be done?"

"Well," Jeff muttered, not quite meeting her gaze. "That's where you come in. We were hoping...you said you have two weeks off, right?"

"Yes, but..." Kate found herself at a loss for words.

"Couldn't you stay here and cover for a couple weeks? We'll take over as soon as we come back from our honeymoon."

Stay in Easy? Kate gulped. Her stomach clenched and a cold sweat rippled along her skin. She couldn't. She'd turned her back on Easy and everything it represented. Just the thought of staying another day made her hands clench into fists at her side.

"You're keeping the shop open?" It seemed easier to concentrate on concrete things rather than the thought of staying in town for two whole weeks—and wearing an apron no less.

"Yes, of course. If you can just keep things running until we get back." He cleared his throat. His eyes shifted away then back again. "It's only two weeks."

Guilt caught her by the throat. Jeff didn't say what Kate knew he could—that he'd stayed when Kate had run off and left them all behind. He'd helped their mother build the business while Kate had been off making a life for herself in New York. For ten years he'd put up with Lillian's domineering ways. It must have been difficult for him. Today was proof of that. He'd had the most important day of his life ruined.

The least Kate could do was repair some of the damage their mother had caused. Was it too much to ask that just this once Jeff be allowed to do what he wanted? He'd never asked Kate for anything before, she realized with another stab of guilt.

Two sets of eyes searched her face. Both Jeff and Sally seemed to be holding their breath waiting for her answer.

Kate's shoulders slumped. What choice did she have? "Of course," she said, leaning forward and clasping her brother's hand. "You and Sally deserve this."

Sally let out a trembling sigh of relief and seemed to melt against Jeff's chest. He pulled her close, smiling at Kate and mouthing a silent "Thank you."

She felt like a heel for wanting to jump on the first available flight back to New York City when there were still so many things that had to be done here. Fourteen days. How bad could it be?

Besides, it was blueberry week.

* * * * *

Later that evening, Kate sat alone in her mother's kitchen. She'd managed to hold herself together as long as she'd kept busy, but with the last hushed goodbye from well-meaning visitors, grief crept in and filled the silence.

The house had changed little. Looking around the familiar kitchen, the years slipped away. She'd known coming home would bring back memories. She'd shored herself up, prepared for the worst. Ten years was a long time, but so much had changed. She'd grown up. Matured. She could deal with a few bad memories.

But she hadn't been prepared for the unexpected rush of *sweet* memories — doing homework at the cracked Formica table while Lillian made grilled-cheese sandwiches on the stove, or sneaking a cookie from the ceramic cookie jar while Lillian chatted on the phone and Jeff built Lego cities on the floor. Those remembrances of happier times hurt almost as much as the more painful ones she'd nurtured over the years. They only reminded her of how much she'd lost.

Walking through the house, Kate focused on the little changes — the new lace curtains replacing the yellow dotted Swiss she remembered, the wrought iron baker's rack in the corner draped with pottery and fresh ivy, a teapot-shaped clock over the window. Each small change pierced her heart with a fresh wave of remorse. Life had gone on here while she'd held it unchanged in her memory. Little by little, Lillian had given up waiting for her daughter to come home.

Home. Kate had thought it would always be here waiting for her. Now that she was back, she wondered why she'd waited so long. How many times had Lillian begged her to come home for a visit? The years had slipped by while Kate had made one excuse after another, too afraid to face the small-town gossip that had sent her running in the first place.

Pushing the negative thoughts aside, Kate busied herself around the kitchen, feeling like an intruder as she opened drawers and cabinets. She tucked the last covered casserole into the freezer, wrapped the cookies and desserts dropped off by neighbors, wiped the counter, then went through the house turning lights on. It was too dark, too quiet.

Her overnight bag rested against the sofa where she'd left it that morning. It seemed so long ago. She hadn't had a moment to herself since she'd arrived, and now that she was alone, the silence felt suffocating. She carried the suitcase into her old bedroom and placed it on the familiar lace-edged comforter. Matching curtains fluttered in the window. Nothing had changed in this room. The linens were crisp and fresh in anticipation of her arrival, and the scent of lemon polish hung in the air. It was almost as if she'd never left.

She unzipped her bag and unpacked the few things she'd brought along. She'd only intended to stay the weekend and realized she'd have to pick up a few things now that her plans had changed. Maybe she'd drive into Phoenix during the week and do some shopping.

The doorbell jangled, interrupting her thoughts. Kate clutched a folded pair of jeans to her chest. Who could that be? She didn't think she could stand another neighbor dropping by to offer condolences. She stood very still, hoping whoever it was would go away. Another buzz convinced her otherwise. She sighed and dropped the jeans onto the bed.

Kate trudged to the door. Every ounce of strength seemed to have been drained from her body, leaving her limp. With a sigh, she opened the front door then blinked in surprise. Standing on the porch step was a boy of eight or nine with tousled sun-bleached hair and tear-stained cheeks. He held up a handful of sagging wildflowers.

"These are for Miz Lilly," he said in a trembling voice. "To take up to heaven."

Kate knelt down on one knee and took the flowers. Only then did she notice the aluminum forearm crutches and metal braces strapped around his legs. "Thank you," she said, feeling her own lip quiver. "What's your name?"

"Bobby," he replied, brushing a fist across tear-smudged cheeks. His shoulders hitched on a quiet sob.

Kate fought the urge to brush her fingers through the boy's tousled hair. She clutched the wilting wildflowers to her chest. Of all the lavish displays that had filled the funeral parlor, this fistful of hand-picked flowers from a child was the most precious.

The boy turned and walked away, the braces on his legs giving him a slow, side-to-side gait. Kate noticed the red pick-up truck idling by the side of the road.

Max?

She couldn't be sure. It was too dark to see inside the truck. Besides, half the male population of Easy drove pick-ups.

Her heart lurched at the thought of seeing Max again. That, more than anything else, convinced Kate it was too dangerous to stay in Easy for long. She couldn't let Max Connors worm his way into her heart again. She'd spent too many years trying to forget, too many lonely nights crying into her pillow for a love that was lost and a trust betrayed. Max was her past. He'd never be her future.

The little boy stopped before reaching the truck and turned back to Kate. "Miz Lilly was my friend," he said, his lips turned down in a brave struggle to keep from crying. "I'll miss her."

"So will I," Kate admitted, watching as the boy made his way to the road and climbed into the passenger's side of the truck. She turned and walked inside, then leaned against the closed door. "So will I."

The boy's simple gesture broke down the control she'd struggled so hard to maintain. She slid to the floor, clutching the flowers to her chest and rocking like a child. How could she have let so much time go by? Who was she really punishing by not coming home all these years?

Her chest heaved and tears of loss and regret flowed unchecked. She'd thought her mother would always be here, that home was a place to which she could always return. Now nothing would ever be the same again.

Sobs clawed her throat raw and she cried until she couldn't cry anymore.

Chapter Two

ഔ

Monday morning Kate drove Jeff and Sally to the airport. Jeff gave Kate the keys to the house, the shop and his car, and promised to call before the cruise ship set sail. His last-minute instructions were lost in a flurry of hugs and kisses as their flight boarded.

The newlyweds glowed. Kate was miserable. *Just two weeks.* She had to keep reminding herself as she drove Jeff's car back into town. She glanced at her watch. It was only eight o'clock, but she decided to swing by the Tea and Crumpet Shop and check it out before the morning rush.

She gave a quick little snort. How much of a rush could there be? Even if the whole town showed up, there would still be enough room left over to square dance. Kate missed the lights and glamour and excitement of New York, the adrenaline rush she felt walking to work each morning along bustling sidewalks. She'd forgotten how deathly boring a small town could be, how monotonous all that wide-open space was first thing in the morning.

Her longing was forgotten when she pulled up to the shop on Main Street to find it not only open already, but brimming with customers. Stepping inside, she was overpowered by scents—a warm mixture of sweet aromas that set her taste buds tingling.

The shop was bigger than Kate had imagined, with enough room for dozens of round, marble-topped tables and wrought iron chairs. Bright gingham swags adorned every window, and a cheery glow came from crystal light fixtures hanging from the ceiling. Two waitresses bustled from table to table, a blur of motion as they delivered orders. The jangle of an old-fashioned cash register fairly sang as Arthur, wearing a white rolled cap over his bald head, rang up orders.

Behind the counter, Nellie slid a tray of steaming, sugar-crusted blueberry muffins into a glass display case already overflowing with scones, muffins and sweet rolls. Her cheeks were flushed as she looked up and smiled at Kate.

"There you are, honey," Nellie called, wiping a streak of cinnamon sprinkles across her apron. "Come on in and let me show you around."

"Who opened the shop?" Kate asked.

"Oh, I did," Nellie said, leading Kate back into the kitchen. "I come in at five o'clock to start baking every day. We don't officially open until eight, but Arthur's usually here early, and if there's a crowd waiting outside we just open the doors and start serving."

"You come in at five o'clock? Every day?"

"Well, I always was a morning person. And we pride ourselves on baking everything fresh daily." She winked. "That's what keeps the customers coming back."

Kate glanced around the kitchen. "There's enough food in here to last a week. You mean to tell me you go through this much in one day?"

"Not always," Nellie said. "When Arthur leaves, he takes a basket over to the fire house. We'll usually send a few bags of goodies home for Max's kids. Whatever's left over when we close up is donated to a local shelter. Then we start fresh the next day."

Kate hadn't heard a single word after "Max's kids". Nellie grabbed Kate's arm and dragged her around the shop, but Kate's mind locked on those two words. Max had kids? A wife? Why hadn't her mother told her? And why had Kate assumed he'd stayed frozen in time simply waiting for her to return?

She found the nerve to ask, surprised when her voice came out in a squeak. "How many kids does Max have?"

"Hmm?" Nellie blinked, as if the question had caught her by surprise. She pursed her lips and gazed off in the distance, counting on her fingers. "Let's see. I think about fifteen or so right now. It changes."

Changes? Kate opened her mouth then closed it again. What was he, a rabbit?

"You'll have to ask him," Nellie said. "He'll be by a little later."

Kate had no intention of asking him. She didn't want to think of Max as a husband and father, let alone populating half of Easy County. She followed Nellie but found it hard to concentrate on her monologue.

Nellie's tour of the Tea and Crumpet Shop included a huge stockroom filled with teas. There was black, oolong and green teas, Chinese and English teas, spiced teas and fruit teas, as well as breakfast, herbal and decaffeinated teas. There were teas with exotic names like Golden Kenya, Mountain Chai and Temple of Heaven Gunpowder. Kate had no idea there were so many different kinds of tea in the entire world, let alone one small corner of Easy, Arizona.

And accessories! Kate couldn't believe the ceremony involved in brewing a simple cup of tea. No tea bags for this crowd. Their selections were brought to the tables on individual serving trays laden with handmade tea cozies covering bone china tea pots, delicate porcelain drip catchers and cloth-lined wicker baskets filled with sweets.

As Nellie finished the tour and led her to a table, Kate realized that the shop was more than just a place to grab a quick bite to eat. It was an event. Somehow the Tea and Crumpet Shop had become the town's social hub.

"Who's that?" Kate asked, pointing to a woman in a gold caftan weaving between tables and occasionally stopping to speak with customers.

Nellie rolled her eyes and leaned close, speaking in a hushed whisper. "That's Adelaide Wilkinson. She calls herself

Madame Zostra and reads tea leaves for a small donation. She's a crackerjack, but the customers love her. Your mother said there was no harm in it. Besides, she's good for business."

"She reads tea leaves?" That was something else her mother had conveniently left out of her letters and phone calls. Before Kate could investigate further, a familiar voice called out from the back room.

"We're up front, Max," Nellie called back.

Max stepped through the doorway, smiling when he spotted them. Kate noticed he'd traded his starched shirt for denim today, but the ever-present jeans remained. And they were still too tight, she noticed. Or maybe it was the way his tool belt slung low on his hips that drew her eye. Either way, he was the last person she wanted to talk to this morning.

Before Kate could stop her, Nellie gestured for Max to join them at the table. She fussed over him like a mother hen. "Why don't I just get you some tea and muffins? I'm sure you two have a lot to talk about."

Kate shook her head, but Max spoke up first.

"That would be great," he said, turning the full force of those baby blues on Nellie. She bustled off, leaving the two of them alone in uncomfortable silence.

Kate cleared her throat.

Max studied her, his lips quirked up in a half smile. He stretched his long legs, taking up most of the space under the table.

Kate felt the brush of denim against her ankle. She shoved her chair back and tucked her feet beneath it, out of Max's reach. He was crowding her. In more ways than one. She glanced around, searching for an excuse to get up and leave.

"It's blueberry week," Max said.

Kate nodded. "So I've heard."

"Everyone in town knows that."

Kate gritted her teeth. Why did that sound like a challenge? "Well, I don't live in town anymore, in case you haven't noticed."

"Oh," he drawled, "I've noticed, all right."

Kate was saved from having to reply by Nellie, who returned with warm muffins and a steaming pot of tea.

Max nearly broke the sound barrier reaching for a muffin the size of a softball. Nellie smiled indulgently and patted his head as if he were ten years old. Kate wondered when Max had become the Tea and Crumpet Shop's official mascot.

Max attacked the blueberry muffin as if he hadn't eaten in weeks. Kate nibbled on her own, looking everywhere but into those challenging eyes. It was hard enough being back in town after all these years, but to be thrown together with the one man she never wanted to see again was intolerable. Especially since he still had an effect on her, making her heart trip and her knees go weak.

That was easy enough to fix. All she had to do was remember how he'd ruined her life.

She'd been in love with Max for as long as she could remember. He was good-looking, popular and could have had any girl he wanted in school. She'd been nobody—just a plain, gawky, invisible girl who hadn't had the right clothes or the right friends. All she'd had was her good reputation. She hadn't realized at the time how fragile that was, how easily her reputation could be ripped to shreds, making her life miserable.

And it all began when Max finally noticed her. She'd given him her heart, her soul and seven glorious months of her life.

In return, he'd lied about her and ruined her reputation. By the time Kate had realized what he'd done, it was too late to stop the rumors from spreading. The story had taken on a life of its own, snowballing with each telling until her reputation was more tattered than her second-hand clothes. *Easy.* That's what they'd called her. And all Max's friends had wanted their shot at a sure thing. The girls in school shunned her. The boys she rejected simply made up more outrageous stories to boost their own reputations rather than admitting they'd struck out.

It hadn't mattered that she was still a virgin. Even if she'd had the nerve to face her attackers, no one would have believed her. And so she'd done the only thing she could. She'd run away, leaving her family and her reputation behind. She'd left the town whose very name reminded her of those mocking taunts.

The pain was as fresh today as it had been all those years ago. She had it all now—a good job, nice clothes and friends who didn't judge her by locker-room rumors—but inside she was still that same insecure girl who could hear the whispers and taunts following her through the halls. Inside she was still the girl everyone called "easy".

She'd never forgive Max for that. Not in two weeks, not in a thousand years. And she wouldn't fall for his charms ever again.

"Kate?"

Max's voice pulled her back to the present. He'd finished wolfing down his muffin and spread a contract out on the table between them. He was explaining what renovations he'd done at the Tea and Crumpet Shop. Pushing the old familiar resentment aside, Kate tried to concentrate on the figures.

"This seems a little high for some shelves," she said, running her finger down to the total at the bottom.

"Not just shelves," he argued, "*cabinetry*. I've put a lot of labor into these built-in hutches and pantries and I'm damn proud of my work."

"Whatever," she said, waving away his wounded pride. "The fact is you could have done it a lot cheaper."

"Cheaper?" His lips pulled into a thin line. "Your mother wasn't interested in cheap. She wanted quality."

Kate felt her cheeks burn. What did he mean by that? Was he still talking about the cabinets or was it a cruel reference to her ruined reputation? She felt the old, familiar paranoia rear up, stiffening her spine.

Kate stared at the papers in her hand. The figures blurred for a moment then cleared again. She fought to regain her composure, unwilling to let Max see her pain. If he'd meant to hurt her, he'd succeeded.

Kate pursed her lips, pretending to study the contracts. Once she had her emotions under control, she lifted her chin and challenged him head on, anger tightening her voice. "Did this job go out to bid? Were there any other quotes?"

Max straightened, tipping his head to stare at her. "Out to bid? This ain't New York City, darlin'. We do things differently here in Easy. Or maybe you've forgotten."

"I don't forget anything," she said pointedly, working hard to ignore the way his casually drawled *darlin'* could still turn her insides to mush. She knew she was goading him but couldn't stop herself. "My mother was not the most business savvy—"

"Oh, you're wrong there," he interrupted. "Look around you. Your mother didn't build this business by cutting corners. Maybe she wasn't some fancy New York executive," he snorted, the derision evident in his voice. "But I can tell you this—Lillian Feathers was one smart cookie. And no one took advantage of her."

"Maybe not," Kate admitted. "But you're dealing with me now."

"Oh? For how long? Until you decide this town's not good enough for you anymore and run off to bigger and better things?"

Kate drew back as if he'd tossed cold water on her face. Is that what people thought? Well, he was right about one thing. Her visit was only temporary. She'd be out of town faster than butter sliding off a hot biscuit. If it weren't for Jeff, she'd already be winging her way back to New York. But she'd made a promise, and as long as she was here she intended to make sure that no one took advantage of her family.

"I want an accounting of all parts and labor by morning," she said, shuffling papers. "And a firm completion date. I don't see anything here about when all the work will be delivered."

"Your mother and I had an arrangement."

"And I'm making a new arrangement. I don't think it's too much to ask for a commitment for work that's already been paid for."

"I see," he said, standing. "Then I guess I'd better get right to work."

She nodded, dismissing him. At least now he'd know he wasn't dealing with some naïve lovesick girl anymore. "Oh, and Max?" she called, putting as much steel into her voice as she could muster.

He turned, his eyes dark and smoldering with anger.

Kate pointed to his empty plate. "Don't forget to pay for your muffin."

His jaw tightened. "I don't have to," he said. "It's in the contract." With that he turned and stormed out.

Kate blinked, wondering if she'd heard right. She flipped through the pages until she found the addendum. There, in Lillian's own handwriting, was a provision giving Max a daily breakfast muffin as part of the legal and binding contract. Wasn't that just like Lillian? Always taking care of everyone, whether they needed it or not.

Kate ran her fingers over the familiar loops and swirls of her mother's handwriting, only now coming to terms with how much she'd miss her letters, the sound of her mother's voice on the phone, the weekly nagging to come home. Maybe she would have come home sooner if she hadn't been so stubborn.

If only she hadn't waited so long.

Fighting back regrets, Kate lifted her cup to her mouth, draining all but a few drops of the cooled tea then absently swirling the dregs in the bottom of her cup. She'd always preferred coffee, and the only tea she'd ever had came from a tea bag. But this was really very good and surprisingly soothing.

Maybe her mother was savvier than she'd given her credit for. If the continuous stream of customers was any indication, Lillian had tapped into a gold mine here. Even the extravagantly garbed woman reading tea leaves was a stroke of brilliance.

As if sensing Kate's thoughts, Madame Zostra drifted over on a cloud of jasmine. She reached out and placed her hand over Kate's cup, stopping the swirling motion. "Enough," she said. "I'll read for you now, Miss Kate."

Kate waved her hand. "No, that's all right."

Before she could argue, Madame Zostra turned the cup upside down, letting it drain onto the saucer. "No charge for you, Miss Kate," she said, settling into the seat, flowing robes of gold and royal purple floating around her.

Kate couldn't muster up the energy to argue. Her confrontation with Max had drained all the fight out of her. She leaned back as Madame Zostra prepared to divine her future in the pattern of tea leaves.

"I see a trip in your future," she intoned.

Kate fought back an indulgent smile. That was a no-brainer. Everyone in town knew she'd be going back to New York soon. She watched the sunlight glitter off Madame Zostra's gold hoop earrings, thinking the whole gypsy outfit was a little overdone.

"There's love. True love. But you have to open your heart to see it." Madame Zostra closed her eyes and tipped her head to the side. "I feel…" She opened her eyes again and studied the cup, both inside and out. "This is your mother's cup," she said. "No one else ever used this one."

"Oh, I didn't know."

Madame Zostra pointed to the elaborate curl of vines and roses decorating the front of the cup. Only then did Kate see the letter "L" hidden in the design. Lillian's cup.

Kate glanced over at Nellie, wondering why she'd given her that particular cup. Perhaps it was a symbolic gesture, passing the reign of power from mother to daughter.

"I can feel your mother's vibrations," Madame Zostra said. "So strong. So clear." The woman gasped. Then her face grew serious — deadly serious. "Your mother is trying to reach you," she said. "It's very important that you listen."

Kate nodded. "Okay, I'll listen." At this point she would have said anything just to get the psychic to leave her table. It was all getting a little too strange for her.

Madame Zostra cocked her head again then laughed. "Your mother said you never listened while she was alive, why would you listen now?"

That comment was so like Lillian that Kate felt a prickle of goose bumps crawl up and down her arms.

"Take this," Madame Zostra said, shoving the cup at Kate. "Take it and keep it with you."

"Why?" Kate asked, feeling a little silly taking the empty cup. She couldn't help sneaking a quick peek inside, half expecting to see her mother's face staring back at her.

"I don't know," the psychic said, a puzzled frown on her face. "I just know you must." Then her voice softened to a whispered hush, her eyes glazed and distant. "And listen," she murmured. "Listen with your heart.

* * * * *

Outside, Max Connors worked in a back lot that served as delivery drop-off, storage space and employee picnic area. He stripped off his denim shirt and tossed it over a bench. The afternoon sun was hot, but it was anger that had his temperature boiling. How dare Kitty — *oh excuse me, I mean Kate!* — accuse him of taking advantage of her mother. He'd taken on this project as a favor to Lillian, and he'd taken it for a damn sight less than he could have too.

His jaws hurt from grinding his teeth in frustration. He shouldn't have been surprised. Kate had a history of underestimating him. But they'd been kids then. He'd always hoped she'd come to her senses. Even Lillian had convinced herself that Kate would tire of living in New York and come back to Arizona. As the weeks turned to months and the months to years, it was only stubborn pride that had kept Max from picking up the phone and begging her to come home. Now he could see he'd been a fool to wait for her.

Max ran a hand through his hair. Even as the thought came, he knew it wasn't true. He'd have waited a lifetime for Kate. She excited him and infuriated him at the same time. There'd been other women over the years, both casual and semi-serious. But none of them had come close to making his nerves sing and his blood sizzle. And none of them had made him forget Kate. Now that she was back, those feelings were stronger than ever, even while she continued to push all his buttons. He could handle the accusations she threw at him if it meant finally clearing the air, but how dare she question his integrity.

He picked up his planer and started shaving a piece of oak, running his thumb along the surface every now and then to test the edge. He'd hand-picked the finest woods, choosing them for evenness of color and grain. He'd consulted with Lillian at every step of the design phase, incorporating pullout pantries and lazy Susans at her request. Together they'd picked out architectural details such as moldings, casings and trim.

It didn't end there. Each layer of finish was hand-sanded between coats to remove even the tiniest imperfections, and the final coat hand-rubbed to the desired luster. Money couldn't buy craftsmanship like this. He'd poured his heart and soul into every piece.

It had been worth it, though. He loved working with wood and building something from nothing at all. So had Lillian. She used to sit out here watching him, asking him questions as he worked and making the time fly by with her stories—mostly stories about what Kate was up to in the big city. Lillian had appreciated and admired every detail of the work. She'd called Max a genius, a true artisan.

Obviously Lillian's daughter didn't share her good taste.

* * * * *

Kate stood in the doorway watching Max work. The muscles of his forearms bunched and flexed as he ran the planer along the wood in long, smooth strokes. The smell of fresh-cut wood mixed with the sweet green scent of new-mown grass. She took a deep breath, holding it in for as long as she could.

Straightening, Max pulled a blue and white bandanna from his back pocket and wiped his forehead. A light sheen of perspiration emphasized the solid strength of his bare back and shoulders. He looked hot — in more ways than one.

Before Max could turn and catch her staring, Kate ducked back inside and reached into the cooler for two cold bottles of iced tea. Max had probably worked up quite a thirst working out in the hot sun — not that she needed an excuse to talk to him or see for herself whether his bare front was half as enticing as the back.

She had a great view of his backside as Max bent over the sawhorse again to sand the wood he was working on. She admired the view, feeling like one of those drooling women in a soft drink commercial. *Not too cliché*, she thought, glad she'd chosen tea instead of cola.

She'd had a chance to look at the work he'd done inside and had to admit that the finished product was both beautiful and functional, taking advantage of every inch of space inside and out. Maybe she'd been a little rough on him. That didn't mean she'd let him walk all over her. He'd taken advantage of her innocence once and it wouldn't happen again.

He hadn't heard her walk up, so when he stood and stretched, she cleared her throat to get his attention. He turned, narrowing his eyes when he saw her.

"I thought you could use something cold to drink," she said, holding out one of the bottles as a peace offering.

He grunted his thanks, took the bottle and held it against his forehead for a moment before twisting the cap off. He tipped his head, drinking half the cold tea in one long gulp. She watched him drink, mesmerized by the bobbing of his Adam's apple as he swallowed. A slow trickle of sweat ran from his forehead to his jaw, glistening in the sunlight. She realized that her own throat had suddenly gone dry as dust.

Grateful she'd worn slacks instead of a skirt, she climbed onto a nearby picnic table and leaned back, lifting her face to the sun. Ignoring her completely, Max finished his drink and returned to his work. Not that she could blame him for being a little peeved after her earlier outburst.

"Max?"

He answered with another grunt, not bothering to look up.

"I'm sorry," she said, rushing to get the apology out before she could change her mind. "I'm sorry for snapping at you."

He stopped what he was doing and turned slowly to stare at her.

"I've had a chance to look at your work, and you were right about the quality. It was unfair of me to compare it to department store furniture."

When he still didn't speak, she rambled on, filling the silence. "I felt overwhelmed and guilty for not being here to help Mom these last few years. I guess I always thought she'd be here if I changed my mind. And now...anyway, I overreacted and I'm sorry."

There, she'd apologized and given him the perfect opening. It was his turn now. And he had a whole lot more to be held accountable for.

He put down his sandpaper, brushed sawdust from his jeans then sat beside her. "Why didn't you?" he asked. "Why didn't you ever come back?"

She shrugged. "I wanted a fresh start. A clean slate." She looked up at him. "Surely you can understand that?"

"No, not really," he said with a frown. "I guess I never wanted more than this." He made a simple gesture, taking in the whole town, his work, the very grass at his feet. "Guess I'm just a small-town cowboy with no aspirations, huh?"

"Why would you say that?" And then she blushed, remembering the night behind the football bleachers when she'd spit those exact words at him. They'd still been dating then, and she couldn't even remember what they'd been arguing about at the time. How long had he been carrying those hurtful words around inside him?

Probably as long as she'd harbored her own personal grudge.

"I guess we've both said things we shouldn't have," she admitted, giving him another opening to come clean and apologize for being a cad all those years ago.

He slapped a palm on each knee and straightened, blocking out the sun as he towered over her. "Yeah, I guess we have."

And that was it. No apology, no excuses, nothing. Well, she'd given him the opportunity to own up to his mistakes. If he had, she might have forgiven him and taken the first step toward putting the painful past behind her.

Pretending she wasn't hurt, she picked up their empty bottles and walked away.

Two weeks. Fourteen days. How hard could it be to avoid Max Connors until she fulfilled her obligations and flew back to New York?

Chapter Three

Ed Tate Jr. strolled into the Tea and Crumpet Shop to the surprised gasp of every customer inside. Heads inclined to whisper and speculation hissed hotter than steam from a teakettle.

"Well, what do we have here?" Nellie murmured, wiping her hands on her apron. "Lillian's not even cold in her grave and the Tates are descending like vultures."

Kate looked up, adding her own questioning gaze to the combined stares of everyone else. Ed Jr. hadn't aged well in the ten years she'd been gone. His hairline was creeping north and his waistline was drooping south. Kate remembered him as an overbearing bully in high school. Apparently he'd found a way to turn it into a career, judging by the khaki deputy sheriff uniform he now wore.

Ed's dull walrus eyes searched the room, finally lighting on Kate. He harrumphed and tugged on his belt then threaded his way through the room toward her, seemingly unaware of the buzz around him.

"Kate," he said, holding out a beefy hand. "It's good to have you back. I'm sorry it had to be under such tragic circumstances."

The sympathy didn't reach his eyes. Kate waved him to a seat across the table. "Can I get you anything?"

He turned to Nellie who hovered protectively beside Kate's chair. "I'll have some of that fancy tea everyone raves about."

When Nellie turned with only a barely disguised snort, Ed called after her. "And one of your famous muffins too."

Having dismissed Nellie, Tate pulled out a chair and turned his attention to Kate. "I just wanted to welcome you home."

Home? No, this was only temporary. Two weeks at the most—just until Jeff came back from his honeymoon. Then she was heading back east again, as far from Arizona as she could go.

Ed looked around, seeming to take in every detail of the shop. "Your mother built quite a little business here," he said with a nod. "Now that we're family, I hope to spend more time in here myself."

"Family" wasn't exactly how Kate would describe it. Jeff's marriage to Ed's sister made them in-laws, but only in the legal sense of the word.

"You're more than welcome, of course," she said, wondering where this conversation was leading. She didn't trust Ed Tate. He was the kind of man who'd run your dog down in the street then drive away without blinking an eye. Maybe he'd changed, but in her mind Ed Tate was still the sniveling little brat who'd tried to kiss her behind the bushes in the third grade. And the fourth and fifth and—

"Kate?"

She shook her head. "I'm sorry. What were you saying?"

Ed puffed out his chest. "I was hoping you'd changed your mind. Since you're in town anyway."

"Changed my mind? About what?"

"About attending our ten-year reunion. The committee sent you an invitation a few months back."

Kate vaguely remembered getting an invitation, which she'd promptly thrown into the trash and pushed out of her mind.

"It's not too late to reserve a spot," he said. "I'm on the committee, so I could squeeze you in."

"No," she protested. "Don't go to any trouble."

"No trouble at all." He gave her that sneaky smile that made her want to hide behind the playground bushes all over again. "I'm sure you'd like to catch up with some friends since you're in town."

What friends? They'd all abandoned her when she'd needed them most. If there had been anyone she'd wanted to keep in touch with, she would have. She hadn't, and didn't intend to start now.

Nellie returned to the table, teapot in hand. She placed a cup in front of Ed and filled it halfway. "Fresh out of muffins," she said with barely concealed contempt, then turned to Kate. "Refill, honey?"

Kate placed a hand over her empty cup and shook her head, then jerked her hand back when a tingling vibration traveled up her arm. It felt as if a mild electrical current had jumped from the cup to her hand.

What the...?

Gingerly touching the cup again sent the same vibrations skittering along her fingertips. She glanced around, but no one else seemed to notice anything unusual. Nellie had already turned to leave, Ed Tate was frowning in annoyance at the packed display case and additional baskets full of muffins sitting on the counter, and the rest of the customers seemed oblivious to everything but their own teacups.

Nerves, she told herself. *Only nerves, nothing else.* She pulled her hand away from the cup, frowning.

Just then the lights flickered.

That wasn't her imagination. Ed saw it too.

"You'd better get that looked into," he said. "Could be a fire hazard."

Kate nodded, waiting for the flash again. But nothing happened. She glanced at the cup, wondering what could have caused the shock and whether it had anything to do with the lights flashing. For just a moment, the letter "L" on the side of the cup seemed to light up with an ethereal glow. Kate blinked and it was gone, a trick of the light or perhaps only her imagination.

Ed cleared his throat. "I was thinking if you'd changed your mind, maybe I could escort you."

Kate forced herself to focus on the man sitting across from her. Was he still talking about the reunion? Even if she was desperate to go, the thought of walking in on the arm of Ed Tate Jr. made her skin crawl.

No sooner had the thought crossed her mind than the teacup in front of her rattled, as if someone had kicked the table. It wobbled on the saucer for a moment then came quietly to rest.

A deep baritone voice pulled her attention away from the cup's antics. "Sorry, Ed. Kate's already agreed to go to the reunion with me."

Kate's eyes widened at Max's announcement. *Since when?* Max shot her a warning glance and she clamped her mouth shut, swallowing the urge to argue. When Max glared at Ed, the air sizzled between them. Kate thought they looked like two junkyard dogs facing off over a juicy T-bone. Something threatening passed between the two men. There was bad blood there—whether old or new, Kate wasn't sure. The teacup remained mercifully silent on the subject.

Ed was the first to look away. He gave Kate a too-friendly nod and stood to leave. "If you need anything, just call." He looked around the room and a dozen gazes shifted away, pretending they hadn't been following the exchange. "This is a nice place you have here. Wouldn't want anything to happen to it."

Like what? Kate was about to ask when Ed turned on his heel and walked away. The unspoken threat seemed to hang in the air. Kate watched until Ed was out the door then turned to Max. "What was that all about?"

"Unfinished business," he said.

"Well, I want no part of it. I have no intention of going to that reunion—with you or anyone else."

Max tipped his head and gave her that slow smile again. "You've got two weeks to decide, darlin'. My offer stands."

"I don't need two weeks. I'm not going and that's final."

"Suit yourself," he said. "But at least you won't have to spend the next two weeks fighting off Deputy Ed."

She knew what he was implying. All she'd accomplished in the past ten years didn't matter. Nothing had changed here. It was still a small town filled with small-minded gossip. As long as she was back in town, she'd have to fight off men who still thought of her as an easy target. She wondered if Ed Tate was only the first of many who'd try to score with the town tramp.

It didn't matter that none of the gossip was true. She couldn't escape her reputation that easily. And standing in front of her — pretending to be her guardian angel — was the person she held responsible for starting the unfounded rumors in the first place.

"Thanks, but no thanks," she said, turning away from Max and all the bitter memories he brought back to the surface. She wanted to run, leave all this behind her. If she hadn't promised her brother to watch over things until he returned, she'd take the first flight back to New York and never look back again.

Her hip bumped the edge of the table as she stood, setting her mother's teacup wobbling again. Both Kate and Max reached to steady it at the same time and their fingers brushed. His hand — strong, hard and calloused in all the right places — closed around hers. Again she felt that low hum, as if the delicate china was vibrating to a tone beyond the range of human ears.

"Do you feel that?" Kate asked.

"Feel what?" His gaze locked on hers.

How could she have forgotten those eyes? They were as blue and wide as the Arizona sky. The intensity of his gaze held her and seemed to plumb the very depths of her soul. His hand relaxed, allowing her to pull free. But the vibration continued, seeming to shiver through her whole body. Only now it seemed to come from some place deep inside.

"Nothing," she said, pulling her gaze from his. "I um..." She tried to focus on anything other than the riotous emotions swirling through her body. "I think there might be an electrical short somewhere. I felt a vibration or something before. Could you check around and see if there's a loose wire?"

He tipped his head, an amused smile on his face. "Don't you think you should call an electrical contractor for that?"

"Aren't you the handyman?"

His laughter was a deep, rumbling vibrato. "No, not quite," he told her. "I said I was doing a job for your mother. It was more like a favor...when I'm not too busy out at the ranch."

Kate was more confused than ever. "You built these cupboards, right?"

He nodded. "I do a little carpentry on the side. I'm good with my hands." His slow smile gave more meaning to the words than Kate wanted to admit. "But it's more of a hobby than anything else. When your mother couldn't find anyone locally who could handle the job, she came to me. I had some spare time and couldn't resist the challenge, so I offered to help her out."

"For a price, right?"

"Of course." He tipped his head, still smiling. "But not much more than the cost of the materials. I told you I liked her ideas, as well as the challenge of fitting together what she wanted in the space we had to work with. Check the books if you don't believe me."

"I'll do that." But she didn't need to. Max Connors might be a heartbreaker, but he wasn't a swindler. "One other thing," she said before he could leave. "Just when did you and my mother get so chummy?"

"A long time ago," he said, leaning closer until his breath was a warm whisper against her cheek. "You see, we had something in common."

"What's that?" she asked, feeling a slow trembling centered deep in her chest.

He held her gaze, his voice a slow, husky drawl. "We both missed you."

Her heart seemed to flip and tumble clear down to her toes. Before she could find the presence of mind to form a snappy reply, he turned and strode out the back door, letting it slam shut behind him.

Kate brushed the back of her hand across her flaming cheek. It was going to be a long, long two weeks.

* * * * *

Max concentrated on his work, trying to push thoughts of Kate out of his mind. He recognized the look on her face when he'd pushed her. She'd been skittish as a colt, ready to bolt if he said the wrong thing. Wouldn't be the first time, would it? She'd bolted before and she'd do it again. It would be plain stupid for him to think otherwise. So why was he even getting involved?

Good question. The last thing he needed was some city girl making him feel awkward and adolescent and not near good enough for her. Well, the hell with that! Little Miss Kitty, or Kate, or whatever the heck she called herself these days, could just head on back to New York City for all he cared. But not until she answered one question—what had he done that was so bad she had to travel eighty gazillion miles to get away from him?

The next swing of the hammer clipped the edge of his thumb and a string of curse words burst from his mouth.

A soft giggle followed his outburst. Clutching his throbbing thumb, Max turned to see Chrissy Roberts, one of the part-time waitresses, standing just outside the doorway.

"Ain't you supposed to be working?" he asked.

"I'm on a break." She sauntered over and sat on the picnic table. "I thought I'd come outside and have a smoke."

"You're too young to smoke."

"Am not," she argued, lighting up a cigarette and taking a deep drag to prove her point. "I'm eighteen now. Graduated last month." She leaned back, her ponytail swinging, and stretched out long, tanned legs.

Max turned back to his work but Chrissy was intent on capturing his attention again.

"So, what was all that commotion with Deputy Ed inside?" she asked.

"No big deal. He was just testing the waters, that's all." Just the mention of Ed Tate's name had him gritting his teeth. Uniform or no uniform, he had a score to settle with Tate, and it was long overdue.

"Well," Chrissy continued, "if Miss Lillian knew there'd been a Tate in her shop, she'd have blown a gasket."

"Yeah, and if Miss Lillian saw you sucking on that cigarette she'd have tanned your hide."

Chrissy scowled and blew out a stream of smoke. "Sheesh, you sound like my father."

"If I was your father, you'd be eating that cigarette instead of smoking it, young lady."

Chrissy pouted then stood and dropped her cigarette to the dirt, grinding it out with the toe of her tennis shoe. "There, happy now?" She stepped closer, tipping her head and giving him a flirtatious smile.

Max took a step back just as Nellie called from the doorway, "Chrissy! Break's over and we've got customers lined up."

Chrissy sighed and called over her shoulder, "Coming Aunt Nellie." She rolled her eyes at Max then turned and headed back, wiggling her hips all the way.

Max shook his head. Nellie had her hands full with that little filly. She was a wild one, all right.

Speaking of fillies, it was time to head home and feed the critters. He put his tools away, locking them in the metal toolbox strapped to the pick-up bed, his mind on the Arabian mare they'd rescued just last month from a slaughter auction. Barely six hundred pounds when he got her, Venus was nothing more than skin and bones, with ribs protruding like umbrella spokes from her once-lustrous chestnut coat. Although the mare was malnourished and infested with parasites, Max knew the animal's physical condition was the least of his worries.

He climbed behind the wheel and slammed the door, his mouth pulled into a thin, hard line as he thought about the horse. Lash marks on her flank were the most obvious signs of physical abuse, but it was the terror in her eyes that clawed at his heart. Abuse had left her fearful and head shy, but Max saw a spark smoldering there. She hadn't given up yet, and with enough love and patience she just might get some of that sassiness back he saw lurking beneath the fear in those big brown eyes.

Thinking of the Arabian mare brought his mind back to Ed Tate. Tate hadn't been any help when Max had tried to find the previous owners of the abused horse. They'd stood toe to toe in the dirt arguing over animal abuse.

"I've got more important things to deal with in this town than chasing down an honest rancher trying to earn a living," Tate had growled.

That had made Max see red. "There's nothing honest about abusing an animal to the brink of death. Look at her!"

But Tate hadn't bothered to investigate. "Damn bleeding hearts," he'd muttered under his breath. "Care more about animals than a man's God-given right to support his family."

Oh, Max knew all about supporting a family and trying to scrape together a living off the ranch. But that was no excuse to mistreat a horse. His latest skirmish with Tate wasn't the first time they'd nearly come to blows. Max knew it wouldn't be the last either.

Anger had him driving carelessly, tires skidding over rutted dirt roads, leaving rooster tails of desert dust in his wake. Long-fingered shadows from saguaro cacti seemed to caution him, but he drove on, unmindful of their silent warning. His thoughts were as swift and fleeting as the whiptail lizards that prowled the desert landscape.

Frustration churned inside him. He knew that for every horse he saved, a dozen more died in miserable squalor, starving and filthy, their bodies battered and their spirits broken. He couldn't save them all. Even doing extra jobs on the side like this, there was barely enough money to cover medicine, feed and veterinary bills for the few he was able to rescue.

The anger was familiar. He felt it every time he saw an animal hurt or abused. But there was more to his broiling emotions than just anger over the horse. Seeing Kate again after all these years had opened up a wound that had never fully healed. He thought he'd gotten over her, but one look into those snapping green eyes told him how wrong he was. His heart had taken a plunge at his first sight of Kate—her soft, silky hair begging to be stroked, full lips ripe for nibbling. Even in anger, her voice had tugged at his heart, pulling a smile from long-unused muscles.

She was back and as intoxicating as ever. But he'd be a fool to fall under her spell again. She'd leave, just like she had all those years ago, and he wasn't sure his heart could stand being left behind a second time.

Taking a deep breath, Max let up on the gas. Driving recklessly wasn't the answer. It wouldn't do anyone any good for him to kill himself. When he reached the ranch, his fingers were stiff from gripping the wheel, and his clenched jaw throbbed. He pulled the truck onto the dirt lane leading to the Triple-R, parked alongside the main house and jumped out of the pick-up, taking the porch steps in three quick hops. Stopping only long enough to grab a couple apples off the kitchen counter, he headed back out to the stables.

Max stood for a moment admiring his surroundings. This was the only world he knew—sweeping views of dry desert dotted with sagebrush and the distinctive silhouette of saguaro cacti, wide-open spaces flanked by the toothy Superstition Mountains in the distance, and sunsets that could break your heart. Why would anyone want to live anywhere else? He knew these were dangerous thoughts that brought him full circle to Kate. How could she leave this? How could she leave *him*? Max kicked at the dust, pushing thoughts of Kate out of his mind, and headed for the stable.

His father stepped out of the stalls to meet him. "Thought I heard your truck," he drawled. "Either that or one of them fighter jets was making a landing in our front yard."

Max shot his father a grin. Otis Connors was a true American cowboy, skin leathered by the Arizona sun, eyes crinkled with starburst creases from years of squinting into its harsh glare. He represented a hundred years of Arizona cattlemen and western tradition—time-honored values such as honesty, hard work and lending a helping hand to your neighbor.

"How's our girl doing?" Max gestured toward Venus' stall.

Otis leaned the muck shovel against the side of the barn. He pulled a red bandanna from his back pocket, thumbed the brim of his Stetson back and ran the bandanna across his forehead before answering. "Had her teeth floated today. She's eating better already." He tucked the bandanna back in his pocket and gave his son a reassuring pat on the shoulder. "We'll have her filled out in no time."

Max nodded. Time and treatment would mend the horse's body, but would they be able to heal her spirit? "I'd like to get my hands on the scum-sucking lowlife who did this to her," he growled.

Otis eyed the apples in Max's hand. "One of those better be for Outlaw. I think he's jealous of the time you're spending with the new horse."

"So I noticed," Max said, heading into the barn. He felt at home with the familiar smells of horse, leather and fresh hay.

Otis picked up the muck shovel and followed. "I'd better finish up here so we can get Venus inside."

Max strolled over to Outlaw's stall. The horse pretended indifference, but his head hung over the stall, ears pricked forward. Max leaned against the gate, playing along. He had a special bond with Outlaw, the first horse he'd rescued and trained.

Max pulled his pocketknife from his Levi's and sliced a wedge from the apple. "Mmmm...sure looks good." He brought the slice to his mouth, smacking his lips.

Just as his teeth sank into the chunk, Outlaw gave a demanding snort and butted his muzzle against Max's shoulder. Max had braced himself, prepared for the gentle assault. Outlaw was a big baby who liked to think he was the one in charge.

"What?" Max feigned surprise. "You want some of this?"

The horse nickered and nudged his shoulder again, harder this time.

Max smiled and cut another slice, holding it out in the flat of his palm. The horse lowered his head, feeling around for the treat with his lips. Only then, happy that he'd gotten his way, would Outlaw allow himself to be nuzzled and stroked.

"You're a big tough guy, huh?" Max said, scratching behind the horse's ear. While Outlaw munched on his treat, he allowed Max to stroke him between the eyes and along his broad neck. Outlaw could put on a good show, but he was gentle and patient with the kids who came to the ranch. Arabians were curious and friendly and had a natural aptitude for nurturing children — qualities that made them perfect for use in animal-assisted therapy. That made it even harder for Max to understand how anyone could abuse such a gentle animal.

Outlaw hadn't been as badly abused as the Arabian out in the field right now. Venus might never learn to trust humans again. He fed Outlaw the last of the apple then ran his hand once more down the horse's muzzle, stroking the coarse expanse between his eyes and nose.

Otis ambled up beside them. "I hear young Kitty Feathers is back in town."

Max grunted. "She wants to be called 'Kate' these days."

"That so?"

"Yep. Guess she's too good for the likes of us now. Big-shot city girl."

"Ain't nothing wrong with that," Otis said. "Your momma was a city girl."

Max had to smile. It was hard to imagine his mother being anything but a rancher's wife. Anne Connors had gotten dirty with the men, pitching in where she could, even helping to birth calves. The Triple-R ranch couldn't have run as efficiently as it had without her at the helm. She'd even been responsible for giving the ranch its name.

The way Max had heard it, a young, love-struck Otis Connors had allowed his new bride to name the ranch where they'd spend the rest of their lives raising children and cattle alike. Eyes sparkling, Anne had clapped her hands together and christened it the Rock Rose Ranch, after her favorite cactus blossom. The fact that the name remained was a testament to how much Otis adored his wife, although for as long as Max could remember, they'd simply called it the Triple-R.

"The difference is," Max grunted, "Kate *chose* to be a city girl." With that, he headed out of the stalls to see if he could coax Venus with the other apple.

He took his time approaching the wary animal, avoiding eye contact. Venus jerked her head aside and stepped back, shying away from him. She moved as far away from the gate as possible, until she couldn't retreat any farther then stood perfectly still, barely breathing as she watched Max approach. Her entire body shuddered to escape. Dark, liquid eyes pleaded with him not to come too close, not to hurt her.

"It's okay, girl," he soothed in soft, slow tones that seemed to calm her somewhat. He stopped a foot away, not wanting her to feel trapped, then began slicing the apple, hoping she'd come to him. She watched him, but her curiosity wasn't enough to overcome her fear. He took a bite then held out the wedge, only to have her look away.

"That's okay," he assured her. "We've got plenty of time. After awhile you'll see you're safe here. No one's ever gonna hurt you again."

He left the apple on the fence rail, turned his back and walked away. Only when he was halfway across the yard did she move forward with a cautious, lumbering grace. He sneaked a peek over his shoulder and saw her hesitate then begin nibbling at the remaining apple he'd left behind.

Chapter Four

§ာ

After the hustle and bustle of her day at the Tea and Crumpet Shop, the house felt too quiet. Kate had been looking forward to the time alone but instead found herself feeling smothered under the weight of memories. Everywhere she looked were reminders of her past. And nowhere was the past more evident than in Kate's old bedroom, which hadn't changed since the day she left. Her high-school yearbook lay open on the scarred oak desk, which had seen years of homework assignments, scribbled girlfriend notes and dreamy diary entries.

As always, the open bedroom window tempted her to escape. How many afternoons had she sat here yearning to be outside running free? For most of her life this small room had felt like a prison. She'd wanted to explore the world on the other side of that window, wanted to run farther than the eye could see. And she had. She'd crossed the Arizona borders, following the rising sun to a city where horses and pick-up trucks weren't the primary means of transportation. But she'd never really escaped. She'd simply carried her prison walls with her.

She flipped through the pages of her yearbook and came to a picture of the three of them—Kate, Max and his twin sister Sue. They looked so young, so carefree and innocent. Kate let out a wistful sigh. If she'd only known then how quickly everything would change.

The book opened naturally to the well-thumbed page with Max's senior picture. Even in the posed portrait, he exuded a relaxed confidence. An unruly curl escaped just-combed hair, making her reach out as if she could touch the past and brush the stray lock from his forehead. Her touch lingered over the cocky half-grin that seemed to mock the camera, fingers tracing slowly over those lips she knew could go from tender to demanding in a heartbeat.

In her mind she could still see him the way he was back then—cocky and sexy and so handsome it took her breath away. She used to stare at him in class for hours like a lovesick puppy. If she closed her eyes she could still feel his lips lingering over hers, could smell the sensual mix of earth and sunshine she associated with kissing Max Connors.

A whimper escaped her lips. *Damn him!* She slammed the yearbook shut and reached for her appointment book, slashing a red "X" through Saturday, Sunday and Monday. That still left eleven more days to get through before returning to her life. Her own life—a cramped two-room apartment in Manhattan that devoured most of her paycheck, concrete and bus fumes and long rides on sticky subways in a cold and lonely city. A city without Max.

Which was exactly what she wanted. Wasn't it?

She was saved from having to analyze that question too closely by a disturbance in the living room. A howling screech followed by the frantic scrabbling of claws on wood. Kate ran to the living room. Her mother's gray angora, Sophie Tucker, crouched in the corner, hissing and snarling. Back hunched defensively, the cat faced the cluttered roll-top desk where Lillian had kept her bills and papers for as long as Kate could remember.

"What's the matter Sophie?" Kate reached down, but the cat scrabbled out of reach and hid under the sofa. Kate shrugged and walked toward the desk. The surface was covered with piles of paperwork, every cubbyhole stuffed full with envelopes and invitations and index cards. Lillian had thrived on disorder.

Her mother's teacup, which Madam Zostra had insisted she bring home, lay upside down on top of an overflowing pile of papers. Kate vaguely remembered setting it on top of the desk when she'd come in. The cat must have knocked it over and scared herself. Kate reached for the cup, again feeling that same light tingling vibration ripple up her arm when she grasped the handle. It was almost as if the cup was trying to tell her something.

"What?" Kate cried out, glaring at the cup. "What do you want?"

Her scream of frustration sent the cat scurrying from the room. Kate lifted the cup, jostling the pile of papers and sending them in a skittering slide across the desk. A slim, buff-colored envelope slid free of the pile. "Last Will and Testament of Lillian E. Feathers" was scrolled across the top in a fancy, gothic script. Kate recognized the name of her mother's lawyer stamped on the bottom.

The cup hummed in her hand.

"Okay. Okay, I got it." Kate set the now-silent cup back on the desktop and sat down at the desk. She stared at the envelope, then back at the cup. "Fine. I'll have to do this eventually anyway." She shook her head and sighed. "Now's as good a time as any."

She read silently. The will was simple and straightforward. Basically, the house and property were to be divided equally between Kate and Jeff, with the request that they keep the business running in her absence. Absence? It sounded as if Lillian was only taking a short vacation.

There were a few small bequests to neighbors and friends. Kate glanced through the list, smiling. She could hear her mother's voice quoted amid the legal jargon. "To Bertha Pitt, I leave my secret hothouse chili recipe, since I told her she could have it over my dead body. To Vinny Keppelwhite, I leave the sum of five hundred dollars, if and when he takes down that stupid eyesore of a birdfeeder he made."

The list went on and on. It looked as if every soul in Easy would have something to remember Lillian Feathers by. Kate scanned to the end of the document. The balance of her mother's estate, which was considerable due to some smart financial planning and stock market windfalls, was to be divided equally between Kate and Jeff...*and Max*?

"What the hell?" Kate jumped up, sending the chair toppling behind her. "Max Connors? You've got to be kidding me," she shouted at the cup, as if it had an answer for her. Great, now she was yelling at a teacup!

"We'll just see about this," she muttered, to no cup in particular. She shoved the papers into her purse and stormed out the door. Max had some answering to do and by god, she was in just the mood to have it out with him once and for all.

* * * * *

Max led Outlaw back toward the stable. Sitting atop the gentle horse, his nephew Bobby chattered nonstop to the soft clop of the horse's hooves on the dry dirt path. Bobby loved riding Outlaw, but more than that, Max knew that the horse's gentle motions helped improve the boy's motor skills.

When Bobby had been diagnosed with cerebral palsy, Max and his sister had studied every article they could get their hands on. A few years ago Max had heard about a new method of treatment for cerebral palsy patients. Hippotherapy, or therapeutic horseback riding, literally meant "treatment with the help of a horse". According to the reports Max had read, the swinging rhythm of the horse's gait transferred to the patient's pelvis in a manner similar to a normal human gait. Hippotherapy improved muscle tone, equilibrium reactions, head and trunk control, coordination and spatial orientation, and was used to improve strength, balance and muscle tone.

All Max knew was that it made Bobby happy. And that made him happy too.

They'd started putting Bobby in a special harness and saddle to ride Outlaw for a few minutes a day. The first time they'd gotten Bobby up on the horse, his little face had lit up with a smile of pure wonder. For that reason alone Max continued Bobby's daily rides. He'd climb a cactus naked for one of his nephew's smiles.

In no time at all they'd seen a change in Bobby's walking. It hadn't happened overnight, but there was definite improvement. When they'd realized how much riding the horses had helped Bobby, Max and his sister opened the ranch to other disabled kids — a few at first, then more as word spread. Some of the children came from as far away as Phoenix for horse-assisted therapy.

Soon they'd had more kids than they could handle and they'd had to ask for volunteers. People from all over town answered the call and helped out in any way they could — sidewalking with the children, grooming the horses, cooling them out, cleaning tack. Lillian had been one of those volunteers. She'd taken a special shine to Bobby and the boy missed her terribly.

Max unbuckled the special harness that allowed Bobby to ride the horse. He lifted the child from Outlaw's back and swung him in the air. The heavy leg braces nearly doubled the boy's weight. Bobby wrapped his arms around Max's neck and giggled.

"Uncle Max?"

"Yeah, Champ?"

"You're almost as good at this as Miz Lilly."

Max helped Bobby out of the protective headgear and tousled his corn-silk hair. "Almost, huh?"

Bobby crinkled his nose. "Yep, 'cept you don't smell as good."

Max lowered his nephew to the ground and smiled indulgently. "If you worked around horses all day, you wouldn't smell so good either."

"I'm not saying you stink or nothin'," Bobby said seriously. "It's just that Miz Lilly always smelled like a birthday party." He curled his small hand around Max's. "You know, like cake and ice cream."

"You're right," Max said, remembering the hint of vanilla that always seemed to follow Lillian. He wasn't sure if it was a scent she wore, or whether the smells from the Tea and Crumpet Shop had settled into her very pores.

"Hey, Uncle Max? You think Miz Lilly can see us from up in heaven?"

Max raised his eyes skyward and smiled. "Oh, I'm sure she's keeping an eye on things from up there," he assured his nephew. "Miz Lilly liked to keep a finger in everyone's pie, right?"

Bobby's face curled up in a thoughtful frown. "Uncle Max?"

"Yeah, Champ?"

"If I get to heaven first, I'll say hello to Miz Lilly for you."

Max's chest tightened and fear gripped his heart, squeezing the breath from his lungs. His heart flipped and tumbled, and it was a moment before he could choke in a breath of dry desert air. "Don't talk like that, Champ," he croaked.

Bobby pursed his mouth, lower lip trembling. "It's true."

"No." Max stopped and knelt in the dirt, pulling Bobby roughly to his chest. "You're not gonna die. Hear me?"

Bobby shrugged. "Been thinking about it since Miz Lilly died. There ain't no cure for cerebral palsy."

That was true. But since Bobby's diagnosis, Max had become an authority on the disease. "Bobby, the damage that caused you to have cerebral palsy was done a long time ago. Probably before you were born. But it's not progressive...that means it won't get any worse."

Bobby searched Max's face, his eyes full of trust.

"Have I ever lied to you Champ?"

Bobby shook his head. "Nope."

"And I never will," Max said. "So trust me. You'll probably live as long as me. And with treatment—like riding Outlaw every day—your condition can improve. You'll always have to work at keeping your motor skills up, but as long as you do that, it won't get any worse than it is right now, understand?"

Bobby nodded, fighting back tears. "Mom doesn't talk to me about this stuff. She acts like it's my fault."

"Or hers," Max mumbled. He knew his sister harbored her own share of guilt over what she might have done or not done to cause her only child to be born with a disabling condition. But Bobby was too young to understand the way guilt, whether real or imagined, made a person act irrationally. "You can always talk to your favorite uncle, okay Champ?"

Bobby grinned. "You're my *only* uncle."

"Then I'm a shoe-in, huh?"

Bobby pretended to give the question some thought. "Maybe," he said, trying to hold back a grin.

Max raised an eyebrow. "Maybe? *Maybe*?" Max dug his fingers into Bobby's ribs, tickling the boy until he squirmed. "Whaddaya mean maybe?"

Bobby lost it then, breaking out in hysterical giggles. "Okay," he shouted. "I give up! You're my favorite uncle."

Max released his grip as Bobby collapsed against his chest. Max clutched the boy tight, wishing he could shelter him from the world. "All right then," he said. "And I don't want to hear no more foolish talk, okay?"

"Okay," Bobby agreed, wiping his eyes. Then more quietly, "I love you Uncle Max."

Max swallowed hard over a lump in his throat. "I love you too, Champ. I love you too."

Chapter Five

ဆ

Even after all this time, Kate still knew the way to Max's ranch. How could she forget the place she'd left her heart so long ago?

Her first glance of the Triple-R ranch came as a shock. Time hadn't been kind to the cattle farm. The once-grand main house had an air of gently fading dignity. In the distance she could see a vacant barn scarred by fire, but battered more by time and neglect.

Kate knew from her mother's letters that the steadily falling price of beef over the years had hurt many local ranchers. Most were losing money on every head of cattle they sold and had to lay off hands and sell acres a little at a time in order to survive.

The Triple-R no longer bustled with activity. It seemed to be slowly vanishing into a distant memory of itself, like a sepia photograph fading with time.

Kate hardened her heart. It was obvious the money from her mother's will would go a long way toward helping the Triple-R regain some of its glory, but she wouldn't let Max's financial plight allow him to take advantage of her mother's generosity, however misplaced.

As soon as Kate pulled onto the dirt road leading to the main house, she spotted Max mending fences out at the corral. The brim of his hat cast cool shadows over his face. Ten years in the city and Kate still couldn't shake the feeling that a man wasn't completely dressed without a Stetson.

She watched him from the safety of her car, each movement sure and smooth, taking as much care with the weathered planks of the corral as he had with the delicately carved moldings of Lillian's pantry cupboards. Then, as if sensing the heat of her gaze, he looked up, tipped the brim of his Stetson back and stared across the field toward her. She felt a jolt ripple through her body, as if he'd physically reached out and touched her.

He straightened and turned in her direction, thumbs hooked in the pockets of his jeans in a casual stance that belied the strength and power of lean, corded muscles beneath taut denim. His body language seemed to dare her to come to him, to make the first move. He seemed prepared to wait forever if he had to, as if warning her with his silent challenge that she was on *his* turf now.

Struggling to hold onto her anger, Kate stepped out of the car. The desert air was hot, dry and dusty, yet her skin felt clammy. Max leaned back against the fence rail and crossed his arms over his chest. His image wavered in the shimmering heat of the Arizona sun. The distance between them could have been measured in miles rather than yards. Kate wanted to turn and get back in her car, the desire to run away as strong now as it had been then.

No. Not again. She was through running from her past.

The first step was the hardest, but momentum carried her the rest of the way. She leaned forward, her head held high, chin thrust forward in defiance. As she drew closer, she tried to read the expression on Max's face, but it was an impenetrable mask.

Then he spoke, that slow, sexy drawl turning her to jelly inside. "Watch where you step, city girl."

She jerked to a stop and looked down at the ground. When he gave a quick snort of derision, she realized it had been a test—and she'd failed.

"Don't call me that," she grumbled. But he'd already broken her momentum and she stood rooted to the spot.

"City girl? Why not? Isn't that what you are now?" He gave her a slow, insolent assessment from head to toe, the curl of his lips saying just exactly what he thought of "city girls".

The cocky look on his face infuriated her. Ten years of suppressed anger seethed inside her, making her stomach churn. She'd lost everything because of him — her dreams, her scholarship and her reputation.

And still, after all this time, she couldn't confront him, couldn't vent the anger she'd kept bottled up inside. Not for herself and not for the innocent teenager she'd been so long ago.

But what she couldn't do for herself, she could find the strength to do in order to defend her mother. She stood up straight, challenging his insolence with her own righteous anger.

"So," she said, gesturing to take in the barns and fields. "Which are you? A rancher or a carpenter?"

He tilted his head, giving her a quizzical stare. "I do a lot of things."

"Oh? And just what did you do to weasel your way into my mother's will?"

He cocked an eyebrow. "Excuse me?"

"You heard me," she challenged, stepping closer. "Obviously you took advantage of her somehow."

"Took advantage, huh?" He seemed to chew on the words, a storm brewing behind his eyes.

Kate took no heed of the warning in his voice. She continued her rampage, poking a finger at his chest. "First you milked her for those fancy cabinets then you talked her into putting you into her will. God only knows what else you got out of her before then. What's your con, Max?"

"Con." He repeated the word as if it was foreign to him, nodding his head slowly. He looked at her, hurt and disappointment evident in his eyes. "You think I conned your mother out of her money." It was a statement rather than a question.

"Yes." But her voice faltered on the word. "Why else would she leave you a third of her estate?"

The statement seemed to surprise him. Either that or he was a better actor than she gave him credit for. Surely he knew just how much his share of the estate amounted to. Her mother had invested wisely, and the business was doing better than Kate ever could have imagined. Max had schemed his way into a nice chunk of money and she was determined to find out how.

"I could tell you why," he said. "But you wouldn't believe me, would you? Never have, never will."

Kate bristled at his tone of voice. Why should she? She'd learned her lesson a long time ago. Believing in Max had nearly been her undoing.

He shook his head. "You've changed, Kitty. You're not the same girl I used to know."

Anger stiffened her spine. "Yeah, I've changed. I'm not gullible anymore. I can't be charmed with smooth talk and pretty words and then…"

Kate stopped. This wasn't about her or what had happened between the two of them. It was about her mother and the money Max stood to inherit.

"And then…?" Max tipped his head, waiting for her to finish.

Kate shook her head, fighting back tears. Damn him! Why did it still hurt after all this time? She stood her ground. She'd run once before. But not this time. She made a sweeping gesture with her hand. "That's water under the bridge."

"I don't think it is," Max said. "You come storming out here sore as a rained-on rooster, accusing me of taking advantage of one of the sweetest ladies I've ever had the pleasure of knowing. You look at me with those big hurt eyes of yours like I'm some kind of monster. Come on, Kitty. You know me better than that. What did I ever do to make you hate me so much?"

Kate trembled. How could he look at her that way? Like *he* was the injured party?

He took his hat off and ran his fingers through his hair. "Okay," he said. "Maybe I wasn't the smartest kid back then. I know I pushed you, but still…that's no reason to treat me like this. And it sure as hell wasn't reason enough for you to leave town the way you did."

Kate blinked, remembering the night so long ago. Pushed her? He'd been all over her. Too many beers combined with too much testosterone. But she didn't blame him for that. It was what came afterward. The lies, the rumors, the snickering behind her back and everybody thinking she was easy—just like the sash she'd worn so proudly. Miss Easy County. Her cheeks burned with shame at the thought of how people must have laughed behind her back at the irony.

By that time the rumors had already been flying. Max must have told half the town he'd gotten lucky with little Kitty Feathers because after that night her name wasn't worth the paper it was scrawled on. The lies had spread like wildfire and by the time she'd realized her reputation was destroyed, it had been too late to take them back. The worst part was she hadn't deserved it. She'd kept her virtue, even to this day. But who'd believe her? Everyone—including Max—had been more than willing to believe the worst of her.

And then it had all come crashing down around her. Her crown, the scholarship it represented, along with all her hopes and dreams—she'd lost it all because of Max's lies. Time hadn't healed those wounds. If anything, it had only left deeper scars.

Kate shook with suppressed fury. She couldn't deal with this anymore. Seeing Max brought it all back, the pain as fresh as it was ten years ago. She wiped a hand over her eyes, as if she could erase the past.

"Kitty?" Max reached out and touched her arm.

Kate jerked away. "No. Don't call me that." It was petty, she knew, but Kate was the name of a woman in control of her life, while Kitty was a girl who let events control her.

Max dropped his hand to his side and stepped back, as if sensing she needed space between them. "Kate," he corrected. "A lot has changed while you've been gone."

"Yeah," she muttered. "Like the fact that you've got fifteen kids now."

Max blinked in surprise, then roared with laughter. "You could say that. As a matter of fact—"

"Look," Kate said, interrupting him. "I'm not here to talk about your personal life. I couldn't care less." The statement rang false to her own ears. She straightened her shoulders, forcing herself to face him without a tremor of regret. "I'm here to look out for my family's interest."

Max narrowed his eyes. "A little late for that, isn't it?"

Kate's jaw dropped. How *dare* he?

Max grabbed her arm, and this time he didn't let go when she tried to pull away. "I'm not the villain here," he said. "If you were so worried about your family, why didn't you come home and see how hard your mother had to work to make a living? If you thought someone was taking advantage of her, why didn't you come back to do something about it? Lillian prayed every single day for you to come home." His voice dropped to a low rumble, like distant thunder. "If you were so worried about protecting your family, then why did you leave in the first place?"

Kate trembled. How could he even ask? "I had my reasons," she said. "You of all people should know that."

She pulled away and this time he let her go, a look of puzzlement on his face. He shook his head from side to side. "No," he said. "I don't know. Why don't you tell me?"

Before she could do just that, however, a woman's voice called out, "Max! Dinner's ready."

Kate glanced at the woman standing at the porch railing. Her sundress fluttered in the breeze and one hand was raised to shield her eyes from the sun.

"Your wife's calling," she said when Max made no effort to move.

"I'm not married." He held her with a penetrating gaze. "That's my sister. You remember Sue, don't you?"

Kate nodded. Of course she remembered Sue. They'd been friends once, then competitors. What Kate remembered most was that when she'd been stripped of her crown, Sue had been waiting in the wings to take her place. Sue Connors' was only one in a long line of betrayals that had kept Kate from coming home again.

She spun on her heel. Escape was only a few feet away. But there was no escape from the bitterness she harbored inside. She knew from experience that no matter how far she ran, the whispers waited for her, nipping at her self-esteem in the darkest corners of the night.

From the doorway, Sue Conners watched her brother and Kitty Feathers arguing. She wished Kitty had never come back. Everything had been going just fine, but ever since Kitty Feathers came back to town Max had that sad look in his eyes again. He spent all his time working, as if he could burn off his frustration with physical labor.

All because of pretty little Kitty Feathers. She'd had it all...looks, brains and any boy she wanted. Everything seemed to come so easy for her—even the title of Miss Easy County. It had been down to the two of them, and Sue had had to fight back bitter tears when they laid the sash over Kitty's shoulder and placed the crown on her head. As first runner-up, Sue had pretended to be happy, while once again Kitty Feathers got everything—the chance to move on to the Miss Arizona Pageant, along with a scholarship and prizes.

Then along came Ed Tate with a grudge of his own. Between the two of them they'd destroyed Kitty completely, publicly stripping her of her title and all that went with it. After all, there could be no hint of a scandal associated with the Miss Arizona Pageant. One of the requirements of being a pageant participant was an unblemished reputation in the community. After Ed was done, Kitty Feathers could no longer claim to have good moral character. She'd been stripped of her crown and Sue had been crowned in her place. But the victory had been bittersweet.

Sue turned away from the doorway, guilt flaming her cheeks. All she'd wanted to do was take Kitty down a peg. But that was a long time ago. She'd been a different person then. And she'd wanted Kitty Feathers out of her way.

How was Sue to know Kitty would leave town in shame? How was she to know it would hurt the person she cared about most, nearly destroying Max?

Besides, it wasn't all her fault. She'd just put a bug in Ed's ear and he'd done the rest. But as hard as she tried, Sue couldn't justify what she'd had a hand in doing to Kitty. And she couldn't think of a way to make it right now. If Max ever found out…

She didn't want to think about it. He'd never forgive her. Sue glanced back to where Max stood shaking his head, watching as Kitty turned on her heel and stormed away. Sue hoped Kitty Feathers left town for good this time.

The sooner she was back in New York, the sooner things would get back to normal here.

Max watched Kate storm off. "Women," he muttered under his breath. He'd never understand them. Only when Kate's car was no more than a shimmering spot on the horizon did he turn and head for the house.

Sue met him at the porch. "Was that Kate Feathers you were talking to?"

Max answered with a grunt. He scraped his boots and headed inside, followed by Sue and a thousand questions.

"I heard she was back in town. How long is she gonna stay?"

Max shrugged. He didn't want to talk about Kate, but knew that Sue wouldn't stop hounding him until her curiosity was satisfied. "Couple of weeks, from what I hear. Then she's heading back to the big city."

Sue exhaled a breath that sounded like a sigh of relief. Max shot a questioning glance in his sister's direction.

She shrugged, color rising to her cheeks. "I just don't want to see you hurt again, that's all."

"I can take care of myself," he assured her.

She turned, but not before Max saw a quick flash of worry cross her face. Geez, what was it with him and women today? He couldn't seem to say anything right. Max washed up then settled down at the table. Unfortunately, his run-in with Kate had spoiled his appetite.

Chapter Six

ℰ

Still seething over Kate's rejection the day before, Ed Tate paced back and forth in his mother's small kitchen, looking for all the world like a lion confined in a too-small cage. And his mood wasn't much better than that of a caged lion either. He turned up the volume of his stereo until the pulsing beat of BTO's "Taking Care of Business" drummed like a war chant through his veins. Oh, he'd be taking care of business all right. Damn straight! And the first order of business was Easy's own prodigal daughter, Kate Feathers.

"Uppity bitch," he growled. "I'll show her once and for all."

And he would too. He'd show Kate Feathers and Max both. Thought they were so much better than everyone else. Always puttin' on airs and acting too damn good for other people. Even other people who made something of themselves, like pulling themselves up by their bootstraps and becoming deputy sheriff — maybe even sheriff someday. And they still looked down their noses. Just who the hell were they, anyway? Some useless cowboy who was long on charm and short on brains, and a city girl who ran away when things didn't go her way. Well fuck 'em both. He'd show them who ran this town.

Ed Tate Jr., that's who. Yeah. He curled his thumbs beneath his waistband, hitched his pants up and stood straighter. Tipping his head back, he slugged down the last of his beer and slammed the bottle on the counter. He was the man — the man with the badge. Edward Lamar Tate Jr. was a force to be reckoned with, and it was about damn time that certain people in this town realized it.

Especially people who hadn't learned their lessons the first time around.

"Ya find it yet, Ma?" he called out.

"Not yet," Ginny Tate yelled back. Her voice was muffled, as if she had her head half buried in a closet, which in fact she did.

"For Christ's sake," Ed howled. "You were married to the man. Didn't you save any of his stuff?"

Ginny stormed out of the bedroom, hands on hips, puffing a limp strand of hair off her forehead. "It was a long time ago," she screamed back at her son. "And we were only married six months before he croaked on me."

"Well, if you'd find that damn paper, those six months might end up being worth it."

"Oh, it was worth it all right," Ginny gloated. She'd never forget the look on Lillian's face when she'd waltzed away with her man. Jebediah Feathers was a handsome scoundrel who knew how to make a woman smile, that's for sure. And Ginny had done plenty of smiling, wallowing in her triumph over Lillian Feathers.

But her victory hadn't lasted long. After only six short months, she'd buried her new husband, along with the pleasure of having something Lillian still wanted. Of course, half the people in town acted as if Lillian were the grieving widow, forgetting that Jebediah Feathers had shared Ginny's bed for the last six months of his life.

"Ma!"

At her son's warning, Ginny turned and stalked back to the bedroom, muttering under her breath. She didn't know why Ed was so intent on finding that slip of paper. It wouldn't hold up in a court of law. If she thought it would, she'd have used it against Lillian a long time ago. She should never have told Ed about it in the first place.

It just rankled her that Lillian had managed to pick herself up and turn that run-down old shop into the classiest business in town. And now, barely cold in her grave, people were starting to talk about her like she was some kind of saint, running a successful business all these years and raising her kids alone — and don't think Ginny didn't see the looks they cast her way when they pointed *that* out. As if she was some kind of scarlet woman or something.

The fact that Lillian was dead didn't dilute Ginny's resentment. If anything, she was even more determined to prove she was the better woman.

If Ed's plan worked, she'd have it all — the shop and the town's respect. They'd forget that Lillian Feathers ever existed.

* * * * *

Kate was still seething from her confrontation with Max the day before. She'd gone to the ranch to confront him and he'd put her on the defensive, making her feel weak and ashamed. But she wasn't done. She'd have it out with him one way or another. Just not today. She was feeling too vulnerable to go on the attack. She needed fortification.

Only two days behind the counter of the Tea and Crumpet Shop, and if Kate never saw another teapot again, it would be too soon. She needed coffee. Straight, black and pumped up with as much caffeine as the law and Juan Valdez would allow. A cup of that sludge they sold at the corner store wouldn't do. She needed fresh-brewed — a whole pot of it. She wanted to drown in an ocean of coffee.

If she had to be here for two weeks, she might as well invest in her own coffeepot. And a thermos, she decided. She could sneak in her own supply of coffee and no one at the Tea and Crumpet Shop would be the wiser.

Kate stood in the center of the department store's appliance aisle. Who knew they made so many brands and types of coffeemakers? Her mind went blank. Suddenly making one more decision was just too much to handle. She wanted to go home, to her own apartment, with a Starbuck's on the corner and not a single cowboy or red pick-up truck in sight. And best of all, no memories to haunt her. No prying eyes watching her every move, judging her and whispering behind her back.

Her fists clenched, fingernails leaving crescent-shaped depressions in the fleshy pad of her palm. How dare these small-minded people judge her? How dare they take away all of her dreams and never even give her a chance to defend herself?

And after all this time, why should she still care?

Kate stood straight, head held high. She wouldn't let the small-town gossip get to her. Ignoring the throbbing at her temple, Kate grabbed the first coffeemaker she saw, not caring if it brewed ten cups or twelve, whether it had an automatic shut-off or timer or came with its own live-in butler. She just needed a decent cup of coffee until she could get out of this backwater town once and for all. And this time she'd never come back.

Not for all the tea in China. She grimaced at her own pathetic joke, choking back a sudden wave of hysteria.

"Kitty? Kitty Feathers, is that you?"

Kate whipped around at the vaguely familiar voice. The woman balancing a chubby baby on her hip was just as vaguely familiar. A name danced around the corners of Kate's memory...*Carol? Cheryl? Carly?*

The woman advanced on Kate, the baby bouncing with each step. "Oh my God, it *is* you! I heard you were in town, but I thought you'd left already."

The woman threw one arm around Kate and gave her a gentle hug, enveloping her in warmth and the scent of baby powder. The baby burped, adding a current of sweet banana breath to the mixture.

And just as suddenly, Kate put a name to the face. Cheryl Quillan. They'd been on the pep squad and yearbook committee together. Little by little, more memories slipped into place—picnics and bonfires and pajama parties. Kate was unprepared for the flood of carefree memories, which had for so long been overshadowed by bad ones.

Kate stepped back and studied the woman before her. The Cheryl she remembered had been younger, thinner. But this older version had the same unruly mass of dark curls and the same sparkling eyes with a devilish glint, as if daring Kate to sneak a cigarette with her in the girls' room of Easy County High.

Kate couldn't help smiling. "Cheryl, you look great!"

"Nah. You do, though. Has it really been ten years? You don't look a day older than you did at graduation."

The baby reached out and gripped a handful of Kate's hair. Without missing a beat in the conversation, Cheryl untangled the baby's fingers with a gentle admonishment. "No, TJ," she said then turned back to Kate. "Are you staying in town for the reunion?"

Kate wondered how many times she'd have to answer that question before the two weeks were over. She couldn't have picked a worse time to be back in town. "No," she said. "I'm only here long enough to help put things in order while my brother's away."

Cheryl shifted the baby on her hip and reached out to squeeze Kate's hand. "I was sorry to hear about your mother."

"Thank you." And then, to avoid the embarrassed silence that always followed whispered condolences, Kate turned her attention to the baby. "And this little fellow is TJ?"

"Named after his daddy," Cheryl said, adoration shining in her eyes as she stroked the baby's strawberry-blonde peach fuzz.

TJ gave Kate a toothless smile. His head bobbed. "Da!" he said, either sneezing or confirming that he was named after his father. Kate couldn't be sure which.

"Not Tommy John Anderson?" Kate asked, remembering a gangly redhead who was a year ahead of them in high school. If she remembered correctly, he was also president of the Chess Club.

"That's the one," Cheryl confirmed. "It took him long enough to get around to asking me to marry him, but he finally did."

"You look happy," Kate said. It was true. Cheryl had been a bubbly teenager, but now she glowed with an inner contentment. Married life and motherhood obviously agreed with her.

"I am," Cheryl said. "Hey, I have an idea. Why don't you come over for dinner Friday night? Unless you have plans…"

Kate didn't, other than brooding around a too-quiet house or remembering how Max looked strutting around the shop in too-tight jeans.

"Isn't that blasphemous?" Cheryl asked.

Kate blinked, afraid for a moment that Cheryl had read her thoughts about Max.

But Cheryl was pointing at the coffeemaker in Kate's shopping cart. "Aren't you in the tea business?"

"Not by choice," Kate admitted with a smile. "And to be honest, I never really cared much for tea. Coffee is my drug of choice." She gave Cheryl a conspiratorial wink. "But that'll be our little secret, okay?"

"My lips are sealed." Cheryl made a locking motion over her lips. TJ mistook the gesture for one he was more familiar with and started blowing bubble-smacking kisses in every direction. He was very good at it.

Let me give you my address and number," Cheryl said, balancing the baby on one hip while leaning in the opposite direction to dig one-handed into her overstuffed purse.

Kate reached out, offering to hold TJ while Cheryl fumbled for pen and paper. The baby held out his pudgy hands, stubby little fingers snapping open and closed in the universal "take me" gesture. When Kate lifted him, he curled perfectly into the crook of her arm, nuzzling his face against the side of her neck. He smelled fresh and sweet in the way only babies and bakeries can, triggering maternal yearnings Kate never knew she had.

As soon as Cheryl finished scribbling her address and phone number, Kate handed the baby back. His softness was too tempting and she couldn't afford to add one more desire to the list of things she couldn't have.

Kate tucked the address into her purse as they said their goodbyes, already looking forward to an evening of home cooking and hospitality. Winding through the department store aisles, she picked up a coffee grinder, fresh roasted beans and a mug. Delicate bone china was fine for tea, but coffee deserved a sturdy mug.

Kate's step was lighter as she finished her shopping and she didn't feel quite so alone in the town she no longer called home. At least there was one person who smiled and offered a hand in welcome.

* * * * *

Max felt like he'd been rode hard and put away wet. No matter how long he worked, there were still too many chores and not enough hands on the ranch to help out. At this rate, he wasn't sure how much longer he could keep the ranch going.

But that was the least of his problems. The work couldn't take his mind off Kate. He kept going over their encounter in his mind, but it didn't make sense. Why was she so angry with him?

Her accusations had left him speechless. She'd claimed he'd taken advantage of her once before, that she wasn't that young, foolish girl anymore. Then she'd stormed off in a cloud of dust and anger, leaving him for the second time in his life. He couldn't help but wonder just who had taken advantage of whom.

He remembered the last time she'd run out on him. They'd been dating seven months, and things were getting serious. It had been a week before the prom and they'd gone to the drive-in. He'd snuck a six-pack into the cooler that night and drank five cans to Kitty's one. The rest of his memory was a little hazy, but things had gotten hot and heavy in the backseat. He remembered wanting her so badly that he thought he'd explode. They'd argued. She'd pushed him away. He'd tried to make up, but his mind hadn't been working right and he'd said all the wrong things. But jeez, she had to know he wouldn't have forced himself on her. Didn't she?

He never did get the chance to prove it. She'd stormed out of his car, angry and in tears. At first he'd just sat there, sure she'd cool off and come back. But she hadn't. He'd waited, but eventually the beer got the best of him and he'd ended up sleeping off the alcohol alone in the backseat. When he came to, the drive-in was clearing out and there was no sign of Kate.

The next day he'd heard she'd gone home with Ed Tate. If it had been anyone else, Max probably would have just blown it off. But Ed Tate? That hurt his pride more than anything. He'd waited for Kate to call and apologize for dumping him for Ed, but she hadn't. A week had gone by. Maybe if *he'd* called, things would have been different.

Stubborn, that's what he was.

Next thing he knew, Kate had stood him up for the prom. Max had stayed home rather than watch her dancing with some other guy—especially Ed Tate. But Sue had told him that Kate had been seen the next morning sneaking out of some seedy motel with Tate. So much for keeping her virginity. She'd made him the laughing stock of high school after that…the only boy who hadn't gotten a piece of the action. He'd tried to ignore the rumors, tried not to believe them, but it seemed every guy in the locker room had a story to tell about Kitty Feathers.

Most of all, he remembered Ed Tate's smug smile afterward, the way he'd looked at Max as if he'd finally succeeded in getting something Max didn't have first. Then the months when Kate wouldn't answer his calls and the snickering and gossip grew and spread until he thought he was the only man left in town who hadn't slept with Kitty Feathers. She'd taken his love and thrown it back in his face. And all the time he was left wondering how she could have changed so completely and quickly.

And yet he'd still hoped she'd come to her senses and they'd manage to straighten things out. But before he knew it, she was gone, changing her plans to attend Arizona State with him and running off to New York City. When had she decided that? And *still* he'd held onto the possibility that she'd come back home after college. She hadn't.

Not until now. And now she was back with a chip on her shoulder, acting like *she* was the injured party, when she'd been the one to dump him and strut around town like some little—

Sue brought him a cup of coffee, interrupting his thoughts. She placed the mug on the table and sat across from him. "So, you never said what Kate Feathers wanted."

Max blew on the steaming coffee then took a deep swallow. *She wanted to tear a strip off my backside, that's what she wanted.* But Max didn't say that out loud. "Something about Lillian's will."

Sue's eyes lit up. "Lillian always said she'd leave something to the ranch someday. I thought it was just idle talk."

"Guess not."

Sue ran one hand up and down her arm. "Did she say how much?"

"Doesn't matter," Max said, setting his mug on the table. "I'm not taking it."

"Max!"

"We're doing just fine without it," he said.

"That's not true and you know it. Every day we fall deeper and deeper in debt. If we keep going the way we are, we'll lose the ranch by the end of the year. What about Bobby? And the other kids?"

That took some of the wind out of Max's sails. His pride was one thing, but he couldn't let the kids down. Not after all the good they'd done here.

"Lillian believed in what we're doing," Sue insisted. "She would have wanted the money to be used to keep the ranch going, to keep the kids in therapy."

"I'll find another way." If he had to work around the clock to keep the ranch running, he would. But he'd be damned if he'd take one red cent from Kate Feathers.

Chapter Seven

೫つ

Kate balanced the bags from the department store in her arms and fiddled with the lock on the front door. The key was stuck. Knowing her mother, Kate figured Lillian probably hadn't used it in years. No one locked their doors in Easy County.

She jiggled the key, one bag slipping dangerously as she tried to unlock the door.

"Need a hand?"

Kate turned, and Ed Tate took a bag from her arms before it could slide from her grasp.

"Thanks," she muttered, finally getting the key to turn in the lock.

She opened the door and Ed followed her inside. She turned to retrieve the bag but he shook his head.

"I've got it," he said. "Just tell me where you want it."

"Put it on the counter there," Kate said, hoping he wouldn't hang around too long. She had a pounding headache and wanted a cup of coffee so bad she could taste it, but didn't dare attempt to unwrap her newly purchased coffeemaker. Ed might take that as an unspoken invitation.

She dropped the rest of her bags on the couch and turned to face him. "Thanks for helping, but I'm a little pressed for time."

He didn't take the hint, instead leaning back against her mother's roll-top desk and settling in for what seemed to be a long chat. "It's good to see you again, Kate. Sorry it had to be under such tragic circumstances."

Kate nodded. Maybe if she just heard him out he'd get to the point and leave that much sooner.

"We had some good times back then."

She hoped he wasn't going to get all nostalgic. She wasn't in the mood for a trip down memory lane.

"Have you thought any more about the reunion? My offer still stands." He winked, as if offering her the moon and the stars and just waiting for her to leap at the opportunity.

"I really don't think so," Kate said. "I'm just here long enough to get my mother's things in order and hold down the fort until Jeff and Sally return from their honeymoon."

Ed's smile vanished. His eyes became cold, sending a shiver down Kate's spine. Her annoyance turned to alarm at finding herself alone with him. Suddenly she didn't feel so safe.

"Funny," he said. "Despite our family's differences, there's always been a connection."

Kate blinked, not sure what he was talking about at first.

"I mean, Jeff and Sally getting married. Who'd have thought there'd be a Tate-Feathers union someday? Of course, that's not the first time…"

Kate knew what he was getting at. The day Kate's father left and ran off with Ginny Tate it had seemed as if their whole world had fallen apart. But Lillian had worked hard to keep their little family together and held her head up high.

Jebediah Feathers had married Ginny Tate and for a few months, Ed had actually been her stepbrother. He was right. Despite the long-standing feud, there'd always been some strange connection between the two families. Now that Jeff and Sally were married, Ed was her brother-in-law. But if the look in his eyes was any indication, he wanted the connection to be even stronger. Kate shuddered. That was the last thing she wanted.

Ed watched her, as if reading her thoughts, a look of animal cunning on his face. "You know," he said finally, "I always thought maybe you and I would be the ones to put an end to the feud once and for all."

He waited for her response. She wasn't sure what to say, so she made a joke instead. "Not gonna happen," she said. "Who would take me seriously if my name was Kate Tate?"

Ed didn't even crack a smile. She should have known better than to try to appeal to his nonexistent sense of humor.

Kate took a deep breath and changed the subject. "There's no more feud," she said, inching farther away from him. "Jeff and Sally are married, Lillian's gone, I'm going back to New York and what happened with my father and your mother was a long time ago. It's over."

Ed watched her carefully. Then, as if coming to a decision, he straightened. "Not quite over," he said.

Again Kate noticed the chill in his eyes. She was glad she hadn't come right out and rejected him directly. There was no telling what he was capable of if pushed too far.

"I'm afraid I have some bad news," he said.

Kate rubbed the bridge of her nose and sighed, trying to push away the headache that had settled there. She wasn't sure she could take any more bad news. Not today, not ever. She just wanted to get back to her quiet, solitary life without all of this small-town intrigue. She wanted to get as far away from Easy as she could.

She took a deep breath then let it out slowly. "What bad news?"

Ed looked away, then back again. "It's about your mother's estate."

Kate shook her head. Did he know about her mother leaving a third of her estate to Max? And why should that concern him? She knew that Ed and Max had always been competitive, but had hoped they'd outgrown that boyhood rivalry by now.

Ed cleared his throat. "I hate to bring this nasty business up at a time like this," he said, not looking the least bit unhappy about it, "but when your father died, he left everything he had to my mother."

Kate nodded. If she recalled correctly, her father hadn't had much at the time other than the clothes on his back. They'd struggled to make ends meet, and if Lillian hadn't opened the Tea and Crumpet Shop on that run-down piece of property...

Kate blinked, comprehension coming slowly. *The property.*

As if sensing the understanding she'd come to, Ed nodded. "Your father's name was on the title to that property."

"No," Kate said, refusing to believe what she was hearing.

Ed nodded. "I'm afraid so. And as his legal heir, the property reverted to my mother on his death."

"But that was years ago," Kate argued. "It wasn't worth a plugged nickel back then. My mother built the shop and turned it into a thriving business. If your mother had any claim to it, why didn't she come forward sooner? Why now?"

"Well, contrary to what your family always thought," Ed explained, "my mother is a tender-hearted person. She felt bad enough falling in love with Jebediah and leaving you kids without a father. She didn't want to take the food out of your mouths as well by claiming her rightful ownership of the property."

That was a load of bull and they both knew it. Kate felt her fury mounting. Her mother's body wasn't even cold and the vultures were circling, picking away bits and pieces of everything she'd worked so hard for. First Max and now the Tates.

"So let me get this straight," Kate said, her voice tight with anger. "Out of the goodness of her heart, Ginny Tate let my mother build a successful business on this property. And in all these years she didn't so much as whisper a word about claiming her share until now? Is that right?"

"Like I said, my mother is a compassionate person. She wanted to leave Lillian with some dignity."

Kate snorted. That was as far from the truth as humanly possible.

"But now," Ed continued, "with Sally and Jeff married... Well, she just figures it would be best to keep the business in the family. We can all work together as co-owners of the Tea and Crumpet Shop."

"Over my dead body," Kate snarled.

"Now, Kate, I assure you it's all legal—"

Before he could finish the sentence, he jerked forward and howled. He pulled his hand away from where it had been resting on her mother's desk. The cup she'd left there began rocking at the sudden motion, clattering in its saucer.

Ed held up his finger. "What the hell? Something bit me!"

Kate looked from his hand to Lillian's cup, a strange and sudden thought coming to her. Hadn't the cup seemed to thrum in her hands when she'd held it? What had Madame Zostra said when she'd looked into it? That her mother was trying to tell her something. And now...

She shook her head. No, that wasn't possible. Her mother hadn't come back to haunt her in a teacup.

"Let me see," Kate said, inspecting Ed's finger. There was a tiny puncture wound and a single drop of blood hovering at the tip of his finger. He might have leaned against something sharp—maybe a pin or the edge of a letter opener. Kate looked around the desk, ignoring the teacup. There was no sign of anything sharp on the desk.

Then she heard a soft mewl. "Sophie?" She knelt and called the cat, who slunk around the side of the desk, her back arched and tail bristling. Sophie gave Ed Tate a wide berth and leaped into Kate's arms.

"It was just the cat," Kate said, feeling relieved and a little silly for letting thoughts of supernatural events enter her mind. "You must have scared her."

Ed narrowed his eyes. "Has that thing had rabies shots?" He pulled a handkerchief from his pocket and wrapped it around his finger.

Kate had all she could do to keep from laughing. What a big baby. Maybe she should offer to call an ambulance or wrap a tourniquet around his finger. "Sophie has had all her shots, I assure you. You'll live."

Kate turned her back and carried Sophie into the kitchen. The cat trembled in her arms. "It's okay, baby. Everything's okay." If only Kate could believe that. It seemed as if the whole world was crumbling around her. She hated the thought of spoiling Jeff's honeymoon, but she needed to talk to him. She couldn't handle all of this on her own.

She'd almost forgotten Ed was still in the house, so when he came up behind her, she nearly jumped right out of her skin.

"There's still a chance we can make this a real family affair," he whispered close to her ear.

Kate felt trapped. His smarmy voice made her skin crawl. She turned, holding the cat between them like a shield. Ed backed off when the cat hissed.

Kate knew she should back off as well, but she was tired of being pushed around and she had a headache and she was sick of being stuck in this town with people like Ed Tate Jr. who still thought she was nothing more than an easy score.

"Look," she said, pressing a palm against his chest. "I thought I made it clear to you a long time ago that I'm not interested." Her voice rose shrilly. "I wasn't interested then and I'm not interested now. I have no intention of going to the reunion, and if I did you'd be the last person on earth I'd go with. Is that clear?"

Ed took another step back, as if she'd slapped him.

"I'm sorry," she said. "It's just been a rotten day and I've had nothing but bad news." She shook her head and sighed, already regretting her outburst.

The fury in Ed's eyes was nothing compared to the chill in his voice as he turned away. "I'll be back with the paperwork," he said finally. "Once we clear up this outstanding lien on the property, you can be on your way back to New York City..."

Kate caught the rest of his muttered threat as he stormed out the door.

"...or to hell for all I care."

Kate knew she'd made an enemy but didn't care. If it meant not having to fend off any more of his unwanted advances, it was worth it. When she was sure Ed had driven away, she closed the door and locked it. She stood there a moment, resting her head on the cool wooden panel.

Who could she turn to? Certainly not Max. She wasn't even sure if she could reach her brother on the cruise ship. She'd have to handle this all by herself. She blinked away tears of frustration. How much worse could things get?

Slowly she became aware of a soft, faraway sound. Music. She lifted her head and listened, wondering where it was coming from. Less than a week away from New York and already she'd grown accustomed to the peaceful quiet of Arizona. Back in her apartment she wouldn't even have noticed the soft tune over the hum of traffic and street sounds. But here the break in the silence couldn't be ignored.

Kate turned and tilted her head, listening. She knew there was no radio or television on in the house. She walked toward the center of the room, trying to zero in on the sound. The closer she got to her mother's desk, the clearer it became.

Kate stared, suddenly sure that the cup was the source of the music. If she didn't know better, she'd swear the cup was singing.

Singing?

She was losing her mind. She always knew staying in town would make her crazy, and here was the ultimate proof.

Kate tried to convince herself she was only imagining the song echoing from the depths of the teacup. She'd been under a lot of stress. There was no other explanation. Even Lillian wasn't stubborn enough to reach out from beyond the grave. Was she?

Kate reached out and lifted the cup. Again she felt that soft, humming vibration, as if the cup was alive. But it wasn't the jolting bite that Ed had felt. This was more like a soothing caress. Without thinking, Kate lifted the cup to her ear, like a child listening to the sounds of the ocean in a seashell.

And there it was — the honey-smooth voice of Roy Orbison singing "Crying" from the depths of her mother's teacup.

That didn't surprise her as much as it should have. Roy Orbison had always been her mother's favorite singer and as long as Kate could remember the house had been filled with his music. A tear trickled down her cheek as the poignant tune played in her ear. This, more than anything else, brought her mother vividly to mind. Kate could almost see Lillian dancing in the kitchen, her Roy Orbison tape playing over and over as she sang along to each and every song, swaying to the slow tunes and kicking up her heels to one of his rockabilly classics. "His voice can break your heart," Lillian had often said. "But his songs make me feel like I can reach out and touch the sky."

Kate felt it too. There was sadness and hope and loss and love and regret, every emotion pure and true. She closed her eyes and swayed, letting the loneliness and pain speak to her. And with the music came healing tears.

When both had run their course, Kate straightened, ready to face whatever challenges awaited her.

The cup was silent and still, as if it had used up every ounce of energy to send Kate a message of hope. She carried it carefully to the kitchen and placed it on the windowsill. If a part of her mother's spirit still lingered in her favorite teacup, Kate was sure she'd want to look out the window and once more feel as if she could reach out and touch the sky.

Chapter Eight

ଛ

Max barely touched his dinner. Sue had made his favorite— red-hot chili and jalapeno cornbread—but he'd sat there staring at it as if it held the secrets of the universe. His mind was a million miles away. Well, not really a million. More like about ten, but it could have been a million.

He'd let three days go by without stopping in to see Kate, hoping she'd come to her senses.

She hadn't.

Time was running out. In one short week Kate would be on her way back to New York with nothing resolved between them. It looked like it was going to be up to him to make the next move.

He hated knowing that Kate thought the worst of him. It was one thing when she wasn't around and he couldn't see the accusation in her eyes. But to stand right in front of her and not be able to touch her or soothe her or tell her she'd misjudged him was unbearable.

He'd thought he was over her, but nothing could be further from the truth. Seeing her again made him realize he'd spent the last ten years waiting for her to come to her senses. So what was he gonna do? Let her get away again?

Hell no. Not without a fight.

He still had a week to straighten things out and convince her to stay. It was either that or toss Outlaw in a trailer and follow her back to New York City. Either way he wasn't going to let another ten years go by without resolving whatever had gone wrong in the first place. If Kate were anything like her mother, she'd be fair and at least hear him out.

Thinking about Lillian, Max smiled. Even though he had no intention of taking the money she'd left, he couldn't help feeling humbled by her good intentions. It was just like Lillian to try to provide for the ranch in her will. And maybe, in a secret place in her heart, Lillian had always hoped that Kate would return to Max and be a part of the ranch. She'd talked about her daughter every chance she had, and he'd often wondered if Lillian was trying to make sure he'd never forget Kate.

Not likely.

"Hey Uncle Max?"

Max pushed his plate away and looked across the table at Bobby. "Yeah Champ?"

Bobby gave him a gap-toothed smile. "Mom made pie. Peach pie."

"Oh she did, did she?" Max glanced over at Sue. "And what's the occasion?"

Sue shrugged. "Nothing. You just looked like…I don't know."

"Like a guy who needed pie?"

She smiled. "Yeah, just like that."

Max stared at his sister. She looked away. Maybe it was just his imagination, but there seemed to be something furtive—almost guilty—in the way she avoided his gaze. Or maybe he was just being paranoid. After his argument with Kate, he imagined all kinds of things he might have done wrong. Damn, he had to clear things up. He was no good to anyone moping around like this, and he'd have Sue baking a mountain of pies if he didn't cheer up.

"Why don't you save me a piece," he said, pushing his chair back and getting up from the table.

"Where are you going?" Her eyes widened.

"Just going into town for a bit. I won't be long."

Bobby perked up. "Can I go too?"

"Not tonight Champ," Max said, ruffling the boy's hair. "Something I gotta take care of alone."

Sue walked him to the door. "Are you going to see Kate?"

"Yeah. I hate the way things are between us. I just want to see if I can figure out how to fix it."

"Maybe there're some things that can't be fixed," Sue said softly.

"Maybe. Maybe not. All I know is I gotta try."

He started to turn but she grabbed his arm. "Max?"

He could feel her trembling. Her lower lip quivered. "Hey," he said. "What's wrong?"

She dropped her hand from his arm and lowered her eyes. But not before he noticed the shimmer of tears.

"Nothing," she said. "I just…I just love you, that's all."

Max pulled her close and wrapped his arms around her. "I love you too, Sis. And I promise to be back real soon for some of that pie."

She put on a brave smile then stepped back and patted his arm. "We'll be here when you get back."

Max climbed into his pick-up and drove away.

Sue stood in the doorway, watching long after he was gone.

* * * * *

Kate picked up a bottle of Merlot on her way to Cheryl's house. After the week she'd had, a little wine would ease some of the tension. She had half a mind to cancel her plans for dinner, sit home with the whole bottle and get sloppy drunk. But the house was too quiet and she was afraid that if she started drinking she'd be holding conversations with a teacup before the night was over.

The week had slipped by faster than Kate expected. Between keeping busy at the shop during the day and putting her mother's affairs in order at night, she'd barely had time to even think about Max.

Well, not much anyway.

He hadn't come into the shop at all. She couldn't count the number of times she'd looked up as a customer came through the door, half expecting to see Max saunter inside. When he didn't, she wasn't sure whether to feel disappointed or relieved. At least tonight she wouldn't be wandering through an empty house, determined not to answer a phone that didn't even have the decency to ring.

Cheryl's house was easy to find. Driving along the outskirts of town, Kate recognized local landmarks—parks, churches and restaurants. Some of the names had changed, and there were more fast-food drive-ins than she remembered, but basically the small town of Easy was almost exactly the way she'd left it.

The house itself was a modest but well-kept single-family home on a quiet road. A covered patio overlooked a private yard with citrus trees, a child's swing set and a slightly dented plastic kiddie pool. It looked homey and happy. Just the kind of atmosphere Kate needed tonight.

Cheryl met her at the door with a warm, welcoming hug. "I'm so glad you could make it."

"Me too," Kate said. And she was. "I brought this," she said, offering Cheryl the bottle of wine.

Cheryl looked at the label. "Oh good. Merlot. This will go perfect with franks and beans."

At Kate's blank stare, Cheryl laughed and pulled her inside. "I was just kidding. Geez, New York sure has spoiled your sense of humor."

"It wasn't New York that did it," Kate admitted. "But we'll save that discussion until after we've opened the wine."

Cheryl's husband met them in the living room. He gave Kate a genuine hug and told her she looked wonderful. Kate wouldn't have recognized Tommy Anderson. He'd lost the gangly, adolescent awkwardness she remembered and matured into a fine-looking man. His glasses had been replaced by contacts and a neatly trimmed beard softened the lines of his face.

"Da!" The demand came from the kitchen.

Cheryl turned, but Tommy patted her shoulder. "I'll finish feeding him. You girls catch up."

The look of adoration on Cheryl's face when she smiled at her husband tugged at Kate's heart. She realized, had circumstances been different, this might be what her own life would have been like if she'd stayed in Easy—a home, a husband and kids, but most of all a feeling of complete contentment.

Cheryl led Kate to a comfortable overstuffed sofa. "So tell me what New York is really like," she said.

"Bigger than I had imagined," Kate said. "It's a lot like any major city—bustling with excitement, humming with activity. You get an adrenaline rush just walking down the street." Kate expected to feel a wave of homesickness for her tiny apartment in the city, but it didn't come. Her life there was already starting to feel like a dream.

They made small talk, catching up on the last few years, and soon Tommy came back carrying TJ. The baby held his arms out to Cheryl as soon as he spotted her.

"The baby's fed and the wine is chilling," Tommy said, handing TJ over to Cheryl.

"Fish are jumping and the cotton is high," Cheryl quipped.

Kate laughed—the first real laugh she remembered having since arriving in town. She felt comfortable, and that feeling extended over the course of the evening. After TJ was put to bed for the night, they enjoyed a relaxing dinner. Tommy excused himself after dessert while Cheryl and Kate loaded the dishwasher.

"He's off to computer land," Cheryl said with an indulgent smile. "Now it's just us girls. What do you say we finish off this wine outside?" She wiped her hands and carried the bottle out to the patio, where they kicked off their shoes and sat back to watch the sunset.

Kate had forgotten how glorious the sunsets were in Arizona, lighting up the sky in a blaze of gold and orange. There were no skyscrapers to block the view, just miles of horizon and fresh, clean air.

She took a deep, cleansing breath and settled back in the lounge chair. "Beautiful," she sighed.

"So," Cheryl said, filling both of their glasses. "Now that you're relaxed, want to tell me what had you ready to jump out of your skin earlier?"

"Where do I start?"

"Usually at the beginning."

But Kate didn't want to go back that far, so she started with her return to Easy and her promise to stay while Jeff and Sally went on their honeymoon."

"They make such a cute couple," Cheryl mused.

Kate agreed, but admitted that helping to run the Tea and Crumpet Shop wasn't exactly what she had planned for her two-week vacation.

"I hear you had a visit from Deputy Ed earlier this week," Cheryl said.

"The rumor mills are already buzzing, huh?"

"When aren't they? This is a small town and everyone knows everyone else's business."

Kate nodded. She knew that first-hand. "Yeah, he showed his face there. Even Madame Zostra was speechless."

Cheryl giggled. "She's a card. So what did the good deputy want? I doubt if he's a big crumpet fan."

"He wants the business," Kate said. "He claims there's a lien on the property…that the ownership reverted to his mother after my father died."

Cheryl sat up straight. "That's ridiculous! Why now, after all these years?"

Kate rubbed her eyes. "According to Ed, Ginny was too good a person to claim her rights while my mother was still living."

Cheryl snorted. "My butt!"

"Exactly."

"You know, the only reason Ginny Tate wouldn't have said something sooner is if she knew your mother could prove differently while she was alive."

Kate nodded thoughtfully. "That makes sense."

Which meant that the proof—if there was any—was somewhere nearby.

She didn't mention her feeling that the teacup was trying desperately to tell her something. If in fact her mother's spirit resided there, Lillian was having the devil of a time getting through.

"Who's your mother's lawyer?" Cheryl asked.

"I already contacted them," Kate replied. "According to her attorneys, the only time they saw my mother was to draw up her will." Kate took another long swallow of the cool wine, feeling a pleasant buzz. "And speaking of wills," she confided, "it seems ' my mother left a third of her estate to Max Connors."

"I'm not surprised," Cheryl said.

Kate's eyebrows shot up at Cheryl's matter-of-fact response. "Really? Why not?"

"Your mother spent a lot of time over there working with the kids. She loved that place."

This was news to Kate. "Max's kids?"

Cheryl gave her an odd look. "Max doesn't have any kids, silly. He's not even married."

Kate blinked in confusion. "What kids, then?"

"The kids who get therapy out at the ranch," Cheryl explained. "They call it a Therapeutic Horseback Riding Program, and your mother was in charge of getting volunteers to work shifts with the kids. But no one volunteered as many hours as your mother did." Cheryl cocked her head. "I'm surprised she didn't tell you about it."

Kate thought back over the letters her mother had sent. She'd mentioned volunteers, but Kate had assumed she was talking about a social committee. When did she start spending so much time at Max's ranch?

"You remember Max's sister, Sue?"

Kate nodded.

"Well," Cheryl continued, "it all started when Sue's little boy Bobby was diagnosed with cerebral palsy. Max discovered that riding horses helped Bobby with his balance and motor skills. Before long they were bringing in kids from all over. Half the town volunteered to help out."

Kate remembered the boy in braces who'd brought flowers for "Miz Lilly". She'd seen him get into a pick-up truck afterward. That must have been Bobby. And Max.

Now it all started to make sense. Why hadn't Max told her? "So the money was to keep the ranch going for the kids?"

"Of course. Some of the patients have insurance to cover the treatment, but Max provides a physical therapist, speech therapist and occupational therapist as part of the program. Most of them volunteer their services, but some of the expense still comes out of his pocket. Max would never turn a child away who needed him."

"Oh God." Kate blushed with embarrassment, remembering how she'd accused Max of trying to con money from her mother. She should have given him the chance to explain before barging in and making wild accusations. She'd let her old resentment rule her heart and now she had some apologizing to do.

"Hey," Cheryl said, snapping her fingers. "Why don't you come out there with me tomorrow? It's my day to volunteer as a sidewalker — walking alongside the horse and rider during therapy. I've got the cutest little girl on Saturdays. Her name is

Nikki and she has Down's syndrome. I'm warning you though — she'll steal your heart in no time flat."

Kate smiled. "I'd like that. I'd like that a lot." She started to sit up, but the wine had made her dizzy.

"Besides," Cheryl said, "the scenery out at the ranch ain't half bad, either."

"Scenery?"

"You know — cowboys in tight jeans and leather chaps."

Kate blushed, thinking of Max. She couldn't agree more. "Hey," she said. "You're married!"

"That doesn't mean I can't admire a tight butt."

Tommy chose that moment to walk out. "I heard that," he said. "And what's wrong with my butt?"

Cheryl reached out and pinched him as he walked past. "Not a thing, sweetcheeks," she purred.

"You girls are tipsy."

"Are not!" they cried in unison.

Kate held up the empty bottle and looked at it with a puzzled expression on her face. "Did we finish this whole bottle ourselves?"

"Nope," Cheryl giggled. "Tommy had a glass with dinner."

"Oh good," Kate replied. "I wouldn't want to think we were lushes."

That struck them both as funny and they collapsed in giggles again.

Tommy balanced on the edge of Cheryl's lounge chair. "I guess that makes me the designated driver tonight."

"Oh, that'll work out great," Cheryl said. "If you take Kate home tonight, then I'll pick her up in the morning and we'll go out to the ranch together. She can grab her car when we get back."

"That's all I want you grabbing, hear?" Tommy said, teasing his wife. "Keep your hands off any tight butts in leather chaps."

Cheryl patted his knee. "Yours is the only butt I need." She winked at Kate, as if to say...*that doesn't mean I can't look.*

* * * * *

Max had been sitting on Kate's doorstep for over an hour. It was obvious she wasn't home, but he kept giving her five more minutes, hoping she'd show up. The sun had set in a brilliant blaze, leaving him alone in the dark with only his thoughts for company.

It was probably stupid of him to come here. He should be used to Kate thinking the worst of him by now, but it still hurt. More than he cared to admit.

Max stood and brushed off his jeans, ready to call it a night. He could still be home in time to read Bobby the next chapter in his Harry Potter book before tucking him into bed.

A car turned onto the road. Max recognized the deputy's car, which slowed down as it passed Kate's house. Ed Tate glared at Max from the driver's seat. He pulled over and called out, "Everything okay here?"

"Right as rain," Max said, walking toward his pick-up. What the hell was Tate doing here? Still sniffing around Kate, Max supposed. Some things never change.

Ed Tate had been a thorn in Max's side since they were kids, making it his personal mission to compete with Max in every school activity. Unfortunately, Tate wasn't all that smart, athletic or popular. He took his frustration out on Max, finding underhanded ways to come out on top. If Tate couldn't win honestly, he wasn't above cheating.

Tate had always been a bully. Now he was a bully with a badge, and that could be dangerous.

Max sat in his truck waiting for Tate to pull away first. Tate apparently had the same idea. The two vehicles idled at the side of the road in a silent contest of wills.

Finally Tate pulled away from the curb, but not before turning on his lights, as if he'd just been called away on official business. Max saw right through the obvious bluff. To show Tate he knew it was a face-saving gesture, Max pulled out behind the patrol car and followed him until reaching the turn-off out of town.

It probably wasn't smart to goad Tate like that, since he had the law on his side, but the deputy made a convenient target for his anger. Max hadn't forgotten that Tate had refused to shut down the ranch where Venus had been abused. It wasn't the first time Tate had refused to investigate a case of animal abuse, calling Max and other animal rights advocates "bleeding hearts."

Max was still fuming about Tate when he pulled up to the Triple-R. He was surprised to see Sue sitting on the porch, as if she'd been waiting for him. She cradled a bowl of snap beans on her lap, but that seemed as much a ploy as Tate's flashing lights had been.

Max leaned against the porch rail. "Bobby in bed already?"

"No, he's working on his new puzzle. He wanted to wait for you to read to him before going to bed. I told him not to wait, but—"

"I said I wouldn't be long."

She nodded, chewing her lower lip. "How'd it go?"

"Kate wasn't home. Saw Tate nosing around there, though."

Max heard Sue take a sharp, indrawn breath. He glanced at her, but her head was bent over the bowl of beans. The rapid sound of snapping filled the air like dancing crickets.

"I'm not worried about Tate," Max reassured her. "He's all saddle and no horse."

Sue looked up, concern evident on her face. "Be careful, Max. Ed Tate can be a dangerous enemy."

Max gave a quick snort of derision. "Tate may not be all that bright, but he's too smart to mess with me." He pushed away from the porch railing. "I'm going to tuck the little guy in. You coming?"

"In a bit," she said, her voice distant. Then she stopped and smiled at her brother. "Don't forget your pie."

Chapter Nine

Kate barely had time to regret her descent into Merlotville the night before. She checked the teakettle-shaped clock on the kitchen wall. Cheryl would be arriving to pick her up in half an hour and she still hadn't taken a shower.

Kate popped a couple of aspirin in her mouth and watched her new coffeemaker bubble and perk. She'd called Nellie to tell her she wouldn't be in this morning, and Nellie had assured her she had everything under control at the Tea and Crumpet Shop.

When the coffee finished dripping, Kate poured herself a full mug. It was hot and black and strong—just what she needed to start her day.

Sipping her coffee, Kate opened a can of cat food, which brought Sophie running from wherever she'd parked herself for the night. Sophie hopped onto the counter and began rubbing herself against Kate's arm, purring softly. Kate scooped cat food into the bowl, crooning to the cat. "You're a little lover when I'm holding your food hostage, huh?"

The cat brushed herself back and forth, meowing and rubbing her head along Kate's arm. Kate scraped the rest of the cat food into the bowl then turned to rinse the can out in the sink while Sophie dug in, acting as if she hadn't eaten in eight of her nine lives.

Kate finished rinsing the can then glanced at Sophie. The cat had stopped eating. She sat perfectly still, her food forgotten, her whole body on full alert. She was staring intently at the window. Kate followed the cat's gaze.

No, not the window—the cat was watching the cup sitting on the windowsill.

"Sophie?"

The cat didn't move a muscle, her concentration focused on the cup. She almost seemed to be listening.

Kate felt a shiver ripple through her body. This was too freaky. "Sophie, stop!"

The cat slowly turned away from the cup and looked at Kate as if she'd lost her mind. Then, haughtily dismissing her, Sophie went back to her food.

Kate shook her head and headed for the shower. "Stupid cat," she muttered, vowing never to touch a drop of wine again.

Twenty minutes later, refreshed by the shower, she poured a second cup of coffee. She'd pulled her hair up in a ponytail and put on jeans and a denim shirt for her trip to the ranch. The aspirin had kicked in, making her feel at least half alive. The second cup of coffee did the rest of the trick. By the time Cheryl beeped the horn outside, Kate was ready to go.

She locked the door behind her and climbed into Cheryl's car. The two women looked at each other and started laughing.

"You look like hell," Cheryl said.

"So do you."

"Next time—"

"Mountain Dew," Kate finished.

On the ride out to the ranch, they laughed like schoolgirls. Kate was amazed how the years slipped away. While they hadn't been best friends in school, they'd been close in the way high-school friends are close when they're constantly thrown together. What surprised Kate was that even though their lives had gone in different directions, there was still enough of a similarity to forge a new bond, an adult bond. If for no other reason, this renewed friendship made her glad she'd come back home.

It also made her think that if she could put the past behind her, maybe there was a chance at mending bridges with Max as well. She thought of the direction his life had taken. While the news about Max's ranch had been a revelation, it didn't really surprise her. He'd always been a caring person. But if someone had asked her ten years ago what she thought Max would do with his life, running a disabled children's therapy center was the last thing she'd have come up with.

When they pulled up to the ranch, Kate noticed the wheelchairs lined up along the barn—all of them empty. Instead of cold metal, the children sat atop horses, their faces glowing with delight, their bodies in motion with the warm, breathing animals. The horses seemed to sense the special needs of their riders, walking a careful and steady pace.

Kate recognized volunteers from town, some leading the horses, some walking alongside and assisting the riders when they needed support. Kate learned from Cheryl that volunteers also tacked and cooled the horses, helped with fundraisers when they could and even handled some of the administrative duties. But she realized that none of it would be possible without Max, and that filled her with a swift surge of pride.

The feeling was quickly replaced by shame when she thought of the way she'd yelled at him. She should have paid more attention when her mother talked about her volunteer work. She should have put the past behind her before jumping to all the wrong conclusions. But most of all, she should have known Max wasn't capable of the things she'd accused him of. She'd attacked him out of anger and pain, and realized now that she'd misjudged him terribly.

She watched him amble around the track, giving each of the children special attention—a smile, a hug, a word of encouragement. Each child's face lit up with pride. It was evident that they adored Max. His attention didn't end there. Kate noticed that he was just as caring and gentle with the horses as he was with the children.

Cheryl leaned close and whispered in her ear. "Chaps."

It wasn't Max's chaps that drew Kate's attention, however. She was too busy admiring his heart.

"Hey, there's my girl," Cheryl said as a chubby little whirlwind came bounding up to them. Nikki wrapped her arms around Cheryl's waist and hugged her tight.

"You ready to go riding today?"

Nikki bobbed her head up and down, wiggling with excitement.

"This is my friend Kate," Cheryl said. "Can you say hello?"

Nikki peeked out from Cheryl's arms and gave Kate a shy smile, then carefully formed the word "hello." The distinctive features of Down's syndrome gave the child a look of pure innocence, and when she smiled it was the smile of an angel. Cheryl had been right. With one smile Nikki had already stolen her heart.

"You two go ahead," Kate said. She could see how anxious Nikki was to get on with her riding therapy. "I'd like to look around a little."

Kate watched Cheryl and Nikki wander off to the stables. She was interested in learning more about the work they did at the ranch. But most of all, she was hoping to find a few minutes alone with Max. She had so much to explain.

"Hello Kate."

Kate spun around at the familiar voice, but when she saw Sue Connors, she couldn't believe her eyes. The bright and shining young woman who'd stood beside her at the beauty pageant ten years ago had changed. Gone was the youthful radiance, replaced by lines tracking the hard edge of life. Her face was thin, her expression defiant, as if she'd learned that the only way to face a challenge was head-on, with no arguments or excuses.

"Sue," Kate held out her arms and gave Max's sister a gentle hug. "It's been awhile."

"You look good," Sue said. "I was sorry to hear about your mother. Lillian will be missed here. The kids loved her...especially my son Bobby."

"I met Bobby," Kate told her. "He's a lovely boy."

Sue nodded and smiled, her eyes lighting up for the first time at the mention of her son. "Yes, he's my special boy."

For a moment Kate glimpsed the radiant beauty she remembered, but then Sue's eyes hardened again, her voice taking on a note of suspicion.

"How long will you be in town?" she asked.

For the first time since she'd arrived, Kate wasn't sure how to answer that. A few days ago she would have given anything to go back to New York. It had always been easier for her to run away from her problems rather than deal with them directly. Now she saw a chance to make peace with her past, if for no other reason than to put it behind her once and for all.

And then there was Max. She hadn't resolved her feelings about him, but she was determined to try. She realized now that running away hadn't solved anything. She'd simply turned her back on her feelings rather than face them. Now she'd been given a second chance to put things right one way or the other and move on. She couldn't spend the rest of her life wondering what might have been.

Kate hesitated. She glanced at Max working with the horses in the field. He looked so at ease in his surroundings, as much a part of the Arizona landscape as the saguaro cactus and desert wildflowers. He belonged on the open range. She couldn't imagine him anywhere else — especially not New York City.

It was hopeless. Max would never leave.

And Kate couldn't stay.

Sue watched Kate's face. She saw the hesitation there, the wistful way Kate glanced at Max working with the horses in the field. It was obvious to Sue that Kate was still in love with her brother.

She knew Max hadn't gotten over Kate either. What if this time he decided to follow her to New York? What would happen to her and Bobby then?

Kate took a deep breath and turned back to Sue, as if just remembering she'd asked her a question. "I'm not sure," she replied. "Another week at least—until Jeff and Sally come back from their honeymoon."

Sue nodded, fear gripping her heart like a tight fist. That would give Max and Kate plenty of time to discover what had happened all those years ago…and the part she'd played in it. Once Max realized Sue had been partly responsible for sending Kate away, he'd never forgive her. She'd lose her brother forever.

"New York is a long way from Easy," Sue said.

Kate nodded thoughtfully. "In more ways than one."

Sue wished with all her heart that Kate would disappear again, go back to where she came from and never return. It had broken Max's heart the first time she'd left. What would it do to him this time if he got his hopes up again only to have her walk out of his life once more?

Stay away from my brother, she wanted to scream. *You don't belong here anymore. Just go away and leave us alone.*

"I was hoping to talk to Max," Kate said. "But I can see that he has his hands full."

Sue nodded, not commenting one way or the other. She knew Max would drop whatever he was doing if he realized Kate was here.

"Why don't you come inside out of the sun," she offered. "I can tell you about the ranch and how your mother helped pull it all together. None of this would be possible without the volunteers who give their time, and your mother coordinated most of it."

"I'd like that," Kate said, giving one more wistful glance over her shoulder before following Sue into the house.

It was cooler inside. A gentle breeze billowed the kitchen curtains. Through the window, Kate could see the children and horses and volunteers in the field. The sound of laughter mingled in the air with the dull clop of hooves over packed dirt.

"I had no idea," Kate murmured, more to herself than anyone else.

"Of course you didn't," Sue replied. "You've been gone." The words came out sounding like an accusation.

Kate turned, but Sue was busy pouring lemonade, her expression hidden from view. She placed a plate of homemade sugar cookies on the table and gestured for Kate to sit down. Although she played the part of a gracious hostess, there was something about Sue's manner that made Kate uneasy.

Kate pulled out a chair, sticking with the only subject she felt comfortable discussing with Max's sister. "How long have you been using the ranch for physical therapy?"

Sue took a slow sip of lemonade before answering. "About five years now. Once Max saw how good it was for Bobby, he spread the word. Pretty soon people from all over were bringing their kids to the ranch for equine therapy."

Kate thought about Cheryl and Lillian and even Nellie. They all volunteered their time at the ranch. "I guess it takes a lot of people to keep things running smoothly around here."

Sue nodded. "That's right. Everybody from town helps out when they can. That's one thing about a small town. You can depend on people." This time there was no mistaking the insinuation in her voice.

Kate couldn't help but wonder why Max's sister was so bitter. Sue had gotten everything that Kate wanted. She'd claimed the title of Miss Easy County and stayed right here in town surrounded by her family and friends. Unlike Kate, she hadn't been ridden out of town on a cloud of lies and suspicion. Why the anger? And why did it seem to be so fresh after all these years?

Before Kate could ask, a small voice interrupted from the doorway. "Did Miz Lilly like my flowers?"

Kate turned and smiled at the boy. "Hi Bobby." She gestured him over, only now noticing how he favored Max. He had the same wide blue eyes and stubborn jaw. He'd be a heartbreaker someday. Just like his uncle.

"I know she's in heaven, but..." He lifted eyes that seemed to plead with Kate's soul then shrugged one shoulder as the sentence trailed off.

It was a gesture she'd seen Max do a thousand times. No wonder Max would move heaven and earth for his nephew's sake. Kate was already half in love with the child herself. A wave of yearning washed over her. Maybe if she'd stayed in Easy instead of running away, she could have worked things out with Max. Maybe she'd have a child of her own with Max's eyes and mannerisms.

Kate reached out and hugged Bobby close. "I think Lillian loved your flowers best."

The boy trembled in her arms. Then, as if realizing that even the littlest cowboys don't cry, he straightened and put on a brave face. "I picked them myself."

Kate ran a finger through his corn-silk hair. "You did a good job, Bobby."

Sue interrupted the exchange. "Shouldn't you be helping Uncle Max out in the field?"

Bobby turned to his mother. "But..."

Sue gave him a look that was all the admonishment he needed. Bobby dropped his gaze and tried another angle. "Can I have a cookie?"

"You can have a cookie when you're done with your chores. You know the rules."

"Yes ma'am." Bobby pouted and cast one longing look back at Kate before turning to leave. "Maybe someday you can help me ride like Miz Lilly did."

Kate's heart lurched. "Maybe," she said. She didn't have the heart to tell him she wouldn't be in town long enough to volunteer at the ranch.

When Bobby was out of earshot, Sue turned to Kate, her lips pulled into a tight, hard line. "Don't make promises you can't keep," she said. "He's already had his heart broken once."

For just a moment, Kate wasn't sure whether Sue was talking about Bobby or Max. Either way, there was no mistaking the warning in Sue's voice.

* * * * *

Bobby wished he could have stayed in the kitchen and talked with the pretty lady about Miz Lilly. Maybe she'd heard from her in heaven. He wondered if Miz Lilly was happy up in heaven. Most of all, he wondered if she missed him as much as he missed her.

He almost turned around and went back inside, but Bobby knew it was no use arguing with his mother when she had her mad face on. He tried to think of another way to find out about Miz Lilly.

Maybe Uncle Max could help.

Bobby headed toward the barn. He knew he wasn't supposed to be back there alone. But he wouldn't really be alone…that's where Uncle Max was.

He made his way slowly, leaning on his forearm crutches and swinging his legs back and forth with each step. The full-leg braces were more cumbersome than heavy, but Bobby would rather struggle with the crutches than have to depend on a wheelchair.

He was sweating from exertion by the time he reached the barn. Inside, he was out of the sun, but the air was still heavy and warm with the thick aroma of hay and horse. His mother always crinkled her nose when she came into the barn, but Bobby loved the smell, and he loved the horses.

Outlaw wasn't in the barn, though. And neither was Uncle Max. Bobby heard Venus whinny from her stall. He knew she was too skittish to put out with the other horses, but Uncle Max thought that with a little time Venus might be as good with the kids as Outlaw someday. Bobby inched closer to Venus' stall. She eyed him warily, snorting and jerking her head.

The horse stepped back as Bobby advanced. Bobby knew not to make any sudden moves. He'd watched his uncle try to coax the frightened animal.

"Easy girl," Bobby crooned softly, just like he'd heard Uncle Max talk to the horse. He unlatched the stall door and stepped inside. "That's it, nice and easy. Not gonna hurt you."

Bobby swung forward, planted his feet then pulled the crutches around. His left crutch swung wide, hitting the bucket of oats someone had left alongside the stall.

Metal clanged against metal, the sound echoing in the closed barn. Venus spooked and reared. Bobby, already unbalanced on one crutch, jerked back and tumbled to the dirt floor as the animal's hooves thrashed the air over his head.

* * * * *

Max had been on his way into the barn when he heard Venus' frightened whinny. He ran inside and took in the scene at a glance, the horse rearing, hooves flailing. Bobby was sprawled on the ground, helpless to get out of the way. Without thinking, Max ran and dove, covering Bobby's body with his own before rolling both of them out of the way.

The sound of hooves hitting the packed dirt was close. Too close. Max felt the ground shudder beneath them, heard the horse's terrified snorts, felt the spray of dirt against his cheek.

He clutched Bobby tight, adrenaline pumping, heart pounding. What if he hadn't gotten there in time? Max couldn't even think about it. Slowly he stood, pulling Bobby to his feet. He checked the boy from head to toe, relieved to see that he was a little frightened but otherwise fine.

"You scared the hell out of me," he said, pulling his nephew close and holding him tight against his chest. Max noticed a nasty cut on the back of his own hand where he'd scraped the edge of the muck rake, but that was a small price to pay. It could have been worse. Much, much worse.

"I'm sorry, Uncle Max." Bobby rubbed his eyes, tears leaving smudged streaks on his dirty face.

"Let's go get you cleaned up," Max said.

Behind them, Venus had already stopped rearing. She cowered in the back of her stall, haunches quivering, nostrils flaring. Max talked softly to the horse, trying to soothe her as he retrieved Bobby's crutches. He saw Venus' bucket lying on its side next to one of the crutches and shot Bobby a stern glance. "What were you doing? You know you're not supposed to be in the barn alone."

Bobby sniffled. "I was looking for you."

"Yeah?" Max closed the stall door then handed Bobby his crutches, not wanting to compound the boy's embarrassment by carrying him back to the house. It was getting harder to strike a perfect balance between his sense of protectiveness and the knowledge that Bobby needed to live like other boys. He was reaching an age when he resented being coddled and treated differently.

Bobby nodded. "I wanted you to talk to that pretty lady in the house with Mom. Wanted you to ask her about Miz Lilly for me."

Kate? Max's heart gave a quick jolt. Kate was here? He wondered if she'd come to ream him out again. The thought actually brought a smile to his face. He loved it when fire lit up her eyes. That was the Kitty he remembered, not the hollow-eyed woman who acted as if nothing mattered. When he'd first seen her, he'd been afraid she'd turned as cold and gray as that city she couldn't wait to get back to. He was afraid she'd lost the passion he'd loved so much.

"I thought maybe she heard from Miz Lilly in heaven." Bobby's feet kicked up petulant puffs of dust as they left the barn. "Mom kicked me out, though. Said I should come find you."

Max couldn't resist the tear-smudged face. "Okay," he said. "But next time don't try to go near Venus without me. She needs more time to learn how to trust people again. We'll work with her together, okay?"

"Really?" Bobby's face lit up. "I been watching you," he said. "I know how to talk to her real gentle-like. She only got scared because my crutch hit the bucket and spooked her."

Max smiled. The kid had horses in his blood. He'd make a good rancher someday. But there was more to it than just loving horses. When Bobby was on horseback, he wasn't just a boy on crutches. In his mind he was a real cowboy, riding with the wind in his hair and the freedom of movement he could only experience on horseback. For that reason alone, Max would do whatever was needed to keep the ranch running.

Max ran his fingers through Bobby's hair. He stopped and frowned, pressing the palm of his hand to Bobby's forehead. "You feeling all right, Champ?"

Bobby nodded, but Max wasn't convinced. The boy's forehead felt warm to the touch. "Why don't we get you inside out of the sun?"

Bobby shook off Max's hand and pointed toward the house. "There she is," he said.

Max followed his gaze and saw Kate walking with Cheryl Anderson. *Oh no*, he thought. *You're not getting away from me again, little darlin'. Not this time.*

"Go inside and get cleaned up," he told Bobby, giving him a gentle nudge toward the house. Then he took off at a lope to catch up with Kate before she could leave.

"Don't forget to ask her about Miz Lilly," Bobby called out to him.

Max reached the car just as the two women did. Kate spun around, her eyes wide with surprise when she saw him. He gripped her elbow, keeping her from getting into the car. "We need to talk," he said, not giving her a chance to argue. "Privately."

Kate glanced from Max to Cheryl and back again.

"Please?" Max knew if she walked away this time, he might never have the chance to confront her. Before he knew it, she'd be gone again, back to a life he had no part of.

He watched Kate's features soften into a smile. "My car is at Cheryl's," she said.

"I'll drop you off there when we're done." He wasn't giving her any excuse to slip away. It was now or never.

He glanced at Cheryl, who nodded and climbed into her car. She waved to Kate. "I'll see you...whenever."

The women shared a secretive smile, and Max thought that maybe, just maybe, his luck was finally about to change.

Chapter Ten

&

From the passenger seat of the pick-up, Kate watched Max. He stared straight ahead at the road, his brow furrowed in concentration. Now that she was actually here with him, she felt suddenly shy. There was so much she wanted to say but she didn't know where to start.

"Where are we going?" she asked.

"You'll see."

His voice was gruff, thick with emotion. She noticed a streak of dirt on his jeans, and a bright red cut crossing diagonally along the back of his hand. He glanced over and caught her staring. "Bobby took a little tumble," he explained, wiping the blood on his jeans. "He's okay."

Kate didn't want to think of how many germs he'd just thrust into the open wound. He was a cowboy, a rough-and-tumble man's man who had little or no use for Band-Aids.

"Max?"

"Hm?"

"I…I'm sorry for the things I said the other day. I was out of line." Now that she'd started, Kate couldn't stop and the words came tumbling out. "I had no idea what you were doing out at the ranch, or my mother's involvement. I think it's wonderful…what you're doing. And I…I was wrong. I'm sorry. Sorry for accusing you of taking advantage of her, sorry for thinking…"

He glanced over at her, one eyebrow raised.

"…you know," she finished feebly.

"That I was conning your mother? Isn't that the way you put it?"

Kate felt her cheeks burn with shame. She looked down at her hands folded in her lap. "Yes."

"Your mother was an attractive woman," he said.

Her head jerked up. *What?* She stared at him, not sure if she was hearing right.

"But I think she had better taste in men," he added, grinning.

It took a moment to sink in. He was teasing her. She smiled and he smiled back and they seemed to slip into a familiar ease that she only now realized had been missing from her life all these years. No wonder she hadn't felt complete.

"I really am sorry," she said softly.

He reached over and gave her hand a gentle squeeze. His hands were rough and strong and warm. She'd forgotten how perfectly her own hand fit in his, how safe it made her feel. But before she could get accustomed to the sensation, he withdrew and she was left feeling alone again.

Suddenly she realized where they were heading. The distant horizon was broken by a familiar outline. Max turned into the abandoned lot that served as the setting for most of her nightmares.

"The drive-in?"

Max nodded. "Until we can figure out exactly what happened, this place will always haunt us. This is where it all started, and this is where it has to end."

Kate understood. If nothing else they'd have closure, something neither of them had had up until now.

She nodded, her heart in her throat. As hard as it would be to dredge up old memories, she knew it was for the best, like lancing a wound and allowing the poison to flow before healing could take place.

They pulled into the two-lane dirt entrance to the abandoned drive-in. Max jumped out, leaving the truck idling as he unlatched the chain blocking the entrance. He climbed back into the cab of the pick-up and grinned. "Kids hang out here sometimes. Deputy Ed chases them out and puts a new chain up, but it never stays locked for long."

Max drove slowly over the ruts and pulled into what could have been the exact same spot they'd parked all those years ago. Kate could feel the weight of memories pressing down on her. Despite the fact that the drive-in was empty, the screen silent and the sun shining, she was struck by a strong sense of déjà vu. With vivid clarity she remembered the movie that had been showing that night, the dancing soda commercials counting down intermission, the smell of buttery popcorn and warm beer. Her throat tightened. Just like that she was propelled into the past. She felt like a teenager again—young, innocent and so vulnerable.

Max turned off the truck and swiveled to face her across the seat. "Don't be afraid," he said. "I think there's been a huge misunderstanding and the only way to resolve it is if we both re-create exactly what happened after you stepped out of my truck that night."

Kate nodded, unable to speak. How often had she imagined doing just that? Getting it all out in a burst of recrimination, freeing herself once and for all. But now that the opportunity had come, she wasn't sure she'd be able to force the words past her throat.

Max reached across for her hand again. "Do you want to go first?"

She shook her head.

"Okay," he said. "Here's the way we're gonna do it. I'll tell you exactly what happened from my point of view and how it made me feel. Then you'll do the same. Does that sound fair?"

She nodded again.

"You are going to speak at some point, right? If not, this isn't going to work."

"Yes," she said, giving him a weak smile. "And that sounds fair. Have you been taking psychology classes in your spare time?"

"Nope. Sis watches a lot of talk shows and she says this is the way to do it. And for the record," he said, "I don't have a whole lot of spare time these days."

He smiled again, and as charming as his smile was, it did little to ease the tension. She looked at the cracked vinyl of the dashboard, her watch, the threadbare movie screen with its metal skeleton exposed…anywhere but at Max, because looking in his eyes would be her undoing.

He took a deep breath and let it out in a rush. "Okay," he said. "It was the week before the prom when we came here. You wore a yellow sundress the exact same color as your hair." He smiled. "You looked prettier than a sunset."

Her heart skipped a beat.

"You were so beautiful and I was so scared." His voice lowered to almost a whisper. "I was going to ask you to marry me that night."

This time she was the one to gasp. "Marry you?"

He nodded. "Had the ring in my pocket and everything. And then I did probably the dumbest thing I've ever done in my life. I thought that a beer would give me the courage to propose. And one beer turned to two and still I couldn't work up the nerve. Then three and four and by that time I'd forgotten what I was gonna say, I just knew you were so beautiful and I wanted you and…"

He shook his head then finally said the words she'd waited so long to hear. "I am so sorry. God. I was all over you and you said 'no' and I kept pushing you and I don't blame you for slapping me and storming out. I was a jerk. A drunken jerk. And when I came to and you were gone, I knew I'd blown it for good."

Kate let out a sigh.

"On top of that," he said, "when I heard you'd gone home with Ed Tate, I felt like an even bigger jerk. I should have apologized right then and there, but Tate said…" He looked away guiltily.

"What did he say?" Kate asked, trying to coax the rest of the sentence out of him, needing to hear it.

"He said you'd slept together. That you'd chosen him over me. And that he wasn't the only one."

"And you believed that?"

"Not at first," Max admitted. "But then you stood me up for the prom. And Sis said she saw you coming out of a motel later that night—with Ed Tate. And then other guys started saying you'd been with them too. I wondered why everyone else and not me? I thought we had something special, Kitty. Then I thought maybe you were punishing me or something."

Kate crossed her arms around her stomach, hugging herself tight. She felt sick. All the old pain was still there, but this time there was the added burden of knowing that Max hadn't started the rumors to begin with, that he wasn't to blame as she'd thought all these years.

"I have to finish," he said. "See, I still hadn't given up hope. I carried that ring in my pocket everywhere I went. I figured once you were done being mad at me, we'd go back to where we'd left off. But then you just up and left. No goodbye or nothing. You just turned your back as if this town wasn't good enough for you. Or maybe it was me that wasn't good enough. But you never even said goodbye, and that's what hurt most of all."

His voice cracked and he turned away. That was the final straw that broke her heart. All these years she'd thought she was the injured one, and he'd been hurting as much as she had. She wanted to crawl into his arms and curl up and make it all go away. She wanted to cry and scream and let all the pain go.

But first she had to tell him the rest. As hard as it would be, it was her turn now.

Max felt drained. His hands were gripped into tight fists at his sides. To spare Kate's feelings, he'd left out the worst—the vicious, hateful things Tate had spit in his face. "I had your girl and she loved it," he'd said, laughing in Max's face. "She couldn't get enough of it and begged me for more. So I gave her what she wanted, over and over and over."

Max gritted his teeth, remembering those words as if he'd heard them yesterday. How many times had they played over and over in his mind since then? How many nights had he lain awake imagining the two of them naked together?

He felt the seat shift and turned to see Kate sliding closer. She rested her hand on his shoulder.

"He lied," she said. "He lied to both of us."

Max wanted to believe that, but the image he'd tortured himself with for so long was burned indelibly into his brain.

"Max, look at me."

He raised his gaze, looking deep into her eyes.

"He played us both," she said. "He told me that you were bragging to everyone that you'd already…" Kate couldn't even repeat the crude phrase Ed Tate had used. She took a slow, trembling breath. Her voice was barely a whisper as she rephrased the words Tate had spoken. "He said you'd told everyone that you'd already taken my virginity."

"I never said that!" Max felt anger burning deep in his belly. His fists tightened again, his body coiled for a fight. Badge or no badge, he vowed to make Tate pay for this.

"He said you'd told everyone I was easy and that now that you'd broken me in, they might as well take their turn."

"And you believed that?"

"You believed what you were hearing, didn't you?"

She was right, but still it hurt to realize she could so easily think the worst of him. Granted he'd acted like an immature jerk, but he wasn't the kind of person who would spread vicious lies. She had to know that.

"So all this…" he muttered. "Ten years wasted. All because you chose to believe him over me? It was a simple misunderstanding you could have cleared up just by asking me."

"I could say the same," she replied. "Did you ever think to ask me if the rumors you were hearing were true? Did you trust me enough to believe in me instead of locker-room gossip?"

He started to argue but she stopped him. "It's my turn, remember? You made the rules."

Max took a deep breath. "Okay."

Kate looked out the window toward the boarded-up snack bar. "When I left your truck," she said, "I hung around at the snack bar waiting for you to come apologize. Some of the gang was there…including Ed. I waited and waited, but you never came. Finally Ed offered to take me home. He could see I was upset, and that's when he started telling me you weren't the person I thought you were, filling my head with his lies.

"He came around every day for the next week, chipping away at my trust in you, convincing me you'd betrayed me over and over again. He even had friends back him up, swearing they'd heard it out of your own mouth."

She looked at him, her eyes pleading. "And you never once called, never came by to see if I'd made it home all right, never said you were sorry. After awhile, I started to believe them."

The heartbreak in her eyes nearly did him in. He pulled her close, feeling her body tremble. She tucked her head under his chin and he buried his face in her hair, losing himself in the scent he remembered so well.

"I'm sorry," he whispered, knowing it was too little too late. "I'm so, so sorry."

A shudder rippled through her body. He ached to hold her tight, to make up for all the hurt he'd caused. They'd been kids—innocent kids caught up in a web of lies and deceit. He shook his head. All the wasted time — time they could never get back again.

With an obvious effort, Kate pulled herself together to continue her story. "I was numb," she said. "He knew all the buttons to push, tearing down my defenses one by one all week long. When he said you'd already asked someone else to the prom, I agreed to go with him. It was awful. I kept looking for you, but you never showed up. Instead of taking me home afterward, Ed said we were going to an after-prom party. But there wasn't a party. Just a sleazy motel room where he thought he'd finally reap the rewards of all his hard work."

Max's fists clenched tight. He wanted to smash something…or *someone*.

"I fought him," Kate said, her voice a monotone as she remembered. "I threatened to bring charges against him."

She grew quiet. When she spoke again, Max could only imagine what she must have gone through that night trying to fight off a bully who was bigger and stronger and more determined than she was.

"He was furious," she said. "I've never seen so much hate in someone's eyes before. But he seemed more upset about you. He asked, 'What does Max have that I don't?' He said I'd be sorry, that he'd have the final laugh."

"And that's when my sister saw you leaving the motel with him."

Kate nodded. "I know how it must have looked."

"Shhh," he murmured, smoothing her hair. "I wish I'd known." But it was too late to come to her defense. The damage had already been done.

"That summer was the longest summer of my life," she said. "Everywhere I went there were whispers behind my back. I saw the way the boys in town looked at me, sneering and confident that they could get lucky too. Why not? In their minds, everyone else had. It didn't matter that I didn't date, never went out with anyone after that night. No one wanted to be the only boy who couldn't make it with the easiest girl in town, so they added more boastful lies to the growing pile."

Max had heard them all. Worse yet, he'd believed them. He was no better than anyone else in that respect, condemning her with his silence.

"I tried to pretend it didn't matter," she said bravely. "As long as I knew the truth, I thought I could hold my head up high. I still had my pride, if nothing else. But even that didn't last long."

Her shoulders slumped, as if burdened with the weight of the world. Max almost stopped her then, knowing that the worst was yet to come. "The pageant," he said, finally understanding.

"Yes. The pageant. I was counting on that scholarship. It was all I had left to hang on to." She raised her eyes, pleading with him to understand. "It was my last chance to regain my self-respect."

Max remembered that night. She had no way of knowing he'd been there, hiding in the wings to watch her. She'd been so beautiful, radiant in a way none of the other contestants could hold a candle to. His heart had swelled with pride when they'd placed the crown on her head. He'd closed his hand around the ring he still carried in his pocket like the remnant of a shattered dream.

"Then why did you give it up?" he asked. She'd left town almost immediately and the title had gone to his sister. That he remembered clearly.

"I didn't give it up," she said, her voice breaking. "The title was taken from me. Someone complained about my reputation. The rumors had come back to haunt me. The committee decided my moral character was in question. There could be no scandal attached to the competition, they said. I was stripped of my crown, my scholarship and what little shred of pride I had left. Can you blame me for running away?"

"Oh God. And in your mind it was all my fault, right?"

"Yes."

Just that one word, but it was enough to break his heart. No wonder she'd run as far as she could and never come back. No wonder she hated him.

He cradled her, trying to rock away their regrets. He'd never felt so helpless in his life. There was no way he could ever fix the wrongs his carelessness had set into motion, no way he could make up for the years they'd lost.

Suddenly he realized where they were. He should never have taken her here. The drive-in was a graveyard of broken dreams and this was the last place he wanted to be, the last thing he wanted her to remember. He was right when he'd said this was where it had all started, but wrong about this being where it would end. It wouldn't end until he'd found a way to make up for all she'd gone through.

But first he had a score to settle with Deputy Ed, and it was a long time coming.

Kate stared out the window of the pick-up truck watching the scenery glide by as Max drove her back to Cheryl's house. The silence was deafening, each of them caught up in their own thoughts and memories. For a little while they'd been close again. Max had held her while she'd cried tears that had been bottled up far too long. The old pain was there, but knowing how they'd been manipulated and lied to added another layer of regrets.

And there was a new guilt to deal with. Each of them had misjudged the other. Yes, they'd been young, but no matter how she tried to justify it, Kate couldn't get over the feeling of betrayal. Max had believed the worst of her. Perhaps a part of him still did. And she had done the same to him. Even though the misunderstanding had finally been cleared up, how could they ever trust each other again?

She glanced over at him. His face was hard, his jaw clenched. Was he angry with her? Or was he already planning revenge on Ed Tate? She had to know.

"Max? What are you thinking?"

He gave a brusque nod. "I'm thinking I've got a score to settle."

"With me?"

He shook his head. "No, with Deputy Ed."

That's what she was afraid of. She didn't want him fighting for her. She just wanted it to go away. "What are you going to do?"

He glanced over at her as if to say *don't you worry your pretty little head about it,* but the look on her face must have changed his mind. "I'm going to handle it," he said. "Man to man."

"Please don't. It's too late to change anything now. Can't you just drop it?"

But Max wasn't listening. "This is personal," he said. "I've got a score to settle, and I'll settle it the only way Tate will understand."

She could see by the determined set of his jaw and his white-knuckled grip on the wheel that he was primed for a fight. "What good will that do?" she asked. "It will only dredge up all those old rumors again. I couldn't stand it. Besides, when this is all over with, you still have to live in this town."

He took his eyes off the road for a moment and shot a challenging glance her way. "What do you mean by that? After all this, you're still planning on running away? Haven't you learned that running doesn't solve anything?"

She looked away. Yes, that was exactly what she was planning to do. Run. Again. She knew she'd avoid confrontation at all costs, while Max, on the other hand, was ready to face it head-on.

"Just promise me you won't do anything stupid," she begged.

"I'm sorry," he said without a trace of remorse. "I can't promise you that."

Maybe not. But there was still a chance that she could talk him out of beating Ed Tate to a bloody pulp. She hoped to enlist the help of Cheryl and Tommy to talk some sense into Max.

When Max pulled into Cheryl's driveway, however, he made no move to get out of the truck.

"Do you want to come in?" Kate asked, her hand on the door handle.

Max shook his head. "I've got some things to take care of first," he said. "But I'll swing by your place later, if that's okay."

Kate nodded and opened the door. It was obvious from the look on his face that there was nothing she could do to change his mind.

Before Kate could step out of the truck, Cheryl came rushing out the front door. "I'm glad I caught you," she called, running toward the truck. "Max, your sister has been trying to reach you."

"What's wrong?" he asked, concern replacing the anger in his voice.

"It's Bobby," Cheryl said. "Sue said he's running a fever. She sounded upset."

Kate glanced at Max and saw her worry mirrored on his face. "Do you want me to go back with you?"

He shook his head. "No." Then his voice softened and he squeezed her hand. "I know what you're thinking, but my first concern is Bobby right now. I promise not to do anything tonight, okay? I'll sleep on it first then decide just what I'm going to do about Tate tomorrow."

"Okay." That was more than she could hope for. She knew his concern over his nephew would put his fight with Ed Tate on hold...for now. Maybe a good night's sleep would take the edge off his anger. She stood there for a moment then closed the door, knowing Max was in a hurry to make sure his nephew was all right. Already his mind was somewhere else.

She barely had time to step away from the truck before Max backed up and pulled out of the driveway. She watched him take off down the road, the red pick-up dwindling in the distance.

After explaining as much as she could to Cheryl, Kate headed home. Her thoughts went out to Bobby and Sue. She couldn't imagine what it must be like to raise a child alone—especially one with special needs. It made Kate's own problems seem trivial in comparison. But most of all she worried about Max. Once he was sure Bobby was all right, he might decide to go after Ed Tate again.

Kate shook her head. Only a week in town and already she was tangled up in everyone's lives. How had that happened? When she'd left Easy, she'd closed a door on her emotions, putting distance between her new life and the one she'd left behind. Now the door had opened a crack and she found herself caring about people she'd turned her back on—Max and his family, Cheryl and Tom, Nellie and the gang running the shop.

At Cheryl's insistence, she'd even considered the possibility of going to the reunion. What was she, crazy? How could she even contemplate that? The last thing she needed was to renew old ties and find more former acquaintances to worry about. She didn't want to care about their lives. That would only make it harder to leave again.

Sophie wove in and out between Kate's ankles, yowling pathetically. Was she hungry already? Kate wasn't sure how often a cat had to be fed, but she was sure she'd put enough food in her bowl this morning before leaving for the ranch.

She lifted the cat, stroking the soft fur. "What is it, baby? You miss Mom?"

Sophie licked Kate's hand, her tongue rough and raspy, like damp sandpaper.

"Yeah, me too."

At that moment, the sound of Roy Orbison came drifting in from the kitchen.

"Not that much," Kate said with a sigh.

The sound traveled clearly from the other room. Whatever was making the cup sing was obviously getting stronger. She didn't even have to hold the cup to her ear to hear it this time.

Kate carried the cat into the kitchen. "At least we have music," she said. "Now if we could only figure out why."

She moved around the kitchen, humming along to a tune about pretty papers. Setting the cat down, she peeked into the freezer, looking for something to microwave for dinner. She pushed aside casseroles the neighbors had dropped off after the funeral. There, tucked way in the back of the freezer, was a package of macaroon cookies.

Kate was the only one in the family who liked coconut. Her mother must have made those just for her. With a smile, Kate opened the bag and broke a cookie from the frozen mass.

She nibbled on the edges, not bothering to thaw the cookie first but breaking off little bits of coconut and letting them soften in her mouth. Her mother had made these with her own hands, baked them just for her. It was like finding a treasure.

"Thanks, Mom," she whispered, savoring the cookie and the love it represented.

And just as suddenly the cup stopped singing. Kate turned, staring at the china cup, so delicate and pretty. The silence now seemed heavy with meaning. As if…

Was it possible? She walked slowly toward the window, holding her breath. She wasn't sure what to expect, but nothing would have surprised her.

"Mom?"

Nothing.

Now she felt silly. Just what had she expected? A ghost in a teacup?

She stepped closer, reaching out, her fingertips only inches away from the cup. Her hand hovered there, afraid to move forward, unable to draw back. The air was still, the house eerily silent.

Closer. Almost touching now. A chill crawled up her spine. Goose bumps prickled her skin.

Then her fingertip grazed the lip of the cup. Gently. Barely touching. And at the exact moment of contact, the air was split by a jarring peal.

Kate jerked her hand away, her heart pounding in her throat. The cat jumped straight up in the air, all four legs lifting off the floor. It took a moment for Kate to realize the sound she'd heard was the telephone ringing.

She let out a shuddering breath and reached for the phone.

"Kate! Kate, you have to come here!"

It was Nellie and she sounded hysterical.

"Calm down, Nellie. Tell me what's wrong." She was afraid the woman would have a heart attack by the sound of hysteria in her voice. "What is it?"

"It's Deputy Tate. He's here with the electrical inspector and wants to close the shop down! You have to come right now!"

Tate. Damn him! She should have let Max kill the deputy after all.

"I'll be right there," Kate assured Nellie. She hung up the phone and glanced back at the cup. "Now what?" she asked.

The cup made no reply.

* * * * *

Max paced back and forth in the kitchen. Bobby was doing better now. They'd given him children's Tylenol, made sure he had plenty of fluids and taken turns sponging him down. The fever had broken a few hours ago, allaying most of their fears. Now Bobby was resting comfortably while Sue prepared dinner.

"Max, please stop pacing. You're driving me crazy."

Max turned, a smart remark on the tip of his tongue. But the look on Sue's face stopped him. He came over and sat beside her. "He'll be okay, Sis."

She leaned her head on his shoulder. "I was afraid. The fever came on so quickly." She pulled away and gave him an odd look. "I'm sorry I spoiled your afternoon with Kate, but I didn't know who else to call."

"It's okay." Max stroked her shoulder. He hadn't told Sue how close Bobby had come to being trampled by Venus this morning. Just thinking about it made him shudder. He'd have a long talk with Bobby about going into the barn alone. If anything happened to him...

"How did it go with Kate today?" Sue asked. There was something furtive about the question. If Max didn't know better, he'd almost think Sue was glad she'd had to call him away.

Max shrugged. He wasn't ready to deal with all the emotions his conversation with Kate had dredged up. "Seems there was more of a misunderstanding than I realized," he said. "And Ed Tate seems to be at the bottom of it all."

"Ed Tate? I don't understand."

"He's had it in for me since we were kids. You know how competitive he's always been. Apparently he saw Kate as one more competition and did everything he could to turn her against me. It would have worked too if Kate hadn't had to come back. I just hope it's not too late to make up for the past."

"What do you mean? Do you think she'll stay here in Easy now?"

"She will if I have anything to say about it," Max said. "But first I'm going to have it out with Tate."

Sue gripped his arm, her eyes wide with alarm. "What do you mean? You're not going to get into a fight with him, are you?"

"Only if he provokes me," Max said then gave a dry chuckle. "By breathing or something."

"Max, please. He's dangerous. You don't want to mess with him."

Max patted her hand. "Don't worry, Sis. I can take care of myself."

"I know you can," she said. "It's just...I'm worried about Bobby. What if his fever spikes again?"

"I'm not going anywhere," Max assured her. "At least not until I'm sure Bobby's all right."

Chapter Eleven

Kate pulled up to the shop and saw a crowd milling around outside. Some still had their teacups in their hands. She'd barely stepped out of the car when Nellie came running up, wringing her hands.

"It's Ed Tate," she said. "He's inside."

"Tell me exactly what happened," Kate said, talking softly to help calm the frightened woman.

"Well, I was making popovers when I could have sworn I heard your mother's voice. She called my name, that way she always did when she needed me up front. I turned around but the room was empty. And just then there was a sizzling sound and the lights flashed." Nellie leaned close, her eyes wide and intense. "It's as if your mother was trying to tell me something."

Kate tried to keep Nellie on track before she had to face Tate. "The lights flashed," she coaxed gently. "And then what?"

Nellie tugged on her apron strings. "And there was a sizzling sound. Did I mention the sizzling sound?"

"Yes."

"And then all the lights went out. Just like that." Nellie snapped her fingers for emphasis. "Everyone was looking around and I was trying to remember where the fuse box was, when just then Ed Tate came in."

Nellie scrunched up her face as if smelling something unpleasant. "I don't know why he's taken such a shine to this place all of a sudden. He never came in here when your mother was alive!"

Kate knew what his sudden interest was all about, but she kept it to herself.

"So anyways," Nellie continued, "he claimed he'd warned you about getting that electrical problem looked at and said now he had no choice but to call in the inspector. He made everyone leave. Including me! That's when I called you."

"So he's inside now with the electrical inspector?"

Nellie nodded, her head bobbing up and down. "Those popovers are going to be ruined."

Popovers were the least of Kate's problems. "I'll take care of it," she said, giving Nellie a reassuring pat on her shoulder before turning to go inside.

The last person she wanted to deal with was Ed Tate. Especially knowing what she knew now about his lies. But she had to put that aside. Right now the business was more important.

She stepped inside and saw Ed Tate in a huddled conversation with a man who looked vaguely familiar.

Ed made the introductions. "Kate, you remember Chuck Hitchcock, don't you?"

Once she heard the name, she remembered Chuck. He'd been a skinny, sniveling kid who'd always hung at the fringes of Ed's crowd of friends. He was one of those eternally simpering boys who'd do anything to be accepted. From the way his eyes kept flicking to Deputy Ed, he hadn't changed. Kate held out her hand and received a limp handshake in return.

"What's the problem here?" she asked, trying to keep her voice calm.

"Looks like you've got a short in the wiring somewhere," Chuck said, glancing at Ed, then back to his metal clipboard. He looked everywhere but at Kate.

Ed shook his head and pursed his lips. "I told you to have that wiring looked at," he said. "An electrical short is nothing to fool around with."

He drew Kate aside and whispered conspiratorially. "Look, Chuck is an old buddy of mine. I think I can get this taken care of without having to close you down. For old times' sake," he said with a sly wink.

Kate fought down the urge to gag. She knew a shakedown when she saw it. "For old times' sake? And just what would you expect in return for this little favor?"

"Now, Kate. Would I expect anything in return?" He drew her close, a lecherous smile on his face. "Of course, if you changed your mind about the reunion…"

Kate could feel his breath on her face, a sour mixture of hot dogs, chili beans and bravado. He tried to pull her closer and she had all she could do to keep from pushing him away.

"We had some good times," he said. "What's the harm in having a little fun while you're here? We can pick up where we left off."

That was about all she could take. Her anger reached the boiling point and she pushed him away. "Oh, I know where we left off, all right," she hissed, barely keeping the contempt from her voice. "We left off with you lying to me and spreading rumors all over town to make up for the fact that I didn't want you then. And guess what? I don't want you *now* either. So you can take your 'help' and cart it the hell out of here. I don't need your help and I don't want to see your lying face in here again!"

Ed stared at her, his eyes narrowing dangerously. But now that she'd started she couldn't stop. "Oh, and you might want to watch your backside, since Max and I compared notes." She jabbed her finger into his chest, forcing him to step away from her. "He's not real happy about your lies either, I can tell you that. And once I report that you're using your badge to intimidate people, you'll be out of a job too!"

Ed gave her a challenging look. "Try it," he growled then turned his back on her. "Close them down," he ordered the inspector.

"What?!" Kate followed him, screaming at his back. "You can't do that!"

He signed the papers on Chuck's clipboard with a flourish, not even looking at her. "I just did."

He handed her the paper and puffed out his chest importantly. "For the safety and welfare of the customers, I have no alternative but to shut you down. You have until Monday to bring the wiring up to code. At that time, if it fails to pass inspection again, the Tea and Crumpet Shop will be closed permanently."

"This isn't about the shop," Kate shouted, grabbing his arm and spinning him around. "It's about you not getting what you want. You haven't changed, have you? You're the same manipulative, vindictive bully you were back in high school."

"Maybe," he replied. His voice lowered ominously, "But I'm also the one wearing a badge, and if you don't want to be charged with assaulting an officer of the law as well, you'd better keep your hands to yourself, little lady."

He started to leave then turned and gave her a victorious smile. "Oh, and you can expect to be hearing from our lawyers too."

"About what? That ridiculous claim that your mother owns half of this property? Is that what this is all about?"

Ed smiled. "That 'ridiculous claim', as you call it, will be settled in a court of law." He turned his back on her dismissively. "You'll be sorry you didn't accept my help," he called over his shoulder.

"Bastard," Kate hissed as the door slammed shut behind him, before spinning on her heel and reaching for the phone.

* * * * *

From the window, Sue watched Max going about his chores outside. He'd been working nonstop since dinner, obviously fueled by anger and frustration. At the rate he was going, he could single-handedly rebuild the whole ranch before sun-up.

"Mom, can I go help Uncle Max feed the critters?"

Sue turned to her son. Bobby was itching from sitting still too long. He liked to keep busy, just like his uncle. "The doc said to take it easy tonight."

Pouting, Bobby went back to his puzzle. "I'm fine now," he mumbled, half-heartedly trying to fit two pieces together.

Sue smiled, letting him grumble. She knew it wouldn't last long. His naturally sunny disposition would break through like sunshine after a storm. His father had been like that too at one time. Until he decided that raising a child with Bobby's needs was too much to handle, and the daily grind of working on the ranch started wearing him down. After awhile she'd forgotten the man he used to be, the man she fell in love with. She'd forgotten his smile and tenderness, and only saw the tired, worn-down man who couldn't take anymore. Then one day he'd driven into town for some supplies and kept right on going. That was the last they'd seen of him.

She knew what it was like to be left behind. She knew how hard it must be for Max to see Kate again, only to wonder if she'd leave just like last time. Sue couldn't bear to see her brother in that kind of pain again. Everything was just fine the way it was, with just her father, brother and son. They didn't need anyone else around.

The ringing phone startled her out of her thoughts. "I've got it," she called before Bobby could snatch it up.

When she heard Kate's voice on the other end, Sue felt a quick flash of guilt, almost as though Kate had somehow read her thoughts. She kept her voice pleasant but couldn't quell the building sense of resentment.

"Max is out working in the barn," she told Kate. "I'll tell him you called." If it were anyone else, Sue would have run out and told Max right then. But she didn't want Kate taking him away tonight. Or any night, for that matter. And she didn't want the two of them getting any closer than they already had. *It was better for Max that way*, she convinced herself. *Better for everyone concerned.*

Without the slightest twinge of guilt, she conveniently forgot to write down Kate's message.

* * * * *

With nothing left to do at the shop, Kate locked the doors and sent everyone home, assuring them it would reopen as soon as possible. On the drive home, she went over the strange series of events. She remembered the first time the lights had flickered in the shop. It was when she'd touched her mother's cup and felt that first vague hum coming from it. Since then, of course, the cup had found its voice.

Nellie had said the second time the lights flickered she'd been sure she'd heard Lillian call out. Maybe the electrical problem *was* some kind of supernatural occurrence rather than a physical one. Given a choice, Kate would prefer something that could be fixed rather than a muddled haunting. If her mother was trying to reach them from the other side, she was doing a lousy job of it.

As she opened the front door, Kate heard the phone ringing. She lunged for it, hoping it was Max. It wasn't, but she was just as grateful to hear her brother's voice on the other end of the line.

"Jeff! How's the cruise?"

"Wonderful! You wouldn't believe the food. I think I've already gained twenty pounds. Sally and I are having a wonderful time and I can't thank you enough for holding down the fort so we could have a honeymoon."

Kate had to strain to hear him, but the contentment in his voice was evident. "You sound good," she said.

"I am. We should have done this years ago."

Kate knew the reason he hadn't, and wondered if she should even bring up the latest battle in the Feathers-Tate feud or just let him enjoy the few remaining days of his honeymoon.

"How are things going there?" he asked, as if reading her mind.

She decided to give him the condensed version. "Nothing I can't handle. We have a little electrical problem at the shop that needs looking into."

"Have Max check it out," Jeff said. "He'll know what to look for and have it fixed in no time. He's good with his hands."

That phrase conjured images Kate wasn't sure she wanted to deal with at the moment. "I'll do that in the morning," she assured her brother. Then, before their call could be cut short, she decided to ask him if he'd ever heard anything about their father's name being on the property title.

"Not that I know of," Jeff said. "Of course, I was pretty young when he left us. But I'm sure Mom would have said something."

Kate nodded, cradling the phone to her ear. "Yeah, I'm sure she would have." There was no sense spoiling her brother's honeymoon with the problem. There was nothing he could do from there. She'd deal with it, and hopefully by the time Jeff and Sally returned, it would all be settled and they'd have a good laugh over the whole misunderstanding.

They chatted for a few more minutes and Jeff promised to get in touch at the next port of call. Kate said goodbye, assuring him once again that she had everything under control.

If only that were true.

Rather than worry about something she had, in fact, *no* control over, Kate made herself a sandwich and grabbed a paperback novel off a shelf. There was nothing more she could do tonight. Tomorrow was soon enough to start calling electricians—assuming she could find one who worked on Sundays. She'd probably end up paying triple to get the job done, but she had no choice with Tate's Monday deadline looming.

Chapter Twelve

ॐ

Kate woke up to the aroma of cinnamon and brown sugar. She rubbed her eyes and smiled, listening to the comforting bustling sounds in the kitchen. She felt lazy and dreamy, but knew she'd have to get up soon or she'd be late for school.

She blinked her eyes open. *School?* She shook dreamy cobwebs from her mind, slowly remembering where she was and why she was sleeping in her old bed again. As she came awake, the homey sounds of cooking and singing drifted in from the other side of her closed door. *If not her mother, then who was in the kitchen?*

Wearing just the boxers and Arizona Sun Devils T-shirt she'd fallen asleep in, Kate opened the bedroom door a crack and peeked out, surprised to see Nellie bustling around the kitchen.

"Did I wake you, sweetheart?"

Kate turned a bleary eye to the kitchen clock. Five-thirty. "No, I was just going to get up," she lied, rubbing her eyes. "What are you doing here?"

Nellie opened the oven and pulled out a tray of cinnamon rolls. "Getting ready to open," she said.

Kate blinked. "Open what?"

"Why, open for business of course! The popovers were ruined, just like I said they would be. But I made lemon pound cake instead. That's always a big seller."

"How...how did you get in here?"

"Oh," Nellie said innocently. "I have a key. Did I forget to tell you?"

Kate joined Nellie and flopped onto a kitchen chair. It was too early in the morning to think. She only had one brain cell working and it was busy firing the "breathe in, breathe out" command. She'd make sense of this later. Right now she needed coffee.

As if answering a prayer, Nellie set a steaming cup on the table in front of her. Kate grunted and reached gratefully for it. Too late, she realized three things.

First, it was her mother's cup.

Second, it wasn't coffee.

And third, shimmering on the surface of the liquid, her mother's face was staring back at her.

Kate jerked back from the cup as if it was alive. Hot tea sloshed in the saucer and the ghostly image dissolved in a liquid ripple. She shook her head, mumbling, "This is why I'm not a morning person."

With trepidation, Kate leaned forward, hovering over the cup. She held her breath and peeked inside. Amber swirls undulated over the surface. The scent of chamomile tickled her senses, warm and sweet and soothing. Her mother had vanished — if she was ever there to begin with. Still, it seemed rude to take a sip now.

The mirage — for that's surely what it was — had simply been a trick of the light, combined with stress and too little sleep. Yeah, that was it.

Pushing the cup away, Kate glanced around the kitchen. There were cinnamon rolls and muffins and cakes and crumpets on every spare inch of counter space. She narrowed her eyes. "Where's my new coffee pot?"

"I had to put it away," Nellie said briskly. "I needed the room. Besides, we wouldn't want the customers to see a coffee pot in here! It wouldn't be good for business, now would it?"

"Customers? Oh no." Kate shook her head. "No, no, no, no, no. We are *not* doing business from here."

Nellie turned, giving her a sweet, indulgent smile. "Of course we are, dear. We can't let people down. Everyone looks forward to their daily tea and crumpets."

"But it's Sunday," Kate said, hearing the whine in her voice.

Nellie simply nodded. "Sunday is our busiest day."

Kate lowered her head into her hands. Who said life was simple in the country? With a sigh, she answered her own unspoken question — *city people who don't know any better.*

"You should get dressed, dear," Nellie said. "We open at seven." She turned back to the counter, swirling creamy white icing over the warm cinnamon buns as if it were the most natural thing in the world to conduct business out of Lillian's kitchen.

"I need a shower," Kate said. She dumped the cooled tea into the sink, rinsed the cup and set it upside-down in the strainer. Hopefully it wouldn't start singing and give Nellie a heart attack.

Fifteen minutes later, showered and reluctantly awake, Kate felt ready to handle whatever the day had in store for her. At least that's what she thought. However, she wasn't prepared for the onslaught of tea-seekers who showed up promptly at seven, complete with Madame Zostra in full gypsy regalia.

Nellie had set up folding metal TV trays, and the Tea and Crumpet Shop regulars were perched on couches and chairs throughout the living room, dining room and even the kitchen. No one seemed to mind the cramped accommodations. For a fleeting second, Kate wondered whether Nellie included some secret addictive ingredient in her crumpets. What else would explain a craving so compelling that customers would crowd her living space for their daily fix?

And just when it seemed things couldn't get any worse, a courier showed up at the door with an official letter. True to his word, Ed Tate was serving notice of a property claim. Not just the property, Kate realized. According to the legal documents in her hand, the "real property" in question consisted of the land

and anything permanently affixed to it—which meant the shop as well.

Kate read through the legal mumbo-jumbo, a sense of foreboding settling in her stomach. *In the matter of the disposition of real property jointly titled to Jebediah and Lillian Feathers, both deceased...*

From what Kate could see, Ginny Tate was suing for half ownership of the business as her rightful share of Jebediah's estate. That would leave the remaining fifty percent to be split three ways between Kate, Jeff and Max, according to Lillian's will.

It didn't help Kate to realize that all this could have been avoided if she'd given Ed Tate what he wanted in the first place. Apparently hell also hath no fury like a *deputy* scorned.

The more Kate thought about it, the madder she became. She was in no frame of mind to be diplomatic when Deputy Ed showed up.

She met him at the door.

He glanced over her shoulder and shook his head. "You can't run a business in a residential neighborhood, you know."

"I'm not running a business," she replied, crossing her arms over her chest and putting on her most innocent expression. "We're just having a few friends over. That's not against the law, is it?"

His eyes narrowed with suspicion.

Kate turned and called over her shoulder. "Was anyone asked to pay for anything here?"

A chorus of "no's" rang out. That was true. Kate and Nellie had decided to open the doors to anyone who showed up asking why the shop was closed. Taking money in her mother's own kitchen would have seemed sacrilegious. Rather than turn anyone away, they'd served complimentary tea and crumpets to customers all morning, promising that the business would be up and running again by Monday morning.

"So," she continued, "business implies the transfer of money. Since no money changed hands, no business has taken place. Correct? Or do you have to check with your lawyer about the legal ramifications of that?"

Tate hitched up his belt. "Maybe I'll just come in and have a look," he said.

Kate stood firm, blocking his path. "I said we were having a few friends over," she said. "*Just* friends."

His face colored with rage. He leaned close and hissed, "You won't have such a smart little mouth when you lose your mother's business, will you missy?" Then he raised his voice, loud enough for everyone inside to hear. "I'll be keeping an eye on you." Without another word, he turned and stalked off.

With his threat still ringing in her ears, Kate closed the door and made her way through the crowded living room to the kitchen. She slumped onto a chair and cradled her head in her hands.

"Deputy Ed seems to have a burr under his saddle these days," Nellie said. "What's gotten into him?"

"Revenge," Kate said with a tired sigh. "He's decided to get back at me for something that happened a long time ago by taking the business away from us."

Nellie straightened, indignation making her voice quiver. "He can't do that!"

"His lawyers think he can." Kate pulled out the letter and showed it to Nellie, explaining Tate's claim to half ownership of the property.

"That's...that's...bull cocky!"

Kate knew that was the closest Nellie would ever get to cussing, but it was pretty strong stuff for her.

"Your mother owned that property. When she got rid of that no-good bum..." Nellie seemed to suddenly realize what she was saying and her voice softened. "No offense, hon, but Jebediah wasn't fit to clean your mother's shoes, in my opinion. He and Ginny Tate deserved each other."

Kate was less concerned with Nellie's opinion of her father than her insistence that Lillian owned the property free and clear. If that was true, then Ginny Tate had no case against them. "How do you know my mother owned the property free and clear?" she asked.

"Well, I remember Lillian saying she'd washed her hands of Jebediah once and for all." Nellie's hands fluttered like trapped birds. "I remember her saying he had no claim on her now, she was free and clear." Nellie gave a brisk shake of her head. "Those were her exact words. *Free and clear.*"

Kate nodded thoughtfully, remembering her similar conversation with Cheryl a couple days earlier. If her father had no rights to the property, that would explain why the Tates hadn't pursued this frivolous lawsuit before now. Obviously Lillian had proof their claim was invalid. But where was it?

"I've been through all of my mother's papers," Kate said, shaking her head. "There's nothing I can find turning over the property to her. And nothing on record with the county either." She'd checked as soon as Ed had made his initial threat. So where did that leave her?

"I wouldn't put it past Ed Tate to destroy the records," Nellie mused. "He's got half the town in his pocket and the other half running scared." Nellie sighed. "If only Lillian were here."

"Yeah, if only..." Kate's voice trailed off and she glanced toward the cup resting in the strainer. *Maybe in a way she was?*

Then Kate remembered the song she'd heard coming from the cup the other day. *Pretty papers?* Maybe her mother was trying to tell her there were legal papers somewhere that proved Lillian had been the sole owner of the property.

Kate shook her head. The whole concept of receiving messages from the great beyond was preposterous. Still, it was the only clue she had. Without giving herself time to reconsider, Kate stood and retrieved the cup from the strainer.

"Okay Mom," she whispered, pouring tea into the cup. "If you've got something to say, here's your chance."

"Did you say something, dear?" Nellie asked.

"Nope." Barely giving her tea time to cool, Kate drank it down, draining the cup until only a few dregs remained, then swirling the remaining liquid and turning the cup upside down on the saucer.

After setting the cup and saucer on the table, Kate poked her head into the living room. "Madame Zostra? Could you come in here for a minute?"

* * * * *

Max had been working since sun-up, so he didn't feel guilty leaving the ranch behind for a few hours. Sue was capable of handling anything that might come up while he was gone, and Bobby was fine, with no visible aftereffects from yesterday's fever. So Max had a few hours to kill and he knew just the person in need of killing.

On his way to find Deputy Ed, he drove past the Tea and Crumpet Shop. Maybe it was force of habit or maybe he was hoping for a glimpse of Kate. He did a double take when he saw that the doors were closed and it was dark inside.

"What the hell?" he muttered.

With an ominous feeling in the pit of his stomach, Max pulled over to the side of the road, everything else forgotten. He hopped out of the pick-up and left it idling at the curb. The shop was empty and silent. The door was locked and no one answered his knock. Something was wrong. He couldn't remember the shop ever being closed during normal business hours—especially Sunday morning, when it seemed half the town gathered there.

Could something have happened to Kate? Heart pounding, he climbed back into the truck and raced to her house. The drive took only minutes, but it felt like hours. He imagined any number of emergencies, each one of them more frightening than the last.

With a squeal of tires, he pulled in front of Lillian's house and hurried to the front door. In his haste to find Kate, he nearly crashed into Bertha Pitt on her way out.

"No need to hurry," Bertha said. "There's plenty of food left. If I know Nellie, she saved you a special treat in the kitchen."

Only then did Max realize that Bertha was carrying a bag that smelled fragrantly of warm baked goods. What was going on here?

Behind the door, he could hear the sounds of voices. Lots of voices. It sounded as if half of Easy was milling around inside. Max rang the doorbell, only a little surprised when Chrissy Roberts, wearing her waitress uniform and apron, opened the door.

"Come on in, Max," she chirped. "I'll find you a seat."

Max's jaw dropped when he surveyed the living room filled with customers from the Tea and Crumpet Shop. "I'm not here for tea," he said. "I need to speak to Kate."

"Well she's in the kitchen right now." Chrissy batted her big brown eyes. "Why don't you let me get you something while you wait?"

Immune to her teenage flirtation, Max brushed right past Chrissy. "That's okay," he said. "I'll find her myself."

Max wove through the packed living room, trading greetings with neighbors and friends, all sipping tea and munching sweets from trays balanced on their laps. If he wasn't so worried about Kate, Max might have found it amusing, like some surreal sugar-addict's cocktail party.

When he stepped into the kitchen, Nellie noticed him first. She gestured for him to be quiet by putting a finger over her lips and nodding toward the table. Max saw Kate and Adelaide Wilkinson, known far and wide as Madame Zostra, huddled over a teacup. Kate's back was to him. At his raised eyebrows, Nellie shook her head, warning him not to interrupt.

"Roses," Madame Zostra intoned dramatically, humming and weaving back and forth. "She wants you to search among the roses."

Kate nodded and jotted a note on a slip of paper already covered with her neat, precise handwriting.

Suddenly Madame Zostra cried out, "Max!"

He jerked when she shouted his name, but Madame Zostra wasn't looking at him. She seemed to be staring at some distant spot beyond the far window.

"He holds the key," Madame Zostra said.

"Max holds the key?" Kate, still unaware that Max was standing behind her, added the cryptic phrase to the slip of paper. "What else?" she asked.

Madame Zostra clapped her hand to her heart. A whimper escaped her lips and Max watched the color drain from her face. "So much sadness," she said. "Sadness and disappointment. There's a snake in the grass. BE CAREFUL!" Her voice rose to an ear-shattering screech, then she slumped in her chair, drained and trembling.

Max didn't buy her act for a minute. Madame Zostra was no psychic. But why would she torment Kate like this? It was cruel. He stepped forward, intent on stopping this psychic farce.

"That's all I can get," Madame Zostra said, her voice quivering. "Lillian's energy is gone now."

"I think that's enough," Max said.

Kate whipped around. When she saw Max, her face lit up. "You're here."

He knelt beside her chair and reached for her hands, cradling them in his own. "Now what's this all about?"

"My mother. She's been trying to tell me something."

Max crooked an eyebrow, but the hopeful look on Kate's face softened his tone. "Well," he said, tipping his head in

Madame Zostra's direction, "from what I heard, she's not doing a very good job of it." He glanced at the notes on the table. "Roses, keys, pretty papers…" He shook his head. "No offense darlin', but if what you say is true, your mother is one of the most cryptic ghosts I've ever heard of."

"She's having a hard time getting through," Kate admitted sheepishly. "I know it sounds silly, but I swear I've been getting strange feelings from this cup. There's an energy there I can feel, see, hear. My mother is trying to send me a message from beyond the grave."

"And if anyone can do it," Nellie piped up, "it's Lillian."

Max took a deep breath. If it made them feel better, he couldn't see any harm in letting the three women believe whatever they wanted.

"Okay, let's forget about Lillian's ghost for now. Tell me why you're serving tea here and not in the shop."

While Kate filled him in, Nellie went back to her baking and Madame Zostra swept off in search of new psychic connections.

The more Max heard of Tate's manipulations, the more furious he became. His entire body tightened with rage, jaw grinding furiously. At least Madame Zostra had gotten the "snake in the grass" part right.

More importantly, though, why hadn't Kate come to him first? Obviously she still didn't trust him. And how could he convince her that she should?

He stood up, his body thrumming with pent-up frustration. He took Kate's hand and pulled her to her feet. "Come on," he said, needing to do something constructive with the rage burning inside him. "First we're going to take care of the wiring at the shop. Then I'll take care of Ed Tate and get him off your case once and for all."

Chapter Thirteen

ଈଠ

Kate watched Max work on the electrical wiring, more relieved to have someone to share her worries with than she cared to admit. She really hadn't needed to come with him to the shop. It wasn't as if she could be all that much help and she could have easily given him the key. Heck, it wouldn't surprise her to find out he already had one. Half the town probably did.

Nope, she didn't need to be here, but she was glad she'd come with him just the same. There was something about watching a man work—all hard, corded muscles and intensely focused concentration. And he came with his own accessories— tools of every size and type for whatever job needed to be done. She watched him crouch and stretch and bend, the movements doing incredible things to the fit of his jeans. Watching him made her feel as giddy as she had back in high school.

But she wasn't a teenager with a crush on the most popular boy in school. She was twenty-eight with a life to get back to—a life that was far away from here. She couldn't be distracted by the fact that the sexiest boy in high school was now the sexiest man in town.

"Which light did you see flicker?"

"Huh?" Kate had to get her mind off Max's butt and back to the business at hand. "Oh, it was...when I was sitting at that table over there." She pointed, remembering that first day she'd come to the shop and found Max sitting across from her. "I felt a shock...like an electrical current. But it came from the cup."

Max rolled his eyes. "Yes, the haunted teacup. Let's just focus on the electrical problems for now then we'll deal with the supernatural ones."

Kate rubbed her eyes. "It was just a flicker. Ed Tate was sitting right here," she said, remembering the moment the cup had jolted in her hand and the lights had flickered. She'd been too stunned by the jolt of energy coming from the cup to pay much attention to which light had flickered. At the time she hadn't suspected that the cup was haunted, but apparently her mother had been trying to tell her something even then.

"So Tate was sitting here when the lights flickered?"

Kate nodded.

"And then suddenly he's here with the electrical inspector?"

"Well, not exactly." Kate was almost ashamed to admit the next part. "Nellie said she heard my mother's spirit while she was in the kitchen yesterday. Then all the lights went out."

"And Tate showed up again?"

"Well…yes," she admitted, suddenly realizing why Max seemed so suspicious. Tate had an uncanny way of being around whenever bad things happened.

Max narrowed his eyes. "Hang tight. I'll be right back."

Kate watched him swagger out of the room, purposely keeping her eyes off his backside. Well, maybe just a quick peek, but that was all.

She glanced around, looking for something to do, anything to get her mind off Max and his derriere. She wandered through the kitchen but it was spotless, not so much as a spoon out of place. Nellie had taken care of everything.

She ran her hand over the gleaming stainless steel surfaces. Funny, when she first came here she couldn't wait to unload this place. Now she'd do anything to save it. Why? Why was it so important now? It wasn't as if she planned to stay in Easy. But there was Nellie and Arthur and Chrissy and even Madame Zostra to think about. They all depended on the shop. There was Jeff and his new wife too.

And there was Max.

Damn, why couldn't she stop thinking about Max? As soon as the question formed in her mind, the lights came on, nearly blinding her with their brightness. Kate blinked in surprise, not missing the symbolism. She held her breath for a moment, waiting to see if Roy Orbison was going to croon a message from the great beyond as well.

"All fixed," Max called, confirming that there was nothing supernatural about the sudden bright light. "There were a few wires loose in the breaker panel, that's all."

Kate noticed the way he broke eye contact with her when he said it. He was hiding something. "Loose?" she asked. "Why didn't the electrical contractor notice that when he was here?"

Max shrugged, still not meeting her eyes. "Maybe they weren't loose when he was here…"

"Or?"

Max took a deep breath. "Or," he finished, "maybe Tate or one of his flunkies purposely loosened the wires just for an excuse to shut the shop down."

Kate considered Max's theory. It made perfect sense, and she wouldn't put it past Tate. "He had to know you'd find it pretty easily," she argued.

Max nodded. "Yeah, he knew I'd find it. And he knew I'd know who did it. He's just thumbing his nose in our faces. Showing us who's boss."

"And he'll keep getting in our way, won't he?"

Max knew for a fact that was true. Tate would use every underhanded, devious trick in the book to get under his skin. Apparently Kate was on his list now as well.

"Not if I can help it," Max growled under his breath. "If he wants a fight, that's just what he'll get."

Kate seemed to sag. "What's the use? He'll find one reason or another to keep shutting us down until the courts decide on the lien. Then he'll walk away with half of everything my mother worked for."

Max didn't like the look of resignation on her face. For awhile there, she'd been all spit and fire, ready to fight for her rights. She'd reminded him of the Kate he used to know.

"So what? You gonna just give up and run away?"

She jerked back as if he'd slapped her. "I didn't say that." Her lower lip quivered.

He could see he'd hurt her, but he didn't let up. She'd lost her spunk somewhere along the line and if he had to provoke her to get it back, he would. "You let Ed Tate win ten years ago. Are you going to let him win again?"

When she tried to turn away, he grabbed her shoulders and gave her a little shake. "Look at me. If you run off with your tail between your legs, Tate wins. If you stay here and fight with me, we both win."

Her eyes widened. "With you?"

"Yes, of course." He grinned. "I have a one-third share invested in this place, right?"

She jutted her chin out, a tiny blaze flaring in her eyes. "We'll see about that," she said, a brave smile taking the sting out of her challenge.

He gave a low chuckle. "That's my girl."

As soon as he said the words—words so familiar it hardly seemed ten years had gone by since he'd last said them—she caught her breath. Her eyes widened, her lips parted, and the air seemed to stretch and pull and wrap around them in an embrace.

Max focused on her lips, watching them soften and part, releasing a whispered sigh. He knew they'd be warm and full and lush. He remembered their sweetness as if it were yesterday. The pull was irresistible. He leaned closer.

Closer.

"Kate." It was barely a whisper, almost a moan. His body tightened with need and he couldn't have stopped even if he wanted to.

He swooped down, pulling her into his arms. Roughly. Gently. Desperately. All at the same time. And when their lips touched, it was everything he remembered and so much more. He pulled her close, sure if he just held her tight enough she'd never be able to leave again.

Her lips parted. He drew her exhalation in, capturing her soul and returning his own in one sweet, combined breath. And it all fell away. Ten years of loneliness, ten years of resentment, all whisked away with one sweet kiss. It was like a rebirth.

And then it was over.

But still he couldn't let go. Her face was soft and sweet and shy, exactly the way he'd held her in his memory all these years. He drew her head to his shoulder, not trusting his legs to hold him.

"Kitty," he whispered.

She didn't correct him this time. Kate was the woman who lived far away. Kitty was the girl she'd left behind. *His girl.* She'd always be his girl.

She just didn't know it yet.

Kate was the first to break away. There were a hundred reasons she shouldn't be kissing Max Connors. Right now she couldn't think of a single one. She took one step back. Max took one step forward. The air seemed to sizzle between them. He held her gaze then reached out and toyed with a lock of her hair. He trailed a fingertip downward along the curve of her jaw, his touch soft and seductive. The curve of his lips held her mesmerized and despite her best intentions she wanted to kiss him again.

"Max." She placed her hands against his chest, intending to put distance between them. His heartbeat pulsed strong and steady against her palm. Heat radiated from his body, searing her soul. She was torn between wanting to pull him closer and wanting to push him away. But even as she cautioned herself that she couldn't risk falling in love with Max again, she knew beyond a shadow of a doubt that she'd never stopped loving him to begin with. All the distance in the world couldn't alter that.

"I have to get home," she said, breaking the spell.

"You are home."

The words resonated deep inside her. *Home.* She shook her head, trying to clear the fog from her brain. "I mean…who knows what Nellie's brewing up in the kitchen?"

Max dropped his hand to his side. "I'll take you back. Now that the electricity is fixed, we'll have the shop open in no time. Then you can have some privacy again." There was no mistaking the intent behind his smile.

Privacy. Kate shivered. The thought of spending time alone with Max was both enticing and dangerous. This time when she stepped away, he didn't close the gap. It was as if he sensed she needed a little distance.

On the drive back, they kept the conversation on safe subjects, but even their casual small talk was buried under the weight of all that was still left unsaid. Max wasn't a man to give up easily, and Kate knew they'd have to face those unspoken subjects eventually.

"Where's Bobby's father?" she asked, desperately trying to fill the silence with something other than longing.

Max shrugged. "He couldn't handle being a rancher. Guess he couldn't handle being a father either." Max made a snort of disgust. "One day he drove into town for some supplies and never came back. None of us have seen him since."

Max glanced at Kate, his expression unreadable. "Guess you might say it's the Connors curse. The people we love have a habit of running away."

Kate turned. She couldn't bear to see the hurt in his eyes. They drove the rest of the way in silence, each harboring their own personal regrets. Max dropped her off at her front door. He made no move to come inside, and Kate didn't invite him in.

After dropping Kate off, Max went searching for Ed Tate. He was frustrated with the way things had ended with Kate and strung up tighter than a barbed wire fence. He was in the mood for a fight and Ed Tate had a bull's-eye smack dab in the middle of his forehead.

The deputy's car was parked in front of the sheriff's office, so he knew Tate was on duty. Max had no intention of letting that stop him.

Tate was sitting at his desk, talking on the telephone. Max caught the tail end of the conversation.

"If I go down, you're going with me," Tate growled into the receiver. "And I'm not—" He looked up and noticed Max standing in the doorway. Slick as a rattler in a mudslide, his expression changed. His look of surprise was replaced by a phony politician smile.

He gestured to Max to take a seat then returned to his phone conversation. Max remained standing. He could see that Tate enjoyed keeping him waiting, proving it didn't take much to make a little man feel big.

Finally Ed hung up the phone, tipped his chair back and crossed his arms over his chest. He looked secretly amused by Max's arrival. "To what do I owe the pleasure?"

Max was in no mood to play games. "I wouldn't call it pleasure," he said. "More like unfinished business."

Tate raised an eyebrow. "If you've got something to say, Connors, just say it. I'm a busy man."

Max snorted. "Oh, you've been busy all right." He held up his hand before Tate could spout some officious bull. "Kate and I have been talking and it looks to me like you're the one who spread all those rumors about her." Max narrowed his eyes, daring Tate to deny it. "And from what Kate told me, none of them were true."

"Well, that's her word against the whole town then, ain't it?" The front legs of Tate's chair slammed down on the floor as he jerked forward. "Innocent people don't leave skid marks hightailing their way out of town, do they?"

"*You* ran her out of town!"

"You still believe that little—"

"Don't say it," Max warned.

Tate stood and faced Max. He wasn't smiling now. His voice was low and menacing. "Are you threatening me?"

They stood eye to eye, separated only by the metal desk between them. Sunlight winked off the badge on Tate's chest. "You might not want to go digging too deep," he warned. "You never know what skeletons you might dig up."

Max leaned forward, palms flat on the surface of the desk. Rage coiled inside him like a snake poised to strike. His voice was a low growl. "Stay away from Kate Feathers. We both know you're using her to get back at me." His eyes narrowed. "You want a fight, Tate? Take off the badge you're hiding behind and we'll have it out man to man. Just name the time and place. But if you try to get to me by hurting Kate, I'll have you drawn and quartered." Max reached out and tapped his finger against the center of the shiny star for emphasis. "Badge or no badge."

Tate spluttered. "I don't know what you're talking about."

"I'm talking about the trumped-up code violation. I'm talking about your cockamamie stunt to take over Lillian's shop. And I'm talking about anything else you've cooked up in that puny little brain of yours."

Tate opened his mouth to argue, but before he could get a word out, Max held up his hand and stopped him. "I've put a lock on the breaker box. Looks as if those wires that *accidentally* came loose are secure now. See that the inspector is aware of it so that Kate can open the shop tomorrow." Max leaned back, straightening on his side of the desk. "Consider this your first and only warning, Tate."

"You can't threaten me!" Tate stepped around the desk, facing Max. "You think you're the Golden Boy, don't you?" he sneered, looking like the spiteful little boy Max remembered.

"You always got everything you wanted—the girls, the awards, the medals. *Mr. All-American Hero*. Well, who's on top now? I'm wearing a badge and you're saddled with a run-down ranch that can't even make ends meet."

"And you're *still* second best," Max shot back. "Face it. You weren't good enough then, and you're not good enough now."

Max watched Tate's jaw clench and continued goading him. "I know what you did, the lies you spread. And even after you made Kate think I was to blame, she still didn't want you. That must have really pissed you off, huh? After all that, you still weren't good enough. You still couldn't compete with me, could you?"

Tate's hands curled into fists.

"Still second best," Max taunted. "That's why you hate me so much, isn't it? Because you know you'll always be second best."

Tate made a low, growling sound deep in his throat. His body tensed and a flush rose to his cheeks.

Max braced himself and waited for Tate to throw the first punch. That's all he needed—one good opening.

Sheriff Jackson cleared his throat from the doorway, breaking the standoff. "Problem in here?"

Max turned, composing his face in an innocent expression. "No problem, Sheriff. Deputy Tate and I were just clearing up a little misunderstanding about an electrical code problem." Max threw an arm around Tate's shoulder. "Deputy Tate has promised to straighten it out immediately. Isn't that right Ed?"

Tate pursed his lips as Max's fingers dug into his shoulder. "All taken care of," he said gruffly.

Sheriff Jackson stared from one to the other then nodded and walked away.

Max turned back to Tate, speaking low enough so no one else could overhear. "If you pull another stunt like the last one," he said, "I'll see that you lose that badge you're so fond of. Trust me."

Then he turned and walked out of Tate's office, nodding to a suspicious Sheriff Jackson on his way out the front door.

* * * * *

With the last "customer" out the door and the final dish washed and stacked, Kate and Nellie plopped down on the sofa and put their feet up.

"Thank God blueberry week is over," Nellie said with a sigh of relief.

Had it only been a week? Kate felt as if she'd been back in Easy for months now. And she still had another week to go before Jeff came home and took over. Then she could get back to her real life.

Except New York didn't seem so much like her real life anymore. She had friends there, but they were all people she worked with. Would anyone even miss her if she didn't come back? Or would the social waters close up around her absence, like a pond around a sunken pebble.

No matter how much she tried to deny it, Kate knew her roots would always be here in Easy, Arizona.

"So," Nellie said. "Where was Max heading off to in such a big hurry? His tires were squealing like a stuck pig."

Just the sound of Max's name made Kate smile. She could still feel the imprint of his kiss on her lips. But her smile quickly faded. "I think he's going after Ed Tate."

Nellie nodded. "It's about time someone did. Ed Tate was a mean, nasty little boy and growing up hasn't changed him much. I tell ya, no one was more surprised than me when he passed the deputy sheriff's exam. I think even Ginny Tate blinked twice when he told her the news."

"How long ago was that?" Kate asked.

Nellie pursed her lips and thought about it. "Oh, I'd say about four years ago. It was just before Sheriff Jackson was elected. He pretty much inherited Tate and was none too happy about it."

"So why does Sheriff Jackson keep him around?"

"Tate's sneaky," Nellie confided, as if it were a secret known only to a chosen few. "There are rumors swirling around him, but nothing anyone can prove." She leaned close and whispered conspiratorially. "But I happen to know Sheriff Jackson's just waiting for Tate to make one wrong move, then..." Nellie made a slicing motion across her throat. "He's outta here."

As much as Kate relished the thought, it didn't stop her from worrying about Max. No matter what people around these parts thought of Ed Tate, going after an officer of the law wasn't a good idea.

Nellie tipped her head. "Do you hear that?"

"Hmm?"

Nellie stood up. "I must have left the radio on."

Then Kate heard it too. The unmistakable sound of Roy Orbison's singing drifting in from the kitchen. She followed Nellie, trying to place the song.

"You hear it too, right?" Kate needed proof that she wasn't crazy.

"Oh yes, I hear it." Nellie tiptoed to the counter, sneaking up on the cup sitting there. "That you, Lilly?" she asked.

The cup went right on singing.

Kate tipped her head. She knew it was Orbison but couldn't place the title. "What's that song? I don't recognize it."

Nellie stood up straight and turned toward Kate. "It's called 'Coming Home'."

Kate felt a strange sensation in her chest, as if she'd been smacked with a pillow. "Coming home," she whispered, feeling a shiver walk up and down her spine. It was almost as if the song was echoing her thoughts of only moments ago—an acoustic affirmation. There was no denying the feeling of coming home, a feeling that was magnified when she was with Max.

Kate reached out and turned the cup upside down in its saucer, muffling the song. It was one thing for her mother to haunt the teacup if she was going to be helpful, but Kate would be damned if she was going to let Lillian run her life from the other side. Whether she stayed or not was her decision alone, not a choice based on the vocal stylings of a teacup.

Nellie lifted the cup and peeked beneath it. For a moment the volume rose, then hushed again as Nellie let the cup fall back with a clatter onto the saucer.

"I'll be damned," she said, shaking her head. "Ain't that just like Lilly?"

Yeah, Kate thought. *Bossy even beyond the grave.* "It doesn't necessarily prove anything," she argued. "There could be some physical explanation for it. I've heard of people picking up radio stations in their fillings."

Nellie arched an eyebrow. "Let's just assume for a minute that your mother's trying to tell us something."

"And she can only use Roy Orbison songs? Wouldn't that limit her ability to communicate?"

Nellie shrugged and raised her eyes heavenward. "Who knows what kind of rules there are up there?"

"I don't know," Kate said. "Even hauntings should make *some* kind of sense."

The cup finally stopped singing, as if not wanting to interrupt their conversation.

"Oh, it makes sense," Nellie replied. "You know your mother loved Roy Orbison." She chuckled. "I remember when Lilly and Anne Connors came back from seeing Roy Orbison in concert…oh, about 1976 I think it was. The two of them were all ga-ga over him and played Roy Orbison songs non-stop, day and night."

"Anne Connors? Max's mother?"

"Yes, they were the best of friends, don't you remember?"

Vaguely. But Kate had been too young to care about the adults, and Max had lost his mother when they were...Kate tried to remember. It was just around the time her father and mother had split up. The two events were tied together in her memory, so that means she would have been about ten or so.

Funny, she'd forgotten how close her mother and Max's mother had been. But now that she thought back, they'd done everything together. No wonder she and Max had grown up so close. They'd probably shared a crib at one point as their mothers had visited and giggled like schoolgirls.

Then everything had changed. Her father had left and they'd had to struggle to survive. Now that she thought about it, Kate remembered Max's mother being at the house a lot back then, offering sympathy and support to Lillian. So she must have died shortly after that.

"Anne Connors," Kate muttered. "It's a clue."

And just like that the cup answered, the decibel level increasing dramatically so that three specific words of the chorus could be heard clearly even though the cup was upside down.

Kate shook her head.

Nellie nodded. "Hear that? Roy says 'you've got it'."

"Got what?"

"Your answer." Nellie's head bobbed up and down with excitement. "Anne Connors. It's a clue, just like you said." She pointed to the cup. "See? Lilly confirmed it."

"No, Roy Orbison confirmed it."

"Same thing," Nellie said, raising her eyes heavenward again and sighing wistfully. "You think they're together up there?"

"God help Roy Orbison if they are," Kate muttered. She turned to leave the kitchen, nearly tripping over the cat. She bent down and picked Sophie up, murmuring softly. "Don't worry

Sophie—you've got eight more lives before having to deal with Mom again."

Chapter Fourteen

න

Max stood on the porch step staring at Kate's door. What was he doing here? The kiss they'd shared at the shop earlier was still fresh in his memory. Too fresh and too sweet to ignore. Kate still made his heart sing. If anything the magic was more powerful than he remembered, and he knew it would be even harder to forget this time if she chose to turn her back and leave him behind.

He should just walk away right now, before it went further than a kiss. Because he knew if he did more than kiss her, he'd never let her go again. If he had to hog-tie her to the hitching post he would, but once he had her — really had her — he'd never find the strength to let her out of his sight again.

He stood on the threshold, paralyzed with indecision. He didn't want to go but was afraid to stay. As his mind argued the logic of leaving, his hand lifted and knocked on the door.

And then she was there in the doorway, as if she'd been waiting for him all along. The light from inside bathed her in a golden aura. Her eyes were wide and misty, her lips looking full and invitingly soft. Again his body responded before his mind could resist the temptation of her smile. He reached out and pulled her close, clutching her tight to his chest. His heart pounded, as if awakening from a deep, dreamless slumber.

He whispered her name as if it was the only word in the universe, the only name he'd ever spoken. He buried his face in the sweet fragrance of her hair, fitting her body to his as if they'd never been apart. She had to know how right this was. She had to feel it too.

She wrapped her arms around him in an embrace that stole his heart. He'd never felt anything so soft and yielding as her body pressed against his, had never ached for anyone as much as he ached for her.

He swooped down, claiming her lips, his arms tightening possessively around her. Her lips parted beneath his and nothing else mattered. He didn't care that they were highlighted in the doorway, kissing like hungry teenagers for all the world to see. All that mattered was the taste, the smell, the feel of her.

With a moan, he lifted her, carried her into the room and kicked the door shut behind him. She trembled in his arms, making him feel too big and too rough around the edges, but that didn't stop him from holding her tight and clasping her against his pounding chest. He tore his lips from hers only long enough to lower them to the couch, covering her body with his before returning to the sweet seduction of her mouth.

He was intensely aware of the weight of his body sinking into hers. He couldn't breathe. Everything became oppressively tight—his chest, his clothes, his skin. He felt ready to burst.

Softly, hesitantly, her tongue met his, sending a jolt through him, only to withdraw again. He groaned, following the shy retreat, meeting her once again in a silky caress that became bolder, hotter, hungrier.

One calloused hand snagged on the silk of her shirt as he followed the curve of her waist, traveling upward to find and cup the swell of her breast. She gasped, the sharp intake of air drawing a moan from his throat.

He tore his lips from hers, wanting to taste every inch of her. Years of frustration throbbed inside him. He wanted to make up for the lost time in one long deep thrust. He needed her so badly he couldn't think straight.

"Max, please," she pleaded.

He was only vaguely aware of the pressure of her hands against his chest.

"Please? I can't breathe."

Slowly the words got through to his foggy mind. He blinked and rolled to the side, taking his weight off her. "I'm sorry. I didn't mean to crush you."

"No," she said. "It's not that…"

Max was surprised to see tears shimmering in her eyes. The sight tore at his heart. "Oh God, I'm sorry. Did I hurt you?"

She shook her head. "No. We just…need to talk."

Talk? That was the last thing he needed right now. He took a deep breath, trying to regain some control. His pulse pounded violently and his breath came in short, ragged gasps.

Kate turned her head, not meeting his eyes. "Everything's moving too fast."

"Too fast?" Max snorted. "I've been waiting years for this."

Kate swallowed over the lump in her throat. So had she — *in more ways than one*. She pulled away from him. There were things she had to tell Max and she couldn't think straight with his lips so close.

She slid to the opposite end of the couch, pulled her knees to her chest and wrapped her arms around them. "Please can we just talk for a minute?"

Max glanced at his watch. "I can spare a minute."

Kate couldn't help smiling at the twinkle in his eyes. "It might be slightly more than a minute."

"As long as it's not going to take ten years…" He held out his hand, trying to bridge the distance between them. "Come on," he urged. "Just take my hand. I promise not to pressure you into anything more than that."

After a moment, Kate reached out and took his hand. He gave her a smile of encouragement, but Kate had a hard time forming the words she wanted to say.

I'm a virgin.

She'd waited so long to throw those words in his face. A virgin. It was the ultimate, indisputable proof that Max and everyone else in town had misjudged her all those years ago.

Her virginity was the one shred of evidence that no one could take from her and she'd held onto it like a badge of honor.

But in a thousand fantasies it hadn't gone like this. In her fantasies she'd used it to punish him for her humiliation, to hurt him the way he'd hurt her. She hadn't planned on needing more, needing forever. She hadn't expected this storm of love to batter the walls of shame she'd erected around her heart.

She hadn't planned on still loving Max. Now, nothing else mattered.

Max gave her hand a squeeze. This was the moment of truth. She cleared her throat. "Do you remember what you said to me that night at the drive-in?"

He shook his head, but didn't release her hand.

Kate couldn't meet his eyes. She took a deep breath, reaching deep inside for the strength to repeat the words that had haunted her for so many years. "'What are you saving it for?'"

Max looked as if she'd pulled the floor out from under him. Maybe he really didn't remember saying those words. But Kate remembered.

And now she knew the answer.

He started to apologize, but Kate stopped him. "No, this isn't about blame. Not anymore." She slid closer. "I didn't know then, but I know now. I know what I've been saving myself for all these years."

She closed the distance, letting his arms close around her. She'd often wondered why she'd waited even after leaving Easy. Why she'd saved herself when casual sex was acceptable and available. Now she knew why she'd remained a virgin. This is what she'd been waiting for, this feeling of rightness. She'd saved herself for Max—not to prove something to him, but because he was then, and would always be, her first and only love.

"I've been waiting for you," she whispered.

Max clutched her tight. He couldn't believe what he was hearing. He slipped a finger beneath her chin and tipped her face to his. "You're a virgin?"

She nodded. Max watched the gentle slide of one tear from the corner of her eye. He reached out and wiped it away with the tip of his finger.

She turned her head and lifted her chin, as if daring him not to believe her. He didn't know what to say. Even though he now knew the rumors that had destroyed her reputation had all been lies, the extent of how wrongly she'd been accused hit him like a blast of ice water.

Maybe a part of him still harbored suspicions. Maybe all those years of resentment hadn't been completely erased by a moment of truth. But still…ten years? She'd been on her own in the city, all alone. Surely there must have been someone important to her?

He scooped her up and draped her across his lap, cradling her head in the crook of his arm as the raging heat of passion dropped to a slow simmer of tenderness.

Kate sighed. When he held her like this, it made her want him even more. It was obvious she'd shocked him. Maybe deep down he hadn't really believed her when she'd told him the rumors had been lies.

He shook his head, staring at her with disbelief. "You should have told me."

Kate remembered all those old feelings of betrayal. How could she? Didn't he know that the fact that he'd believed the lies had hurt her most of all? All she'd wanted to do was run away. She'd been wrong. They'd both misjudged each other.

She reached up and pressed the flat of her palm against his chest, feeling the pulse and pound of his heartbeat. "There was only you." She looked up, capturing his intense gaze. "You were the only man I ever loved, the only man I ever wanted."

He made a sound that was part sob and part moan, pulling her tight against his chest. He buried his face against the side of her neck, muffling his voice so that she was barely able to make out the words.

"I don't deserve you," he said, his voice heavy with emotion. "I should have had faith in you, should have believed—"

"Shh…" She ran her fingers through his hair. "We each made mistakes. We misjudged each other. I was as much at fault as you were."

His grip tightened possessively around her. "Ed Tate," he growled. "I'll kill him for what he did to you. For what he did to us!"

"That's in the past," she whispered. "Let it go." And she was surprised to realize that she already had. All the anger and pain and hurt seeped away. It was enough to be back home in Max's arms where she belonged. They'd wasted too much time already and she wouldn't let another moment slide away into the shadow of past regrets.

He reached up and cupped her face, staring into her eyes. "I let you down once, Kitty. I swear I'll never let you down again. You can count on me. You can trust me."

She did. His eyes burned with intensity, promising everything she'd always wanted and so much more. "I believe you," she whispered."

He let out a long sigh of relief then kissed her face, her cheeks, the tip of her nose and, finally, her lips. "I'm sorry," he whispered. "So sorry for all the time we lost. I'll make it up to you, I swear."

He would, too. Max wasn't sure how, but he'd make it up to her somehow. He'd make her trust him again and win back her love.

He rocked Kate in his arms, wishing he could give her back those years, the loss of innocence. "How do you feel?"

She gave him a tremulous smile. "Lighter," she said. "I've been holding so much bitterness inside. It feels good to let it go."

Max combed his fingers through her hair. "Thank you for telling me."

She took a slow, deep breath. "Are you disappointed?"

His heart swelled in his chest. How could he ever be disappointed in her? "Not in a million lifetimes," he said, brushing his lips over her temple. "And as much as I want you, I'd rather just hold you tonight."

Kate gave him a puzzled look. "But we don't have to wait anymore. I'm ready now."

"I know darlin'. I'm ready too. You have no idea how ready. But I want your first time to be special. I want it to be memorable. And I want to be sure that this is what you want."

"I do," she assured him.

"Good. Then it'll keep. Let's take this one step at a time, okay?"

Kate nodded, relaxing in his arms.

"First things first. How would you like to go out with me tomorrow night?"

"A date?"

"Yes, a real date—with candles and champagne and soft music. I want to show you off to the world and give you all the things we missed out on. I want to court you properly."

Kate made a soft, purring sound. "I'd like that. I'd like that very much."

Max rocked her tenderly, content to simply hold her in his arms. He realized that Kate wasn't the only one who'd been saving herself all these years. He'd kept his heart locked up tight, waiting for the only woman who held the key. Now that she'd come home to him, he'd cut his heart out before letting her go again.

Max had been watching Kate sleep for hours. The fact that she trusted him enough to sleep in his arms touched him more deeply than if they'd spent the entire night making love.

Her face was even more beautiful in sleep—soft and sweet and innocent. This was exactly how he remembered her, without the hard edge of mistrust she'd spent the last few days trying to hide from him.

The delicate skin under her eyes had a translucent bluish tint, as if she'd spent many sleepless nights since returning home. He realized she must have been exhausted to drift off so easily.

As if awakened by his thoughts, her eyes fluttered open. Disoriented, she looked at him first with surprise, then a slow smile of recognition. "Hi there," she said in a voice husky with sleep.

"Hey sleepyhead."

She tried to sit up, but his arms tightened around her. He wasn't ready to let her go yet.

"What time is it?" she asked, rubbing her eyes.

"A little past midnight."

"Oh no! You've been here all evening." She broke free of his embrace and sat up. "I know you need to get up early to work at the ranch."

He smiled. "Don't worry about me. I don't need much sleep." He winked then laced his fingers together and stretched his arms out in front him. Holding Kate close all night was well worth a few kinks.

While his arms were otherwise occupied, Kate slipped off the couch. He reached out to grab her and pull her back, but she'd already scrambled out of reach and stood looking around the darkened room as if searching for something she had to be doing.

"Stay," he called after her.

They stared at each other across the room, the simplicity of that one word separating them. Not "stay now," but "stay *forever*, stay *here*, stay *with me*."

And that was a promise she couldn't make. Not yet.

"You have to get back to the ranch," she said, as if that explained everything. He stood up, every long, lean inch of him uncoiling from his sitting position and taking up so much space in the room, which suddenly felt too small, too intimate, too private. Kate's heart fluttered in her chest.

When he moved closer, she stepped out of his reach. Her entire body trembled. She wanted him to touch her but was desperately afraid that he would. She needed space to get her thoughts straight. Everything was happening so fast.

Sensing her hesitation, he stopped where he was and shoved his hands in his pockets. Neither said a word for a long, long moment. Then they both spoke at once and stopped at the exact same time.

Their nervous laughter broke the tension. Suddenly the room didn't seem as oppressive. This wasn't just any man, Kate reminded herself. This was Max, her childhood friend, her high-school sweetheart and the man who'd cradled her so protectively while she'd slept. Just Max.

"You first," she said.

"I was just wondering if you were serving tea and crumpets here again in the morning?"

"Nope. I talked Nellie into taking a day off while we straightened things out. Lord only knows how the town will survive."

"Good," he said with a chuckle. "I talked to Tate and cleared up the little misunderstanding. You should be able to open the shop again Tuesday morning."

He looked away and she didn't dare ask him what was involved in "clearing up" the misunderstanding. There was no blood on his shirt, so she figured Tate was probably still alive.

Max reached out and fingered the wilting yellow flowers sitting on the mantel. It seemed so long ago that Bobby had knocked on the door with the handful of flowers. At the time, Kate hadn't even realized Bobby was Max's nephew.

"He's a sweet boy," Kate said, grateful for a safe subject.

Max nodded. "You know he searched all over for these rock roses. They were my mother's favorite flower."

"Rock roses?"

"Yeah. She named the ranch after them—Rock Rose Ranch. We just call it the Triple-R though. It's a pretty name for a flower but kind of a sissy name for a ranch."

Kate stifled a laugh. There was nothing sissy about anything having to do with Max Connors. She had to force herself not to stare at him, but even without looking she was aware of every hard line of his body, the way he carried himself with casual cowboy grace, the snug fit of his worn jeans. Okay, that was dangerous territory.

She cleared her throat. "Won't your sister be worried if you're not home?"

He tipped his head and grinned. "Are you trying to get rid of me darlin'?"

"No, it's not that…it's just getting late, that's all." The truth was she was weak. It was hard enough seeing him in broad daylight, but at night when the shadows were like velvet and her resolve as weak as a midnight dream, she didn't know whether she could fully resist Max Connors' charms.

"Walk me to the door?" His voice was soft and coaxing, making her feel foolish.

"Of course." She moved closer and he draped his arm around her shoulder, as if it were the most natural thing in the world. And that's exactly how it felt. Natural. Right.

At the door, he didn't try to kiss her again. She didn't know whether to be relieved or disappointed. "I'll see you tomorrow?"

"Of course. We have a date, remember?" He tipped his head and winked. "You haven't forgotten already have you?"

"No, of course not." She felt suddenly shy, like a schoolgirl on her first date.

"I'll pick you up at seven." He leaned over and kissed her forehead. "See you then darlin'."

When she closed the door behind him, she leaned against it and took a deep breath, trying to regain her equilibrium. He was dangerous—dangerous to her resolve, and even more dangerous to her intention to leave Easy in one short week and return to New York City.

She locked the door and walked across the room, catching sight of the flowers on the mantel. She fingered the petals that Max had fondly caressed. Rock roses, he'd called them. His mother's favorite. She'd forgotten to talk to him about the friendship their mothers had shared and what that might mean. Rock roses…

Then it struck her.

Hadn't Madame Zostra said something about roses? But Kate had envisioned the long-stemmed velvety florist roses, not these wild desert flowers.

Roses. Anne Connors. Again that connection. Could the roses refer to Rock Rose Ranch? And hadn't Madame Zostra said something about Max holding the key? She had to be referring to the ranch!

Kate ran to the door and threw it open, intending to call Max back. But it was too late. His truck was already disappearing around the corner.

Tomorrow, she thought. There'd be time to talk to him about it tomorrow.

Chapter Fifteen

๛

Max had no sooner sat down at the breakfast table Monday morning when Sue started grilling him.

"You got in late last night."

Max pulled his chair up to the table. "Yep." He piled bacon and eggs onto his plate, hoping she'd take the hint.

"I suppose you'll be spending a lot of time with Kate while she's here, right?"

"Reckon so. Least when I'm not here at the ranch doing chores."

Bobby piped up. "I can help with chores, Uncle Max."

Sue turned to her son. "You're still running a slight fever. Best if you stay indoors for a few more days."

Pouting, Bobby went back to his breakfast. "I'm fine," he mumbled. "Don't see why I can't just hang out with Uncle Max."

"Well, Uncle Max has other people to hang out with these days."

Max glanced at Sue. Her shoulders were set and her face pinched with disapproval. Max figured she had something on her mind, but this wasn't the time or place to discuss it. He'd talk to her alone later when Bobby wasn't hanging on their every word. Maybe she just needed some reassurance that Kate wasn't going to take him away. Sue should know better than that. His heart was here at the ranch, not in some faraway city.

As if reading his thoughts, Sue hammered home her point. "She's only going to be in town another week. Don't forget that."

Max hadn't forgotten. But he intended to make the most of the entire week. By the time it was over, he'd convince Kate to stay. He had to. He realized that he'd been lost all these years. He'd loved her for so long that he couldn't remember a time when he didn't love her. She wouldn't slip away so easy this time. Now that he'd found her again, he'd do whatever it took to make her stay.

"That reminds me," he said. "I won't be home for dinner tonight."

Sue glanced up and held his gaze for a long moment. "Be careful," she said, lowering her voice. "She broke your heart once before. I just don't want to see you go through that again."

Max reached out for his sister's hand. Now he realized why Sue was so upset about Kate. She was simply being protective. He could understand that. He'd feel the same way in her situation. "Things are different now," he assured her. "We're not kids anymore. And this time we know who the enemy is."

Sue glanced away, her lips turned down in a frown. "You don't want to mess with Ed Tate," she warned Max. "He can cause a lot of trouble for us."

Max got up from the table and carried his plate to the sink. Just hearing Tate's name had spoiled his appetite. "Let him try. He won't get away with it."

Sue didn't argue, but Max could tell by the look on her face that she wasn't convinced. He didn't have time to worry about soothing his sister's fears right now. There were chores to do and a long day ahead of him before his date tonight.

"I'll be out in the barn if you need me."

* * * * *

Kate wasn't sure what to do with the whole day ahead of her. It felt strange not to be going to the Tea and Crumpet Shop. In just one short week she'd started looking forward to sharing news and gossip with the regulars, working side by side with Nellie and the gang and, most of all, seeing Max.

But she'd see him tonight. And that thought kept creeping in, surprising her at unexpected moments. She wondered what she should wear for their date. She should have asked Max where they were going. What if he planned to take her someplace fancy? She only had casual clothes with her.

Luckily she'd gone shopping when she realized she'd have to stay a couple weeks. She pulled out a simple black skirt and white silk blouse. That would work. She could always dress it up with some of her mother's jewelry. Then Kate remembered the lavender pashmina she'd sent her mother for Christmas. It would be the perfect accessory to her simple outfit.

Kate rushed to her mother's room and threw open the closet door, then stopped, her eyes widening in shock. She took one step back, her heart racing.

There, hanging right in front of the closet, was *the dress*.

Not just any dress. It was the strapless, clingy, siren-red dress that her mother had made for the beauty pageant. The dress had fit her like a second skin, hugging her in all the right places then falling in a regal train behind her. Kate had felt beautiful and proud wearing it. She'd had no way of knowing that that dress would come to symbolize both the best and worst night of her entire life.

Trembling, she reached out and touched the clear plastic covering the gown. It seemed to whisper to her, carrying echoes from the past. If she closed her eyes, Kate could hear Aubrey Carlisle, the pageant director, breaking the news to her only moments after the ceremony.

"I'm sorry, Kate. We have to take your title away. You know the rules. There can be no hint of impropriety attached to the pageant. It's come to our attention that you've been...indiscreet. I have no choice but to disqualify you from the competition."

Kate nearly doubled over, feeling the same punch to the gut she'd felt hearing those words the first time. Indiscreet? Impropriety? They were wrong. So wrong. The dress she'd been so proud of had become a symbol of her disgrace—her own private scarlet letter.

She'd never worn the color red since.

Kate clutched a fistful of material. Her stomach churned and her head spun. She turned away from the closet, forcing herself to take slow, deep breaths as she tried desperately to bring her emotions under control.

She'd known coming home would bring back memories. She'd shored herself up and tried to prepare herself for the worst. And now that she'd faced it, she could admit that there was another side to the coin, good along with the bad. There was the quick rush of bittersweet remembrances that came at unexpected moments—the first sight of the house where she'd grown up, the way the air smelled uniquely like home, the familiar landscape and remembered faces. How could she have buried the most important years of her life? How could she have let one cruel memory tear apart the very fabric of her youth? And why had she waited so long to revisit her past and heal the wound?

Kate knew that healing was within her grasp. When she'd left town ten years ago, she'd been sure that Max had been behind the rumors—that he'd been the instrument of her final humiliation. Now she knew the truth, and that made all the difference in the world. They'd both paid a price.

But they could move forward from here.

Suddenly it didn't matter whether she had the right clothes to wear for their date tonight. She decided that when Max showed up at the door, she'd be wearing as little as possible. She'd had half of her life stolen from her. Now the time had come to reclaim it once and for all.

She'd waited long enough.

* * * * *

Max had taken a long, hot shower until there was no trace of ranch left on him. Just to be safe, he'd added an extra splash of Old Spice. It wouldn't do to show up at Kate's door smelling like horse and sweat on the first date of the rest of their lives.

He'd dressed in his best duds. She was probably used to slicker-looking men in the city, but he couldn't pretend to be something he wasn't. He was a simple cowboy—no more, no less.

He pulled up in front of Kate's house and hopped out of the pick-up truck. He was halfway to the front door when he remembered the flowers he'd left on the front seat. He ran back, grabbed the clutch of yellow roses and ran one nervous hand through his hair until he felt halfway presentable. At her front door, he took a deep breath, his heart racing like a prize-winning stallion, and rang the doorbell.

He heard the bell echo inside, saw a flicker of light as a curtain twitched in the window. Then the door opened and his pulse went from a trot to a gallop.

The room glowed with soft pools of candlelight. Romantic music played in the background. In the center of it all, Kate stood like a vision in white, wearing a long, flowing, silky nightgown that managed to be both sweet and seductive at the same time. A row of tiny pearl buttons drew his gaze downward.

Max felt the air rush from his lungs. He closed the door behind him then leaned against it, afraid his legs would give out beneath him. He knew he was staring, but he couldn't take his eyes off her.

She lowered her gaze then peeked up at him in a way that made his stomach flip. "I couldn't decide what to wear tonight."

Max gulped. "Mighty fine choice."

Her smile held more than a hint of flirtation. "Have I shocked you?"

He closed the distance between them and slid one arm around her waist. "A little," he admitted. "But I recover quickly." He brushed his lips over her forehead, whispering softly. "I thought we were going to take things slow?"

"I changed my mind." She tipped her head, her eyes twinkling. "It's a woman's prerogative."

He looked around the room. "You sure know how to set the mood."

"Max, I'm a virgin, not a cloistered nun. I have cable television." She slid her hand along his chest until her palm rested over his heart. "I know what sex is and how it's done. I just haven't made the leap to first-hand experience —*yet*."

There was no mistaking the promise in her voice. It was a promise that Max was more than willing to explore. He wrapped his arms around her and pulled her tight against his chest, dizzy with need. Her mouth was soft and yielding beneath his, parting at the first brush of his tongue. He dove deeper, the heat of her mouth enflaming his desire for more. He held her tighter, closer, one part of his mind cautioning him to go slow, the other, more insistent part aching to bury himself deep inside her.

She wiggled against him, sending a spike of heat straight to his groin. He moaned and held her tighter.

"Max," she whispered, a tremor in her voice. "There's a thorn in my back."

"Huh? Oh!" He loosened his grip. The roses he'd brought were nearly crushed in the heat of their embrace. He'd been half out of his mind with desire, like a randy teenager in heat. That's what had gotten him into trouble the first time. He had to remember to go slow, to ease her gently into this. He handed her the roses with a sheepish smile. "Where should we put these?"

She took his hand. "How about in the bedroom?"

That was all the invitation Max needed. Dropping the flowers, he scooped her up and carried her to the bedroom. She nuzzled against the side of his neck, her lips leaving a fluttery trail of heat along his skin that was pure torture. *Slow*, he reminded himself.

He draped her across the bed then sat beside her, wondering if he'd ever seen anything more beautiful in his life. Her skin glowed in the flickering candlelight. Her lips were full and inviting and her eyes dark with desire.

A moan escaped his lips as he leaned over and trailed a fingertip along her cheek. "You're so beautiful, so perfect." His hand traveled over skin as smooth as silk. He caressed her shoulder, her arm, tracing downward along her waist and over her stomach, then back up to cup the curve of a breast that fit perfectly in his hand.

Kate trembled, any doubts she'd had forgotten with the tenderness of his touch. A current of heat traveled from her chest to the pit of her stomach, making her weak. His hand slipped inside the bodice of her nightgown, caressing bare, sensitive skin. It was a man's hand—strong and gentle, calloused and hard. She craved the roughness as much as the tenderness.

Her body bowed upward, wanting more. She'd spent a lifetime preparing for this moment, a lifetime of waiting for Max.

She reached up and unbuttoned his shirt. His skin was hard and smooth and hot. Acting on instinct alone, she brushed a fingertip across his chest, teasing his nipples. A moan escaped his lips and he leaned over her, capturing her mouth in a kiss that set them both on fire. She shifted to make room for him, feeling the mattress sink as he stretched out beside her. How many nights had she fantasized about having Max here in her bed like this? But no fantasy could ever compare with the reality.

Coolness touched her skin as he slid her nightgown upward, stroking the length of her leg, her thigh, her hip. Her skin tingled where he touched her, a flurry of vibrations that left her hot and weak and wanting. His mouth became more demanding, his touch more possessive. She moved with him, opening herself to new sensations.

He cupped her possessively, as if staking his claim. A sound—part moan and part prayer—escaped her lips. He dragged his mouth from hers and held her gaze. "Yes," she whispered.

And then his fingertips slipped inside her—stroking, teasing, pleasuring in ways she'd never experienced before. She opened for him, giving him her body, her heart, her soul. He lowered his face to her breast, claiming it with his hot, demanding mouth and sending a shimmer of heat from her breast to her groin. She rose up, hungry for more. Her fingers slid through his hair, clutching him to her breast as the pressure rose to an aching pinpoint of need.

And just when she thought she couldn't take another second of sweet torture, he brought her over the edge, sending her spinning in a rising torrent of pleasure. She arched against him, crying his name as he held her there, kept her strumming, aching, flowing under his touch. With a hoarse moan, he slid his fingers from her body and rolled on top of her, his weight pressing her into the bed. She gasped and cried out again, feeling the hard, throbbing bulge beneath his jeans pressed tight against her, intensifying the ache at her center. She gripped his bottom, rocking against him as she discovered for the first time what it was to really need a man with every fiber of her being.

Her breath came in short, tremulous gasps. "I want you!" She slid her hands up along his back, fingernails raking his skin. "I need you!" Her mind was a jumble of emotions, but she knew that to be true. She'd never wanted anything or anyone as much as she wanted Max Connors…in her bed and in her life. She knew that giving herself to Max meant more than simply a one-week affair. It had to be forever—body and soul and 'til death do us part.

In answer, he eased off and stretched out alongside her. He reached for her hand and placed it against his body, holding it tight to his jeans. Her eyes widened, feeling the extent of his need, the throbbing heat of him. Along with that need came a sense of power, and an awareness of her own blossoming sexuality. She became bolder, dragging moans from his throat as she touched and explored the length of him and found she still wanted more. She wanted all of him, naked and hot and ready.

Her fingers fumbled at his belt buckle, desperate to uncover more.

He reached down and helped her, slipping out of his clothes, then sliding her nightgown over her head until they were twined together, naked and hot. Although his body quivered with need, he took his time, kissing every inch of her, teasing her with words of love and the long, hot slide of skin on skin. And then he was over her, between her, easing into her with a tenderness that nearly broke her heart. He held her gaze, his movements achingly slow, crooning soft, comforting words as he slid smoothly inside. She gasped at the incredible fullness, holding her breath when he met resistance.

He stopped, his entire body trembling, holding her gaze with an intensity that was more intimate than the physical joining of their bodies. Then he whispered the words she'd waited a lifetime to hear.

"I love you, Kate. I've always loved you."

She sobbed, arching upward to meet his thrust, breaking through every barrier between them. They moved as one, completing the journey as if they'd made love like this in a thousand lifetimes, then coming together in a blazing heat that rocked her to her very soul, spiraling out of control until she couldn't think, couldn't breathe, couldn't remember a time when she wasn't loving Max.

And even when they were both spent, he continued to move within her, as if he still couldn't get enough. He cradled her, rocking slowly, sending ripples of pleasure through her entire body.

She drifted then slowly floated upward through waves of awareness, only now realizing what she'd been missing for so long. She reached up to brush a lock of hair from his forehead, staring at him in wonder. "Is it always like this?"

His lips turned up in a lazy smile. "It's never been like this before." He brushed his lips over hers, slow and sweet. "I won't lie to you darlin'. I've had a few sexual relationships over the years. Not many, but enough." He laced his fingers through hers and brought her hand to his lips. "But that's all it ever was—just sex. I've never made love before. Not like this. Never like this."

He rolled over, taking her with him until she was lying on top, their bodies still joined together. She thought she could stay like this forever. With a sigh of pure contentment, she melted into the comfort of his arms.

Chapter Sixteen

ഔ

As it turned out, she and Max had had their first date Monday night, after all. First they'd showered together then driven to an all-night diner about midnight. After refueling, they went back to her house for dessert. She couldn't get enough of him. Luckily he had plenty of stamina because she had every intention of making up for lost time.

Max had stayed with her until dawn. He'd had early morning chores to get to, but promised to be back as soon as he could get away. Before leaving, he'd assured her that she wouldn't have any problems opening the shop. He was right. There had been no more suspicious incidents and Deputy Ed hadn't showed his face. Whatever Max had said to him had apparently done the trick.

But Kate wasn't ready to let her guard down yet. She still had the property dispute hanging over her head. She realized that she'd forgotten to talk to Max about the clues that seemed to point to his mother. It wasn't as if they hadn't had the opportunity, but talking to Max led to kissing Max and kissing Max led to wanting Max and wanting Max left room for nothing else.

She'd spent the next couple days with a smile on her face. The time flew by—days filled with tea and crumpets and nights filled with passion. By Thursday, Kate had settled into a routine that felt comfortable, a routine she could easily envision stretching out to fill the rest of her life. But she didn't have the rest of her life. She only had the rest of the week. Her flight back to New York was scheduled for Sunday…only three days away. How could she leave now with so much left unfinished? Her life in New York was becoming nothing more than a distant memory. Her reality was right here in Easy.

She couldn't put it off any longer. She had to call her boss and ask for an extended leave. She waited until things were slow in the shop, then closed the office door and placed a long-distance call to New York.

She tried to explain the situation to Lester Crumb, but he wasn't interested in her personal problems. He told her that if she wasn't back at her desk Monday morning, she wouldn't have a job to come back to. His inflexible demands made the thought of going back to her menial job at Stoller, Crumb and Crumb even less appealing.

As he blustered and threatened, Kate realized that her pompous, overbearing boss reminded her a whole lot of Ed Tate. She hung up the phone and drummed her fingers on the desk. Now what? Jeff and Sally would be back Sunday to take over running the shop. There was no reason for her to stay in town.

No reason other than Max.

As if summoned by her thoughts, Max poked his head in the doorway. "Am I interrupting?"

Kate glanced at the phone then back at Max. She shook her head. "No, not at all." She pushed away from the desk and met him at the door. She'd worry about her job in New York later. Right now she didn't want to waste a minute of the time they had left.

She wrapped her arms around his neck and stretched up on tiptoe. "Can I get you a muffin, cowboy?"

He nipped her bottom lip. "For now," he said. "I've got my sights on something sweeter when we're alone."

Her heart did a little jig. Only a week and a half and already she was addicted to him...morning, noon and night. They walked from the office hand in hand. Nellie did a quick double take then smiled and nodded her head, as if everything was finally falling into place.

That evening Nellie sent her home from the Tea and Crumpet Shop with an entire apple streusel crumb cake. Kate figured she'd have to buy a whole new wardrobe if she stayed here much longer under Nellie's protective culinary wing. She'd gotten no sympathy from Max, who said her city-slim figure needed a little filling out anyway.

Just thinking of Max made her smile as she balanced the crumb cake in one hand and wiggled the key in the lock with the other. Sophie met her at the door, winding between her feet with a pitiful mewl, as if she'd been abandoned for weeks instead of hours.

If Kate hadn't looked down to avoid tripping over the cat, she might not have noticed the envelope someone had slipped under the door. Her name was scrawled across the front in block letters that reminded her of a ransom note. Her first instinct was to simply toss the envelope into the trash. Something told her that whatever was inside couldn't be good.

Ignoring her intuition, Kate bent over and picked up the envelope. It felt heavy, ominous, dense with sinister secrets. Following Sophie into the kitchen, Kate dropped both the coffeecake and envelope onto the counter. She waited for some comment from her mother but the teacup remained silent. The cat, however, had plenty to say and it all sounded like "Feed me...NOW!"

"All right, all right. Hold your horses," she said, reaching for the canister of dry fish-shaped kitty kibble. *Yeah, that should fool the feline community,* she thought. If it's shaped like a fish, it obviously must be from the sea. Sophie sniffed at her bowl then gave Kate a plaintive look, not fooled for one second. Then, as if realizing this was the best she was getting, dug into her faux fish with something less than gusto.

Kate glanced at the envelope on the counter, a feeling of dread rippling down her spine. Some sixth sense warned her not to open it. But like Pandora's Box, it beckoned seductively. With a dismissive huff, Kate turned her back on the temptation.

She puttered half-heartedly around the house. Sophie followed her nervous pacing, waiting for Kate to settle in one spot so she could curl up on a soft, warm lap. But Kate didn't feel like sitting. And she didn't feel like wandering around the house all alone with just a cat and a singing teacup for company.

She wanted to be with Max.

Kate heard a clattering sound in the kitchen. She looked around, but there was no sign of Sophie. *Uh oh.* She ran back into the kitchen and saw the cat on the counter, rubbing her whiskered cheek along the rim of the teacup. The cup wobbled on its saucer and Kate reached out just in time to save it from toppling over the edge.

Lord only knew where her mother would turn up if her spirit was released from the cup.

Kate shooed the cat off the counter and stored the cup safely inside the cupboard. Her gaze flicked back to the envelope. Despite her misgivings, she picked it up. She fought down a ripple of apprehension and chided herself. This was silly. It was probably a note from a neighbor requesting an extra order of crumpets in the morning or something.

Before she could talk herself out of it, Kate tore open the envelope, surprised to find pictures inside. Her heart jumped when she recognized where the pictures had been taken. It was the ballroom where her life's dream had ended and her personal nightmare had begun. The pageant. She gasped as memories came flooding back.

The first picture was a close-up showing her on stage wearing her crown and sash and the infamous red dress. She winced seeing "Miss Easy" emblazoned across her chest. The words took on a double-edged significance in light of the incidents to follow.

Kate stared at the picture, surprised she'd ever been that young, that happy. She flipped to the next picture and saw Max standing on the sidelines watching. He hadn't told her he'd been there. She hadn't known he'd been witness to what would soon become her darkest moment.

She turned to the next picture. Max had his back to the camera. He was talking to someone. He seemed to be gesturing, but Kate couldn't tell who he was speaking to. She flipped to the next and last picture, taken from a different angle. And then she knew who Max was talking so intently with. It was Aubrey Carlisle, the pageant director. She'd been the one to privately inform Kate that they had to take her title away—probably only moments after talking to Max.

It could simply be a coincidence. There was nothing unusual about Max talking to Aubrey. They could have been discussing anything at all. Still, the timing was suspicious.

Kate tore at the envelope, looking for an explanation. Nothing. Then she noticed the words printed on the back of one of the pictures.

"Who do you think turned you in?"

Her heart sank, taking all her newfound hopes and dreams with it. No. It couldn't be true. Not Max. He wouldn't. He couldn't. Maybe he'd believed the lies, but he would never do something so vindictive, so cruel, so mean. More than anyone else, he knew how much she'd depended on that scholarship. Even if he hated her, he wouldn't have ripped her dream away. Would he?

She didn't want to doubt him, but pictures didn't lie.

Then she remembered who'd stepped in to take her place when she'd been stripped of her title. Sue Connors had been first runner-up. Max's sister and Kate's one-time friend. Growing up, Max had always been protective of Sue. They'd always been close—perhaps closer because they were twins—and had become even more dependent on each other after their mother died. Kate knew he'd do anything for her. Anything.

Had Max sacrificed Kate for his sister?

"Trust me," he'd said. Was it only a few nights ago? "I promise I'll never hurt you...again." He'd said *again*. As if admitting he'd purposely hurt her once before. If that were true, he'd made a fool of her once more by allowing her to believe his empty promises.

Kate felt as if someone had her heart in a two-fisted grip, squeezing and tugging in opposite directions. It hurt. It hurt more than she could say.

Her first urge was to run—back to New York and her uncomplicated life there. Let Jeff worry about saving the shop. Let Max go back to his ranch and his lies.

A rattling sound came from the cupboard and Kate lost it. "Shut up," she screamed, pressing her hands over her ears. "Just shut up. I can't take anymore!" Tears streamed down her face as she shouted at the cupboard. "First you get me back here under false pretenses, then you die without even giving me the chance to speak my mind, so I don't know whether to hate you or miss you. And now you're trying to run my life without giving me a clue as to what you're trying to say. If you're going to haunt me, either do it right or go away!"

The rattling stopped.

Kate exhaled a quivering sigh, drained from her outburst. She rubbed her eyes with the back of her hands then opened the cupboard, reaching in to tentatively grab the cup. "I'm sorry," she whispered. "I didn't mean it." Her shoulders slumped. "I miss you so much and I don't know who to trust anymore."

The cup thrummed in her hands like a living, breathing entity. Kate closed her eyes, her body still racked with sobs. She held the cup to her chest and for a brief moment could almost feel her mother's arms around her, giving her strength, love and support.

It might have been simply her imagination, but Kate clearly heard Lillian's voice in her mind.

"Don't make the same mistake twice."

Hadn't she said the same thing to herself? No, she had convinced herself she'd already made the same mistake twice by trusting Max. Her mother was telling her *not* to make the same mistake again. Deep down, Kate knew the difference. She'd doubted Max once without giving him a chance to defend himself. She'd believed the worst of him and wasted ten years of their lives because of it.

Don't make the same mistake twice.

Kate took a deep breath and straightened her shoulders. She knew what she had to do—what she should have done ten years ago. Running wasn't the answer then and it wasn't the answer now. She had to give Max a chance to explain. As hard as it would be, she had to confront him with this so-called proof. Maybe there was an explanation. God, she hoped he had an explanation. She wanted to trust him. She wanted to believe he was the man he said he was.

But most of all, she wanted a reason to come back home for good.

* * * * *

When Kate pulled up to the ranch, Sue was standing on the porch. She got out of her car and, shielding her eyes from the sun's glare, looked up and asked if Max was around.

Sue stood where she was on the top porch step looking down. "Max isn't here. I don't expect him back for a few hours." She wiped her hands on the dishrag in a dismissive gesture. "I'll tell him you stopped by."

Kate nodded and turned to leave, then changed her mind. The longer she waited, the harder it would be. Straightening her shoulders, she turned around again. "Would you mind if I waited for him?"

Sue gave her a long, hard stare. "Suit yourself," she murmured, then turned and went back inside.

Kate stood at the foot of the steps, watching Sue's retreating back. Turning around had been one of the hardest things she'd ever done. Her first instinct had been to run. But if she'd learned anything these past weeks, it was that running from your problems didn't solve anything. Problems and misunderstandings fed on being ignored, growing bigger and stronger and more toxic with time.

Pursing her lips and mustering every ounce of courage she had, Kate followed Sue inside. She knew the old Kate wouldn't have had the gumption to do that. Something inside her had changed over the course of the last several days.

Acting braver than she felt, Kate pulled out a chair at the kitchen table and sat down. She looked around at the simple kitchen and realized that despite winning the pageant, Sue's life hadn't been easy or glamorous these past years. No wonder she seemed so bitter and resentful.

"Where did you say Max went?" Kate asked, determined to break through the wall of silence.

"I didn't," Sue replied curtly, turning her back on Kate. Water sloshed carelessly over the edge of the sink as Sue scrubbed the pots harder than seemed necessary.

There was something else going on here, Kate realized. Sue was being more than rude. There was something suspicious in the way she wouldn't—or couldn't—meet Kate's eyes.

"You don't think he went after Tate again, do you?"

"It wouldn't surprise me," Sue said, keeping her back to Kate. "You've shaken things up since you've been back."

Kate blinked, surprised by the statement. "I didn't mean to," she said.

Sue glanced over her shoulder. "Didn't mean to come back, or didn't mean to shake things up?"

Kate shrugged. "Both, I guess."

Sue turned her attention back to the sink. "Maybe you shouldn't have." She sounded more resigned than angry.

For a moment Kate wasn't sure she'd heard right. Why should Sue care? She'd been the one person in town who'd directly benefited from Kate leaving. So where was all this anger coming from?

As if answering the unspoken question, Sue turned to face Kate, shaking her head slowly. "I don't know why you came back," she said with a tired sigh. "Everything was fine before. Now Max is out for Tate's blood and the whole town is all riled up."

"Maybe you're right," Kate replied. "Maybe I shouldn't have come back." Hadn't she thought that herself often enough? "But I *am* back now. And there are things that I need to deal with while I'm here—things I should have dealt with a long time ago."

Sue only stared at her, eyes narrowed with suspicion. Or was it fear? "Easy was never good enough for you," she sneered. "You always wanted something bigger and better." Her voice rose, becoming shriller. "You turned your back on Easy once and you'll do it again. So maybe you should just go on back to that city life you chose before someone gets hurt."

Kate was too shocked by Sue's accusation to answer. Neither of them realized Max had come in until he cleared his throat.

Sue gasped, her eyes widening with guilt when she realized Max had overheard her.

Max didn't say a word, just tipped his head and waited for an explanation.

"It's true!" Sue blustered in defense of her outburst. "I don't want to see you hurt again, Max, that's all." She shot a hateful glare in Kate's direction. "She broke your heart. The last time she left you were a wreck...wouldn't eat, couldn't sleep. You moped around here like you'd lost your best friend."

Kate's heart skipped a beat. She stood and faced Max. "Is that true?" she whispered.

Max swallowed hard and tipped his head in a slow nod.

Sue continued, imploring her brother. "I just don't want her to break your heart again." Tears streamed down her face. "You were so hurt and I felt so guilty."

"Why should you feel guilty?" Max asked. "It wasn't your fault."

As if catching herself, Sue nodded vigorously. "That's right. It *wasn't* my fault." She pointed an accusing finger at Kate. "It was her fault! She's the one who dumped you and left town, remember? And she'll do it again. Just you wait and see."

"That's enough," Max said, his voice dangerously quiet. "What I do is my business. And Kate had her reasons for leaving town." He walked to Kate's side and put an arm around her shoulder. "Now I think you should apologize," he warned his sister.

Sue looked shocked that Max would take Kate's side. Her lower lip trembled and her cheeks flushed. "Max?" she pleaded. "I was just looking out for you."

"I've told you I can look out for myself." His voice held a warning impossible to miss.

Sue lowered her eyes. "I'm sorry," she mumbled in Kate's direction, then rushed by them and fled from the room.

Kate felt suddenly shy alone in the room with Max. She'd been nursing her own grudge for so long that it was still hard to get used to the idea that Max had been hurt as well. That would make it even harder to ask him about the pictures she'd received. But she had to ask. She couldn't let this suspicion fester below the surface.

When she turned to face him, his arm stayed on her shoulder protectively, intimately, making her forget what she'd come to say. He drew her closer, shutting out the world around them. There was only the two of them, the way it was always meant to be.

She whispered his name, her lips barely moving. He dipped his head until their lips met briefly, brushing hers in a soft caress. Just that simple touch made her knees weak and she leaned against his chest for support. His arms came around her, strong and gentle at the same time. She closed her eyes, letting her body mold to his. Her lips parted and she felt the warmth of his breath, the heat of his kiss.

His arms tightened, lifting her and pulling her closer at the same time. He smelled fresh and real, like sun and wind and man. When he held her like this, she felt as if she'd truly come home. Home wasn't a town or a place. Home was wherever Max was, and that's where she was meant to be.

The kiss ended as gently as it had begun. With a soft sigh, Max cradled her head against his shoulder. Kate closed her eyes, content to lean on him, secure in the shelter of his arms. She wanted nothing more than to stay like this forever. For a fleeting moment she thought she could. Then reality came crashing back.

There was still the matter of the pictures. This time she wouldn't jump to conclusions without talking to him first. But she had to be sure. "Max," she said, her voice still husky with desire. She pressed a palm against his chest, gently putting some distance between them. "We have to talk."

His lips curled in a sexy smile. "I'd rather kiss."

Her heart gave a lazy little flip. The truth was she'd rather kiss him too. She could easily envision a lifetime of kissing Max. And more—much, much more. Her body tingled with desire and she knew that if she kissed him much longer the tingle would turn to a simmer, the simmer to a blaze.

With a sigh of regret, she stepped out of his arms. "Max," she said, "there's something I have to talk to you about first." She moved to the kitchen table where she'd left her purse and retrieved the envelope she'd found earlier today. A quick glance at the pictures was like a blast of ice water over the heat of her emotions. Not meeting his gaze, she turned and handed them to Max. "Someone slipped these under my door today."

Max studied the pictures, his brows pulled together in a puzzled frown. He looked up from the pictures and shook his head. "I don't understand."

Kate chewed on her lower lip. "Someone..." Her voice cracked and trailed off. She cleared her throat and began again.

"Someone complained to the Pageant Committee about my moral character ten years ago. Someone insisted that I wasn't qualified to represent Easy County." She reached for one of the pictures in his hand and turned it over, exposing the words on the back. "That *someone*," she said again, emphasizing the word, "is the reason I lost the scholarship and left town in shame."

He nodded slowly, reading the accusation scrawled on the back of the photo. "And you believe it was me?" His face took on a hard, guarded look as he waited for her response.

"Someone sure wants me to believe that," she said.

"I have an idea who, too." His voice was a dangerous growl. When he looked at Kate, his voice softened. "I didn't do this," he assured her. "I would never do that to you. Believe me."

She wanted to. Oh, how she wanted to believe him. But it meant leaving her heart vulnerable...again. Those old feelings of insecurity and betrayal still churned below the surface, threatening to erupt.

He cupped her chin and lifted her face until their eyes met. "I swear to you, Kate. It wasn't me."

There was no hint of deceit in his clear blue eyes. With a rush of relief, she knew that Max was innocent. Once again she'd almost let her doubts destroy something good and pure. But if not Max, then who? Someone had deliberately set out to destroy her.

"We'll find out who did this," Max said, as if reading her thoughts. "And when I find out, I'll make them pay. I swear I will." He pulled Kate tight against his chest, his voice no more than a whisper. "You just have to trust me, okay?"

Kate nodded. She wanted to trust him, but it was hard to break a ten-year habit.

He curled a fingertip under her chin and tipped her face up to his. "Was that a yes?"

She couldn't help but smile back at him. "Yes."

"Good. Since you're in such an agreeable mood, how about staying for dinner?"

The smile melted off Kate's face. "I'm not sure." She glanced at the doorway where Sue had disappeared. "I don't think your sister approves of me being here."

"Don't be silly," Max said. He leaned over and planted a kiss on Kate's lips. "I'll go talk to her."

Chapter Seventeen

ॐ

Kate sat at the kitchen table and watched Otis Connors shuffle a worn deck of cards. His hands were rough, work hardened, yet he manipulated the cards with precision and dexterity. Each time he made an ace appear from the deck, she shook her head in wonder. No matter how hard she watched, she couldn't detect the sleight of hand.

"See?" Bobby giggled. "It's magic."

Kate nodded. "It sure is."

Max chose that moment to step into the kitchen and gently admonish his nephew. "Real magic would be if you set the table before your mom told you to."

"Oh, I'll do it," Kate said, starting to rise.

Max laid a hand on her shoulder. "That's Bobby's job, isn't it Champ?"

Bobby nodded, beaming with pride. "I get two dollars a week for doing all my chores," he said. "Wanna see?"

Kate nodded and Bobby scooted over to the refrigerator, surprisingly agile with his arm braces. He took down a list covered with stars and brought it to Kate. The chores were simple, geared toward his abilities yet important enough to make him feel like a productive member of the household.

A wave of tenderness had Kate fighting back tears. Her first instincts would have been to protect and coddle the child, not realizing how important it was to give him a sense of self-worth. Max understood, and the pride on Bobby's face as he explained his chores was proof of that.

Kate realized that was also a large part of the work Max did here on the ranch—letting the children take part in the grooming and feeding of the horses, giving them something to care for and an outlet for pride in a job well done. All of these chores contributed to the children's emotional and mental outlook.

Cheryl had told Kate all this that first day she'd showed her around the facility. At the time Kate had been nurturing her personal grudge against Max and hadn't wanted to be swayed by this insight into his character. But she couldn't help but be touched.

The therapy, she realized now, involved more than simply physical rehabilitation for the children. They formed a bond with the animals as well—touching, stroking, whispering their innermost secrets to the horses as their bodies strengthened. The horses didn't judge them or tease them for being different. They gave unconditional love in return.

And Max provided all this with no compensation. If anything, he was struggling to stay in the black. No wonder Lillian had gone out of her way to keep money flowing to the ranch. No wonder she'd provided for Max and the ranch in her will. There were no ulterior motives on Max's part. He hadn't asked for anything or manipulated himself into inheriting a share of her mother's estate.

If anything, that realization made her even more determined to see that Ed Tate didn't get his hands on half of the business. He'd be stealing the dreams of these children with his greed. Watching Bobby go about his chores, Kate knew she wouldn't allow that to happen.

"So," Max said, pulling up a chair. "I see Dad's been entertaining you with his card tricks."

"I'm convinced he's a real magician," Kate said with a smile.

"That would be nice," Max replied, a momentary frown creasing his forehead. "We could use a little magic around here."

Kate heard the frustration in his voice. She wanted to tell him that things would be better soon, but there was no way she could make that promise. If Ed Tate had his way, there'd be nothing left for any of them in the inheritance.

Otis gave a sharp riffle to the cards in his hand. "Ain't no magic about it," he said gruffly. "Ranchin' is all sweat and hard work."

Max slapped his hands on his knees and leaned forward. "Speaking of work, I guess we'd better help Sis with dinner."

"What can I do?" Kate asked.

Max sauntered over to the stove and lifted the lid off a pot on the back burner, releasing a fragrant cloud of steam. "Looks like stew tonight. How are you at peeling potatoes?"

"I think I can handle that," Kate replied, joining him at the counter.

Max brought her a bag of potatoes and a paring knife and she set to work, barely noticing the moment Sue joined her. They worked side by side quietly. Sue mixed buttermilk biscuits while Kate peeled and quartered potatoes, accompanied by the homey sounds of kitchen clatter. It felt good. She'd been living alone for so long that she'd forgotten the simple pleasures of preparing a hearty meal for a hungry family.

Kate felt some of the tension she'd been under ease as they went about their separate chores. For the first time in a long time, she felt like part of a family. Bustling around the kitchen, it struck her with amazing clarity that the things she wanted most were the very things she'd been running from.

Home. Family. A place to belong.

Kate rinsed the potatoes then added them to the pot of simmering meat and gravy. Slowly she became aware of the silence around her. She turned from the sink and found three sets of eyes on her.

Otis blinked, Max gave her a puzzled look and Sue frowned then quickly looked away.

"What?" Kate asked. She looked at the empty strainer in her hands wondering if she'd made some grievous potato error.

Max cleared his throat. "You were humming."

"I'm sorry," Kate said. She hadn't even been aware she'd been humming. "Humming is bad?"

Max smiled. "No. It's just that you were humming one of my mother's favorite songs. It was just a shock, that's all. She used to stand at the sink just the way you were and hum that Roy Orbison song while she cooked."

Kate felt a chill crawl down her spine. Of course. Hadn't Nellie said that both Lillian and Anne Connors were big Roy Orbison fans? Kate must have been humming one of the songs from the teacup, not even aware it was one of Anne Connors' favorites. Or was this just another sign?

Maybe it was time to take the teacup's message more seriously. She glanced from one person to another. "We need to talk," she said.

Sue wiped her hands on a dishtowel. "I'll be in the other room," she said.

Kate stopped her. "No. This is important to all of us." She gestured for Sue to join them at the table.

While Max poured coffee, Kate briefly filled everyone in about her mother's will and how Ed Tate was trying to take over half of the Tea and Crumpet Shop. That part was easy, although Max seemed surprised when Kate insisted that he had a right to the share Lillian had stipulated for the running of the ranch and she was determined to see that he got his full share.

"Yes," she said, noticing his surprise. "Your share. This place is too important to you and the kids," she said. "Lillian knew that, and so do I. I'll be damned if I'll let Ed Tate's vendetta spill over onto innocent children."

Sue made a soft sound and looked away. Kate reached over and clasped the other woman's hand. "I won't let Tate's vindictiveness hurt these kids," she assured her.

Sue lowered her eyes. "Thank you," she whispered, her voice choked with emotion.

"Now," Kate said, turning to Max and Otis. "This next part is a little strange but bear with me. I think we're closing in on something here and maybe if we all put our heads together we can figure it out."

She took a deep breath, refusing to think about how silly it might sound, then told the group at the table about Madame Zostra's reading and the singing teacup.

Otis spoke up. "Anne gave Lillian that cup a long, long time ago," he said.

His comment didn't surprise her. It was another connection, another piece of the puzzle. Kate was sure she was finally on the right track. "I know it sounds strange," she finished, "but I think my mother is trying to tell me something important. There are definite clues here, but I'm not getting them."

"A rose," Sue said, leaning forward with excitement. "That must mean the ranch. Rock Rose Ranch."

"Yes!" Kate replied. "I realized that after Max left the other night and it totally slipped my mind. Rock roses are what Bobby brought me after my mother's funeral."

Regardless of how anyone might have felt about Kate's explanation, she was relieved to see that they seemed to be taking her seriously enough to at least give it some thought. Or maybe they were simply humoring the crazy city girl.

"So it has something to do with the ranch," Kate insisted. She glanced at Max. "And something to do with your mother." She thought back on what Nellie had told her about how close Anne and Lillian were. She turned her attention to Otis. "Your wife and my mother were close friends, right?"

He nodded. "Close as can be," he said, his eyes softening with remembrance. "They had the same taste in everything, right down to the music they liked."

Kate nodded thoughtfully. "I thought the Roy Orbison songs were clues, but maybe they were only meant to lead me here."

"Or both," Otis said.

"One of the songs was 'Pretty Papers'," Kate said, turning back to Max. "Would your mother have left any papers here? Something that might prove Ginny and Ed Tate's claim on the property is false?"

Max seemed more puzzled than convinced. "If she did, I'm sure we would have found them by now. We've gone through all of my mother's things."

"I wonder," Kate mused. "When Madame Zostra said 'Max has the key' I assumed she meant the key to the puzzle." She turned her gaze to Max. "What if she meant it literally? Maybe there's a physical key that opens something...a safe or a desk?"

"What about Mom's jewelry box?" Sue asked.

Max shook his head. "No, the jewelry box doesn't lock. There's no key that I know of."

Kate fought down a wave of disappointment. For a brief moment there, everything had seemed to be falling into place. She'd almost believed some supernatural force was leading her to the answers they sought.

She shook her head. "There's got to be something. All the clues are leading me here."

"Roy Orbison...in a teacup." Otis chuckled. "Who'd have thought it?" Suddenly he sat straight up and snapped his fingers. "That's it!"

"What?" Max and Kate both asked at the same time.

"Those records," Otis said. "Anne would listen to them all day and night." He rubbed his hand over his forehead. "Now where did I put them?"

Kate tried not to get her hopes up. She wasn't sure how some old records would help save the business, but it felt right. If nothing else, she could search the song titles for more clues.

Before she could question their direction any further, Otis jumped out of his chair. "The attic," he cried out. "Max, get the key."

As soon as Otis asked Max for the key, nearly echoing Madam Zostra's words exactly, Kate felt a jolt to her chest. This was it. She was sure of it. Although why the attic was locked and what Roy Orbison had to do with saving the Tea and Crumpet Shop, she couldn't begin to guess. But the fluttering in her stomach assured her they were finally on the right track.

"I'll stay down here with Bobby," Sue said. "You all go check the attic."

While Max went to hunt up the keys, Kate followed Otis upstairs. They passed a small game room littered with comic books and video cartridges. Kate smiled. Obviously that was Bobby's private domain. At the end of a long hallway, Otis stopped in front of a locked door.

"Why do you keep it locked?" Kate asked, gesturing to the doorway.

Coming up behind them with a jangling ring of keys, Max answered her question. "Bobby used to think the attic made a great hideaway. We didn't think it was safe for him to play in there and Sue freaked out the first time he came out covered with cobwebs and insulation. So we locked up the attic and gave Bobby his own private game room."

After fiddling with the keys, Max finally unlocked and opened the attic door. Kate followed the men inside and looked around. The attic was actually a full-length unfinished dormer with barely room enough to stand but plenty of nooks and crannies for storage space. And nearly every inch of it had been utilized. Plywood covered the floors, but the spaces between the ceiling beams and wall studs were stuffed with cotton-candy pink insulation.

Dust motes danced in the air as Otis made his way down the length of the attic. "Now where did I put those old records?" he muttered, peeking in corners and cubbyholes along the way.

Kate waited, surprised when Max gave her hand a reassuring squeeze and grateful when he didn't let go. She smiled at him, her heart fluttering in her chest. She didn't want him to let go of her hand. Now or ever. Suddenly New York seemed very far away, almost like a distant dream. She realized that her life—her heart—had always remained right here.

"Here we go," Otis cried, bending over a small stack of cardboard boxes.

Kate and Max joined him as he finished opening the flaps of the uppermost carton. Neatly stacked inside were dozens of albums, reminding Kate of a time before compact disks, audiotapes or even eight-track tapes. The album covers were faded with time, the records inside protected by crisp paper sleeves.

Kate only half-recognized names from another era—names like Johnny Horton, Del Shannon, Brian Hyland, Johnny Rivers, Gene Pitney and Bobby Vee. Kate wondered if there was an identical pile of these same albums tucked away somewhere in her mother's attic, a symbol of a past dimly remembered, a time of youth and friendship and secret dreams.

Impulsively she reached for Max's hand again, feeling safer when his fingers closed around hers, connecting her to her past and perhaps her future. As if recognizing the yearning she felt, he leaned closer, his lips only a heartbeat from hers.

Otis cleared his throat, breaking the silent stillness of the moment. "Why don't you kids search through these boxes and see what you can come up with," he said, straightening and wiping his hands on his jeans. "I'll be right downstairs."

He winked and Kate felt a flush rise to her cheeks. Caught like a guilty teenager.

Max chuckled when Otis shut the door behind him, closing them both together in the dim recesses of the attic. "Wanna make out?" he asked.

"Yes," she said, feeling that familiar ache blossom deep in her belly. "But not here in the attic. Let's find what we came for and then sneak away someplace quiet where we can be alone."

"Sounds like a plan," Max said, kneeling in front of the open box. He pulled out albums, stacking them carefully alongside the box. "Let's see if we can figure out what the teacup wants us to find."

Nothing.

Disappointment rushed through Kate, pulling her stomach into a tight knot. They'd gone through all the record boxes and a dozen others. She'd been so sure the clues had led them to this hiding spot, but they'd torn the attic apart and found nothing at all.

Heaving a sigh, she sat back on her heels and looked around at the empty boxes scattered around her. It was hopeless.

Max put an arm around her shoulders and pulled her head to his chest. They knelt together while he whispered soft words of reassurance.

"I was so sure," Kate whispered, her voice choked with emotion.

Max combed his fingers through her hair, slow and soothing. "I know. Don't give up, though. We'll keep looking."

Her shoulders slumped. "Where? We've looked everywhere already."

"I'm sorry," Max said. He cupped her chin and lifted her face until their eyes met, then brushed his lips over hers.

As sweet as the kiss was, it couldn't dispel the lingering shadow of disappointment Kate felt. She'd wanted to do this for Max as much as herself, to somehow make up for all the lost years and misunderstanding. And maybe deep down inside she'd wanted to build something new for herself too. A new home, a new life, a new love to make up for the one she'd thrown away in her haste to leave her soiled reputation behind her.

She wrapped her arms around Max, lingering over the tenderness of his kiss. Maybe it wasn't too late to salvage something from the dusty recesses of the past. And maybe that's where her mother's restless spirit had been leading her all along—*to Max*.

He was the first to break the embrace. "I need to ask you something," he said.

Her heart swelled with anticipation. Was this it? Would he ask her to stay? She held her breath, waiting.

"I want you to come with me to the reunion tomorrow night," he said.

It took Kate a few moments to grasp what he'd said. The reunion? Her heart plummeted. Absolutely not. The thought of facing all those old classmates sent chills through her body. They'd believed the worst of her. She remembered the way they'd avoided her, the suspicion on their faces. She'd been defenseless, ambushed by innuendo and lies. No. She shook her head. There was no way.

Max stopped her with a finger to her lips before the word could be said aloud. "Just hear me out. You've said yourself you'd made a mistake, that running away wasn't the answer. Isn't it time you stopped running and put the past behind you?"

She nodded, not ready to admit where her thoughts had been leading her when she'd made that comment. Certainly she hadn't been thinking about attending her ten-year reunion.

"The reunion is as good a place to start as any," he said. "You can face the ghosts of your past all at once and put them to rest. You can walk in there with your head held high and show this town once and for all what you're made of."

Kate remained unconvinced.

"Not everyone believed the lies about you," Max assured her.

The words were like a spike through her heart. "*You* did," she whispered.

He lowered his eyes. "Not really. Not deep in my heart where I knew the real you. But it was easier than thinking that you didn't love me."

"But I *did* love you," Kate cried. "I…" Her voice cracked and she left the sentence unfinished.

Max held her gaze, the moment stretching out uncomfortably. "Say it, Kate," he urged.

And there in his arms, she realized she could finally admit aloud what she'd been running from all these years. "I…I still do."

Max crushed her tight against his chest and this time the kiss was more possessive. "I never stopped loving you," he whispered between hungry kisses that claimed her as completely as his words. "I love you. Only you."

Kate felt a piece of her soul slip back into place, a shattered fragment that had been missing far too long. She held on tight, afraid to let go. She knew now how easy it was to lose the one true love of your life. She wouldn't make that same mistake twice. This time she wouldn't let love slip away.

"Yes," she said. "I'll go with you." And just like that, a weight fell away — the weight of shame and guilt and resentment she'd been carrying around all of her adult life. She'd face them all, with her head held high, just like Max said. She had nothing to hide, nothing to be ashamed of. With Max by her side, she could do anything.

Anything.

Even go back to high school if she had to.

A muffled cry of "Dinner's ready!" came from outside the attic door.

Max turned and called out that they'd be right there, while Kate knelt down and started putting things back in the empty cartons. She reached for one of the albums stacked beside her and brushed her finger over Roy Orbison's face, trying to penetrate the secrets behind those dark shades. "What?" she whispered. "What are you trying to tell me?"

She turned the album over and scanned the list of song titles. She had to be missing something obvious. She had the niggling suspicion that the answer was staring her right in the face, like one of those pictures where you tried to find the hidden objects. When you finally found the images, it was hard to believe they had been hidden inside all along.

Hidden inside?

Kate's breath caught in her throat. No, it couldn't be that simple. Could it?

She slipped the vinyl record out of its sleeve, her heart galloping with excitement. She knew she was on the right track now. She'd just had to shift her focus, look deeper inside for the answer.

She pulled another record off the stack then stopped as words on the album cover beneath it caught her eye—Roy Orbison's album titled *The Other Side*. Her heart leaped and she knew without a doubt that she'd struck gold. Of course! If she'd had her wits about her, she would have looked inside this one first for a message from her mother. The clues had been there all along, she just hadn't seen them.

She grabbed the album, her heart pounding with excitement. "Yes," she pleaded, half afraid to get her hopes up again. "Be here, be here."

And it was.

With a squeal of excitement, she found what she'd been searching for. Tucked between the record sleeve and the album jacket was an envelope. "Max," she called, slipping out some folded papers. "I think I've found it!"

Her hands shook as she grasped the envelope. It was stiff and brittle with age. Max peered over her shoulder, watching as she opened the fragile packet.

Folded inside was a receipt and cancelled check, both made out to Jebediah Feathers. The letter explained everything. Anne Connors had bought out Jebediah's share of the property, which later became the Tea and Crumpet Shop. Then she'd turned the title over to Lillian, free and clear.

Max rocked back on his heels. "My mother bought out Jebediah's half of the property?"

Kate shook her head in disbelief. "Look," she said, pointing to the other piece of paper. "She held it in trust for my mother. Apparently they'd planned on being partners, but..."

Max nodded. "My mother died shortly after these papers were signed."

Kate glanced at him, her vision misty with tears. "They were really good friends, weren't they?"

Max pulled her close. "The best," he said. "And your mother never forgot. She was always around, watching out for us in whatever way she could. All the time she was building that business from the ground up, she'd made arrangements to see that we'd eventually get a share of it."

Kate felt all the pieces of the puzzle beginning to slip into place.

"You know," Max said, "Lillian tried to give me a loan when I was having financial problems. I wouldn't take it." He jutted his chin, showing a trace of the pride that had kept him from accepting that long-ago offer. "Then suddenly she had all this carpentry work that had to be done." He smiled with the memory. "I told her she was paying me far too much, but she insisted."

"She owed your mother a debt and was determined to repay it one way or the other."

"You know what this means, don't you?" Max asked.

Kate beamed, thrilled with their discovery. "It means we're free of Ed's claim on the property. My father sold his share of the property before he married Ginny Tate." She gave Max a victorious smile. "It also means you'll inherit your fair share of my mother's estate — enough to keep the ranch running for a long, long time."

"Yes," Max said, lifting her off her feet and swinging her around in the tight space. "Let's go downstairs and tell everyone the good news." He nuzzled the side of her neck. "Then we can go off and find that quiet space you promised me for some serious make-out time."

Kate's heart pounded with excitement and anticipation. They'd won an important victory today, but that was only the beginning. With the past finally untangled, it was time to begin looking forward to the future.

"Oh Max, could I use your phone? I have to tell Nellie. She's been worried sick about this." She glanced at the papers in her hand. "Now we can all relax and get on with business."

"Of course," he said. "But after that, you're all mine. Deal?"

"Deal," she agreed with a smile. She couldn't think of anything she'd rather do than put the worries behind her and concentrate on Max.

He took her hand and led them out of the attic, down the hallway to his room. "There's a phone in here. I'll meet you downstairs." He kissed the tip of her nose, then turned and left the room.

Kate made a low, appreciative sound as Max swaggered away. She couldn't decide if it was more fun to watch him coming or going.

Coming. Definitely coming.

Kate's cheeks burned. The man was corrupting her.

She glanced around Max's room. It was a man's room, neat and orderly, with little or no adornment. The only exceptions were the pictures on the wall—pictures of Bobby and Max, Bobby and Outlaw, Bobby and Max and Outlaw.

The bed was neatly made. Kate was struck by a mental image of Max stretched out naked on those very sheets, his hair rumpled sexily from sleep. She fought the urge to bury her face in his pillow and instead reached for the telephone on the nightstand. She couldn't wait to tell Nellie that their problems were solved.

Kate brought the phone to her ear and quickly realized that someone was already on the line. She would have hung up immediately if she hadn't heard her own name mentioned.

"It's over. I'm telling Max and Kate everything."

Kate recognized Sue's voice, but the one that answered shocked her.

Ed Tate was on the other end of the line.

"Like hell you will. If I go down, you're going right down with me."

Kate gently replaced the receiver. She sank down onto Max's bed. What was that all about? What could Tate possibly be holding over Sue's head? There was no mistaking the warning in his voice.

The question was — what should Kate do about it?

Chapter Eighteen

ଚ୍ଚ

Otis slathered a biscuit with butter, shaking his head in wonder. "Who'd have thought," he said, then popped half the biscuit into his mouth and chewed thoughtfully.

"Where did Mom get the money to buy out Jebediah's share?" Max asked.

"Oh, she had a nice little nest egg when we got married," Otis replied. "I was stubborn enough to insist it was the man's job to support his own family with no help from anyone else. I didn't much care what she did with her pin money and never asked."

Kate had to smile at Otis referring to thousands of dollars as "pin money," as if Anne Connors had been tucking away spare change in a jelly jar.

"You know," he said, "now that you mention it, I remember Lillian coming to me claiming she owed Anne money and wanting to repay me." He glanced at Kate. "Told her at the time that wasn't necessary. We were getting along just fine and Lillian was struggling alone with you kids and that shop of hers. I couldn't see taking money I didn't need from a little lady who did."

Kate felt a pang of guilt. She hadn't thought much about how hard it must have been for her mother all those years ago. She'd lost her husband and her best friend. She'd bucked the odds and built a thriving business from nothing, all while raising her children alone. Lillian had been a single mother and successful businesswoman long before it was fashionable to be so.

Yes, she'd also been headstrong, stubborn and controlling. But the flip side of that was she had incredible drive and determination. For a woman alone in the world, those qualities were necessary for survival. Kate wished she could turn back time and tell her mother how much she appreciated her. There were too many words left unsaid. If anything, that gave her one more reason to regret the years she'd lost.

Kate pushed her dish away. "My mother never forgot that debt," she said. "That's why she provided for the ranch in her will." She shot Max a warning glance in case he was having second thoughts about accepting the money. "That's what my mother wanted," she said. "And she'll probably haunt me forever if you don't accept."

"Stubborn," Max muttered.

Kate chose to believe he was talking about her mother's restless spirit. He certainly couldn't mean her. But she wasn't about to belabor the point. Besides, she knew how much good that money would do, and she also knew that Max cared too much about the welfare of the kids who came to the ranch to let his pride get in the way.

She also intended to call her office in the morning and tell Lester Crumb she wouldn't be back to work on Monday. She had too much unfinished business here in Easy, and the few days left of her vacation weren't enough to sort out the pieces of her life. She owed at least that much to her mother. And to Max.

Otis pushed his chair away from the table. "So what are you kids going to do next?"

It took Kate a minute to realize that she and Max were the "kids" Otis referred to.

"Besides kick Tate's ass from here to Phoenix?" Max asked.

"Watch your mouth," Otis admonished. "There are ladies present."

Kate bit her tongue and glanced at Sue. They shared a quick, secret smile at Max's expense as he muttered an apology.

"Sorry ladies," he said before turning back to his father. "Actually, as much as I'd love to throw this in Tate's face tonight, I have other plans. Kate and I had a misunderstanding as wide as the Grand Canyon." He gave her a wink that made her heart flip over in her chest. "I want to be sure that's *all* behind us now."

He stood up and took Kate's hand, pulling her to her feet. "Tate's not going to come between us ever again, darlin'," he promised.

Kate followed him out the door. At that point she would have followed him anywhere just to hear him call her *darlin'* in that slow, sexy southern drawl.

"Don't wait up for us," Max called over his shoulder as he led Kate out to his truck.

It didn't take Kate long to realize where they were headed. "Do kids still come here to make out?" she asked as Max turned onto the secluded dirt road leading to Whiskey Creek overlook.

"How would I know?" he asked. "I haven't been here since you left town." He put the pick-up in park beneath the shelter of a stand of aspens and held out his arms. "Come here," he said. "You promised me kisses."

Kate slid across the seat and into his arms. This was perfect. This was where he'd given her his high-school ring and asked her to go steady. It was *their* spot, the ideal place for starting over. They'd come full circle.

He pulled her onto his lap so she was straddling him. Kate watched the teasing play of moonlight and shadows over the strong angles of his face. A gentle breeze drifted through the open windows and the only sound in the closed cab of the pick-up truck was the whispered rasp of denim along denim as she settled onto his lap.

He tucked his face against the side of her neck, taking slow deep breaths. "You smell so good," he whispered. "I've never forgotten the way you smell. Like sunshine and fresh flowers."

As he spoke, his hands slid along her thighs. Kate melted into his embrace, her curves fitting perfectly along the hard lines of his body.

He nipped the underside of her chin playfully. "Where's my kisses?"

She slid her hands up along his chest and pushed herself back a bit so she could look into his eyes. She cupped his face between her palms, fingers brushing along the ridge of his jaw. "I love you," she said, the words rushing straight from her heart before her mind had a chance to weigh and consider them.

Max moaned, her simple declaration unraveling his self-control. Ten years of emotions held in check erupted like a volcano, turning him to heat and fire. "Oh God, Kitty. I love you so much." He pulled her tight against his body, needing to be closer.

Want and need battled with caution as her lips yielded beneath his. He'd meant the kiss to be sweet, but when she parted her lips and moaned, his heart kicked into overdrive and his body reacted instantly, hardening, thickening, throbbing. He swept his tongue over the softness of her lips, letting his body speak for him. He had to have her — again and again and again.

He cupped her breast and a whimper escaped her lips as he gently squeezed the soft mound. Then she ground against him, her hot tongue darting into his mouth. That was his undoing.

With a husky moan, he tore at the buttons of her blouse, uncovering soft, warm skin. He knew he was acting like a teenager in heat but couldn't help himself. He arched upward, grinding against her. The friction of his jeans stretched tight across his erection was nearly unbearable. The answering heat of her body drove him half crazy with desire.

She tore her lips from his and pulled her shirt off, as if impatient with his fumbling attempts. He only had a moment to try to catch his breath as she reached behind her and unclasped her bra, leaning forward and shrugging it off in one smooth motion more erotic than anything he'd ever seen in his life.

Kate sent him a sultry smile. "I've never forgotten what it felt like to make out with you here."

"Darlin', if you keep this up, we'll be doing more than just making out."

She arched an eyebrow. "My thoughts exactly." Then she slid her fingers through his hair and pulled him to her breast before he could object. He was long past the point of objecting anyway and feasted on her like a starving man, his tongue teasing and circling her nipple into erection, then suckling hungrily.

She whispered his name and rocked against him until he thought he'd explode right then and there. "Easy baby," he whispered. "I'm not sure how much more of this I can take."

That was an understatement, for sure. All he knew was that if he didn't have her, he'd surely go mad. But a woman like Kate deserved better than a quick tumble in the front of a pick-up truck. She deserved hearts and flowers and silk sheets and candles.

He pulled her roughly against his chest and laid his head back on the seat rest, struggling to catch his breath. The windows were fogged with steam and the air inside the cab heavy with the heat of their sexual yearning. He cradled her, letting the throbbing ease enough to clear the fog from his brain. But he couldn't stop touching her, one hand gently stroking up and down her back as he held her close.

As much as he wanted her physically, he needed more. He needed *forever*, and that's what he had to tell her. But he was just a cowboy. How could he ever find the words pretty enough to romance her? How could he convince her to give up her glamorous world for life on a dusty Arizona ranch?

"I want you so much," he groaned.

She peeked up at him, her eyes soft with desire. "I want you too, Max."

"Not just like this," he said, brushing a fingertip along her cheek. Her skin was so soft against his calloused fingers. He was almost afraid to caress her, as if his touch was too rough for skin so delicate. "Not just for one night in the front seat of my pick-up truck." He wanted her to understand that she deserved so much more.

"Stay," he pleaded, putting his heart in her hands. "Stay and let me court you. We deserve to discover what could have been, what could *still* be if we give ourselves a chance to find out. Please, Kate. Stay here with me."

Kate felt her heart slam against the walls of her chest. Max wanted her. But he wanted more than her body—he wanted her to stay. And more than anything in the entire world, she wanted that as well. The realization hit her like a blast, sending shock waves through her body. The world seemed to spin and lights flashed before her eyes.

Lights?

Before she could answer Max, she realized that the lights were coming from outside the truck. And they were coming closer. She reached to the seat beside her and grabbed her shirt, barely able to clutch it against her naked breasts before the truck door was yanked open.

The glare of a flashlight beam blinded her, but she recognized the voice at the other end of the light.

"Well, what have we here?" Deputy Ed snickered. "Thought I was gonna catch me a couple of frisky teenagers neckin' in the woods." He flicked the light over Kate, who desperately tried to cover herself with the material. "I suppose I shouldn't be surprised to find you here," he sneered. "Once a slut, always a slut."

Max made a dangerous sound, pushed Kate off his lap and lunged for the deputy. "That's it!" he growled. "Badge or no badge, you're a dead man, Tate."

Kate made a grab for Max. "No!" she cried. But it was too late. She heard the dull thud of Max's fist connecting with Tate's jaw, then the flashlight went spinning end over end and she was all alone in the front seat of the truck. She managed to get her shirt on, pulling it closed with whatever buttons she could reach as she scrambled across the seat to Max's aid.

Outside on the ground, the two men rolled around in the dirt. Blinking her eyes to adjust to the darkness, she could just barely make out blood on Max's face. Tate's hands were tight around Max's throat. The sight paralyzed her at first then sent her into a white-hot rage.

Without thinking, she dove for the flashlight. The sound of grunts and thrashing filled the air as her hand closed around the metal handle and she turned it heavy side out.

"Stop!" she screamed, raising the flashlight over her head like a bludgeon, ready to bash Tate's head in if she had to.

"Kate, NO!" Max called out, wrenching away from Tate's grasp. He scrambled to his feet, planting himself between her and the deputy.

"He hurt you," she sobbed. "You're bleeding."

"Shhh…I'm okay."

"Drop the flashlight," Tate shouted behind Max.

Kate glanced over Max's shoulder and saw Tate crouched on one knee, pointing his gun at Max's back. "Are you crazy?" she screamed. "You can't shoot him!"

"Drop the flashlight," he warned her again. "And move out of the way."

"Do what he says," Max cautioned.

Slowly Kate backed away. "Don't shoot him," she pleaded. "Please don't shoot him."

Tate ignored her. He rose to his feet and motioned Max over to the patrol car. "Lean over the hood and spread 'em," he snarled. "One wrong move and I'll do what I shoulda done a long time ago."

Max shot a warning glance at Kate then did what he was told.

Still aiming the gun at Max's back, Tate advanced on him. "You should know better than to attack an officer of the law, Connors."

Despite Max's warning, Kate couldn't stand still and watch him being humiliated. She rushed toward the car, screaming at Tate. "Get away from him!"

Tate pushed her out of the way and she fell sprawling in the dirt.

"Leave her alone," Max shouted over his shoulder. "This is between me and you."

"Not anymore," Tate growled, slapping handcuffs over Max's wrists. "It's between you and the courts." He laughed, an evil snickering sound. "I told you not to mess with me, Connors. Now you're gonna pay."

Then he turned to Kate. "Stay out of my way or I'll haul you in for obstructing justice." He snorted. "Might not be a bad idea, now that I think of it, since you're nothing more than a cheap piece of ass."

Max made a sound of outrage, but Kate was too stricken to respond. The words shouldn't have mattered. Not now after all she'd learned. But even coming from Tate, that was a low blow.

Sitting in the dirt, she dropped her head into her hands and let the tears flow, wishing she'd never come back to town, never dragged Max into this mess. What had she done?

She heard a car door slam and realized Tate was really hauling Max off to jail. She couldn't waste time feeling sorry for herself. She wiped the tears from her eyes with the back of her hands and stood up, watching in disbelief as Tate started the patrol car and backed up, dome lights flashing as if he had a hardened criminal in tow.

She stood there for a moment, dazed, fighting the temptation to rush off after the patrol car and throw herself onto the hood. That would only make things worse. Tate seemed to get a perverse thrill out of tormenting Max in front of her. She needed help if she was going to get Max out of jail.

Even in her muddled state, it hadn't taken Kate long to realize she had to get to Otis if she wanted to free Max. The drive took less than ten minutes, but it felt like hours before she finally pulled into the driveway. She shifted into neutral and set the parking brake then jumped out without turning off the ignition.

Sue met her at the door. Her eyes widened in shock as she took in Kate's appearance. "What happened to you?" She looked behind Kate at the empty truck idling in front of the house. "Where's Max?"

"He…Tate…fighting," Kate stuttered, trying to make sense of what happened.

Otis came rushing in, pulling on his suspenders as he entered the room. "What's going on out here?"

Kate rushed to him. "Ed Tate arrested Max!"

Otis led her to a chair and helped her sit. "Arrested Max? For what?" He turned to Sue. "Get her some tea or something."

Kate shook her head. She never wanted to see a cup of tea again in her life.

"It's okay," Otis said, patting her back as if she were a hysterical child. "Just calm down and tell me everything."

She did, blushing as she admitted that she and Max had been parking out at Whiskey Creek. When she reached the part where Ed Tate stormed in and called her names, Otis swore under his breath.

"And then they fought," Kate said, nodding gratefully as Sue placed a glass of water on the table. "Max was bleeding. I tried to help, but then Tate pulled a gun on Max and hauled him off to jail. He said…he said…" She couldn't go on. It seemed like a surreal nightmare. She looked at Otis pleadingly. "Max was just defending me, defending my reputation. He shouldn't be in jail."

Otis nodded. "That Tate boy's been holding a grudge close to his chest for a long time."

"What are we going to do?" Kate asked.

Otis stood and hitched his pants up. "First I'm going to make a phone call. I think Sheriff Jackson might like to know what his deputy's been up to."

Sue stood nearby, her lips pulled into a tight, disapproving line. "It's not your fault," she said, but the words were as sharp as shattered glass.

Kate couldn't help blaming herself, but her own feelings weren't important now. They had to get Max away from Tate.

She could hear Otis recounting the entire episode over the phone to Sheriff Jackson from beginning to end. Hearing it again filled her with shame.

Sue turned her attention to Kate. "Did I hear Max say you were going to the reunion with him tomorrow night?"

Kate nodded, puzzled as to why Sue would care about something so trivial when Max was in jail. Who cared about the reunion? Who cared about anything except getting Max safely home?

* * * * *

Kate and Otis arrived at the County Municipal Center in record time. The sheriff's car was in the parking lot. He'd made even better time than Kate and Otis.

Kate was relieved to see that Max wasn't stuck in a jail cell. Both Max and Tate sat in chairs, looking like two truants who'd been called into the principal's office. Sheriff Jackson, a grizzly bear of a man, paced back and forth in the office.

He looked up as Kate and Otis entered the room. "Good, we're all here. Now maybe we can get this mess straightened out." He motioned Kate to a chair and took his place behind the desk. "Let's see those papers Otis told me about."

Kate dug through her purse until she found the cancelled check and deed signed over to Anne Connors. Along with that, she handed him the judgment lien that Tate had served her with.

Otis read the papers carefully. Then he turned to his deputy. "You had these papers served in your official capacity as deputy sheriff?"

Puffed up with importance, Tate agreed that he had.

The sheriff made some notes on a yellow lined tablet and then pinned Ed Tate with a steady glare. "First, that's a conflict of interest. You should have gone through the proper channels. Those channels being *me*."

"But—" Tate started.

"Second," the sheriff continued, holding up his hand for silence, "the claim is null and void according to these documents. I'll have the lien removed from the docket and you're hereby notified to cease and desist any and all spurious claims on the property."

Tate's mouth dropped open. "You're going to take their word over your own deputy's?"

Sheriff Jackson shook his head. "I'm not taking anyone's word. I've got a signed and notarized deed and cancelled check for payment of Jebediah's share. That's all the proof I need. You have no claim on the property." He turned to Kate. "I'll have these documents filed and put on record at the courthouse."

Kate nodded gratefully, ignoring Tate's narrow-eyed glare. If looks could kill...

Sheriff Jackson turned to an open folder on his desk. "Now, it says here that the business in question was closed for a period of two days due to an electrical hazard."

Tate, obviously feeling more sure of himself in this area, leaned across the desk. "The paperwork is all in order. The shop was closed because of faulty wiring. You can see the electrical inspector's notes right here."

Sheriff Jackson nodded, flipping through the paperwork and noting it was all in order. "Chuck Hitchcock," he said, reading the name at the bottom of the document. "Friend of yours, Tate?"

Before Ed Tate could answer, Sheriff Jackson turned to Max. "It says you were able to fix the wiring. What exactly was the problem you found?"

"The main breaker panel had been tampered with," Max noted. "A lead wire had been stripped, which caused the wires to short out. I repaired the wires and put a padlock on the box." Max's gaze shifted momentarily to Tate before he added, "That way the wires can't be tampered with again." He came just short of accusing Tate of directly causing the problem, and the implication wasn't lost on anyone in the room.

Sheriff Jackson leaned back in his chair, glancing from Max to Tate thoughtfully. "Seems to me that if Max was able to find the problem with these wires easily enough, your electrician friend should have been able to do the same, right? Was it really necessary to close down a tax-paying business for a problem that could have been fixed in a matter of minutes?"

Tate shrugged, his eyes shifting back and forth. "That was out of my hands. The electrical inspector made the call, I just followed through."

"Followed through," Sheriff Jackson repeated. His voice was deceptively low, the voice of a man who wasn't easily fooled. "This is beginning to sound an awful lot like harassment to me, Tate. We don't do things that way in my department. Anyone who thinks that they can use the law for their own personal agenda has got some serious rethinking to do."

He made some more notes on the tablet as Tate sunk a little lower in his chair. More papers slid neatly into his folder. It was obvious to Kate that Sheriff Jackson was building a case against Tate and collecting all the evidence he needed to make it stick.

Kate wondered how long this confrontation had been coming to a head. Sheriff Jackson wasn't a stupid man, and he looked like he'd about reached the end of his rope as far as Ed Tate's interpretation of the law was concerned.

Sheriff Jackson stood up, dwarfing everyone else in the room. Kate smiled, realizing he wasn't above using his size to intimidate others when it was necessary.

"Now," he said. "About this little episode tonight—"

Tate leaped to his feet and pointed at Max. "He attacked an officer of the law. I was within my rights to bring him in."

"Sit down," the sheriff yelled, pointing his finger dead center in Ed Tate's chest. "I've about had enough of you and your so-called rights. After the things you said to this little lady, Max Connors would have been a coward not to take you down a peg. I'd have done the same thing, only I'd have made you get down on your knees and apologize to her first. Now this may come as a surprise Tate, but for your information, a badge doesn't put you above the law."

Tate flushed, his lips pulling into a thin, hard line. But he sat down and shut up.

"Now, as I was saying," Sheriff Jackson continued, "seems to me this is a personal problem, not police business. If you boys want to have a pissing contest, take it outside. Don't bring your personal problems into my department."

He signed some papers and handed them to Max. "You're free to go home with your family. All charges against you are dropped."

Then he turned back to Ed Tate. "As far as you're concerned," he said, "you're walking a thin line, and I'm not so big a fool that I can't see it." He planted his palms flat on the desk, leaning forward until he was nose to nose with Tate. "You can be sure I'll be conducting an official investigation into this whole matter. Until then, consider yourself on probation. You'd better watch your step," he warned. "One more wrong move and I'll have your badge. Trust me on that."

Tate stood with his jaw clenched. A vein throbbed on the side of his neck and his face was flushed with fury, but he didn't dare speak back to his superior.

Kate realized that all of his anger—which included being chastised in front of "civilians"—would now be directed at her and Max.

This wasn't over yet. Not by a long shot.

Chapter Nineteen

&

After dropping Otis back off at the ranch, then explaining the evening's events to Sue, Kate gathered up her things to leave.

Max walked outside with her. "I'll drive," he said.

"But my car—"

"It'll be fine right here for the night," he insisted. "I want to be sure you get home safe and sound."

Kate started to argue, but Max shushed her with a finger to her lips. "Humor me, okay?"

Kate nodded then climbed into Max's pick-up and wrapped her arms around herself. Now that the danger had passed, she was more embarrassed over being caught than afraid of what Ed Tate might do.

Max settled in beside her then pulled her into his arms. He ran his hands along her back. "You're trembling."

She wrapped her arms around him, holding on tight. Although she'd lost her desire to make out in the front seat of Max's truck, she hadn't lost her desire for Max.

"Maybe we should go someplace more private next time," he said.

Kate slid her hand to his chest, resting her palm over his heart. "Take me home." The words came out even before she realized what she was saying. Yet nothing had ever felt more natural before. Home was wherever Max was.

"Buckle up, darlin'," he said. "I'll have you home in no time."

Instead of returning to the passenger side, Kate strapped herself in the middle so she could stay close to Max. He put the truck in gear with Kate's head on his shoulder and her hand resting on his thigh. They drove in silence, yet the air sizzled with sexual desire.

"Are you coming in?" she asked when they pulled up in front of her place.

He shot her a heart-stopping grin. "I thought you'd never ask."

He unbuckled her seatbelt and lifted her out of the truck, holding her close for a long moment before setting her on her feet again. She slid down the length of his body, feeling his immediate response.

Whether it was adrenaline, hormones, nerves or just plain lust, the minute they stepped inside Max and Kate were all over each other. Everything else was forgotten in a tangle of arms and legs and hot, hungry kisses. They left a trail of discarded clothes from the front door to the bedroom, falling onto the bed naked and ready to pick up where they'd left off.

Over the past few days, Kate had been making up for lost time, discovering ways to pleasure and please, to give as well as take. Max was an excellent teacher, and Kate was a more than willing student. She'd discovered ways to touch him that drove him half mad with desire, and was adventurous enough to search for new sensations—a tug of his hair, the scrape of fingernails along his skin, a swirl of the tongue, the dip and flicker of fingertips. Hearing the way he groaned when she touched him only made her bolder. She couldn't get enough of him.

With a low moan, she rolled him onto his back. He stretched out, letting her take charge easily, effortlessly. Kate felt that familiar moment of breathless wonder as she admired the long, hard line of his body. She could eat him alive, starting from his toes and working her way up.

Neither one of them would last that long.

She stretched across him, reaching for the condoms on the dresser. This was another thing he'd taught her and already she was an expert at turning a necessity into foreplay. She knelt between his legs, her fingers feathering along his inner thighs. His body jerked as she worked her way upward, exploring his contours with a possessiveness that surprised them both.

When she curled her fingers around him, he sucked in a harsh gasp. "Baby, you're killing me."

She peeked up and smiled. "Not yet." Then she leaned over, teasing him with a swirl of her tongue. His body arched, rising to meet her, and still she teased, loving him in a way that was part instinct and part lifelong fantasy. The quivering along his body was all the encouragement she needed and his moans were a testament to her newfound skill.

When she felt his body tighten she eased off, waiting until his breathing settled again before finding new ways to please him. And when she couldn't take another second of sexual torment, she sat up and curled one hand around his base, using the other to ease the condom onto the tip of his shaft. She stroked and smoothed, working it downward with a deft, teasing touch. She took her time, feeling him throb in her hands.

"Mine," she whispered, holding him tight.

With a low growl, he reached for her, pulling her up until she was straddling his hips. "All yours," he replied. "Only yours."

She gripped his shoulders and slid onto him, taking him hard and fast, hungry for him in a way she'd never known before. Their mating was primal, bodies moving together in a rhythm as old as time. She rode him hard, grinding and thrusting and slamming her body into his.

Max couldn't take his eyes off her. He'd never seen anything more beautiful in his life. Through a rising tide of passion he watched her lose all semblance of control, driving them both to a thundering peak. Her skin glistened, her hair whipped around her face and the sounds she made—*oh Lord!*

She was every man's most erotic dream and carnal desire. And she was all his.

He plunged upward, repeating the word with each deep thrust—*"mine, mine, MINE!"*

He felt her tremble, saw her eyes widen with surprise, as if each time was the first time. Then every thought fled and they tumbled over the edge, coming together in a blinding, thundering explosion.

His heart raced, his pulse pounded and his vision blurred. Only when she went limp in his arms did he roll her over and continue thrusting, bringing her over again, intoxicated by the way her body responded to him. Time stretched and spun out around them, carrying with it the promise of a lifetime of loving Kate.

In the quiet afterglow, they held each other, murmuring soft, sweet words. This was the best of all times, when the physical needs were met but the passion remained. Max ran his fingers through her hair, cradling her against his chest. No woman had ever given him the incredible sense of intimacy and fulfillment that he felt holding Kate in his arms.

He snuggled her close, feeling sleep wrap around them like a soft blanket. At some point—it might have been moments or hours later—Kate mumbled something. Max forced one eye open and tried to concentrate, but his mind was a misty haze.

"How close are Sue and Ed Tate?" she asked.

"Hmmm?"

"I was just wondering…"

Max pulled her tight against his chest. "Don't be silly. My sister wouldn't have anything to do with that jerk."

Kate considered that for a few moments, chewing on her lower lip. Maybe she should just tell Max about the phone conversation and see what he made of it. But before she could bring up the subject, he'd already drifted off to sleep and she didn't have the heart to wake him again. He'd had a long, exhausting day and needed his rest. She'd talk to him about it tomorrow. For now, she was content to spend the night in Max's arms.

When Kate awoke Friday morning, Max was already gone. He'd left a note telling her to sleep late and that he'd already told Nellie not to expect her in right away. She smiled and stretched, feeling the luxurious laziness that came with contentment. Maybe she'd take Max's advice and pamper herself this morning. Nellie was sure to have everything under control and Kate had a lot to do before the reunion that night.

It was nearly noon before she ambled into the shop. Everything was running smoothly, just as she'd known it would be.

In the kitchen, Nellie looked up from her baking and gave Kate a sly grin. "You look refreshed."

Kate smiled back. "I slept late." She kept right on going to the front of the shop, ignoring Nellie's knowing chuckle. A line of customers waited at the counter. Kate tied on an apron and started taking orders. When Jeff came back, she'd have to talk to him about hiring more help. Unless, of course, she decided to stay.

Kate turned to Arthur Zimmerman at the register. "Where's Chrissy today?"

"She's out back keeping an eye on Bobby."

Kate's head jerked up. "Bobby? Max's nephew?"

When Arthur nodded his head, Kate asked where Sue was.

"She came by and said she had a few errands to run. Asked if Chrissy could keep an eye on Bobby for a few hours. Didn't see no harm in it."

Only in a small town, Kate thought. Still, it seemed odd that Sue hadn't just left Bobby home with Max. Unless...

Suddenly Kate had a moment of blinding clarity. She should have been more suspicious when she'd overheard Sue and Tate on the phone, but she'd been so excited about their discovery in the attic that she'd ignored the warning signals. Now everything clicked into place—Sue's hostility, the snippet of phone conversation Kate had overheard and the fact that Sue obviously didn't want Max to know where she was going today.

"Like hell you will. If I go down, you're going right down with me."

Kate was convinced that Sue's errands involved a clandestine visit with Deputy Tate. There was something suspicious going on and Kate was determined to get to the bottom of it.

She whipped off her apron and turned to Arthur. "I have to run out for a bit. Can you handle this alone?"

He waved her away with a smile. "Sure. Take your time. I've got everything under control."

Kate went out the front door to avoid having to explain to Nellie. Her heart was pounding. The more she thought about it, the more convinced she became that Sue and Tate were involved in something devious.

Kate practically ran the four blocks to the sheriff's office. It wasn't long before her suspicions were confirmed. The outer office was empty. Millie Clifton, the receptionist and part-time dispatcher, must have been on her lunch break. But there were voices coming from behind Ed Tate's closed door. One of them was Tate's. The other definitely belonged to Sue Connors.

Kate had no intention of eavesdropping. Whatever the two of them had to say, they could say right to her face. She lifted her hand to knock on the door then stopped when she heard Sue's voice rising in anger.

"How was I to know Kitty would leave town in shame, nearly destroying Max? And how was I to know that she'd come back and threaten to expose everything?"

"That didn't stop you from stepping in to fill her shoes, did it?" Ed Tate yelled back. "You didn't mind representing Easy County in the Miss Arizona Pageant after we got Kate out of the way, did you?"

Kate stepped away from the door, stunned beyond belief. Sue and Tate had worked together to get her thrown out of the pageant? She shook her head, not wanting to believe it. Why? Why would they do that to her?

With a sinking feeling in the pit of her stomach, Kate realized that she couldn't trust anyone in this town. What about Max? Did he know his sister was in collusion with Ed Tate? Had he been protecting her all along?

Kate backed up. She had every intention of slipping away. *Running away.* She couldn't deal with this, couldn't face the shame and humiliation all over again. It hurt too much, uncovering old wounds that had never completely healed.

Before she could escape, the door flew open. Sue came rushing out. Her eyes were red and swollen. She took one look at Kate and stopped in her tracks. Her body sagged. She held out one hand in a move that looked like supplication. "Kate," she said. "I'm…"

Sorry? Ashamed?

Whatever Sue had intended to say, one glance in Ed Tate's direction had her reconsidering. "You shouldn't have come back, Kate. Everything was fine and you just stirred it all up." She sounded more hurt than angry. "You're only going to hurt Max again."

Kate shook her head. "I'm not the one hurting Max. How do you think he'll feel when he hears what you've done?"

Sue seemed to deflate before Kate's very eyes. Then she raised her chin defiantly. "What makes you think he'll believe you over me?"

Kate's stomach dropped. Sue was right. Max hadn't believed her ten years ago. Why would he believe her now? But things were different now…

Sue started to say something, but Ed shot her a warning glance. Sue looked from one to the other then gave Kate a look that seemed to contradict the venom that fell from her lips. "No one wants you here, Kate. Everyone is talking behind your back." She kept glancing at Tate as if she was afraid of him. "Why don't you just go back to New York City where you belong?" She gave Kate one final imploring look then rushed out the door.

"She's right, you know." Ed Tate curled his thumbs beneath his waistband and hitched his pants up. "Hear you're planning on going to the reunion after all. That should give the town something to talk about...again. Guess you didn't learn your lesson the first time did you, Little Miss Easy?"

He practically spit the words out, each one another blow to Kate's already bruised heart. All those old insecurities came rushing back, nearly smothering her under the weight of old shame. Maybe they were both right. Maybe she shouldn't have come back.

She spun on her heel and rushed through the door. The memory of Deputy Tate's smug laughter followed her all the way home. In her mind, Kate could still hear the whispers that had chased her out of town the first time. Nothing had changed. Nothing ever would.

Still reeling from Sue's accusations, Kate locked herself inside the house. What was she thinking? How could she ever have considered staying here? She'd been blinded by her feelings for Max, but even those were like quicksand beneath her feet. Ten years of feeling betrayed didn't just vanish overnight simply because he said all the things she wanted to hear and threw her hormones into overdrive.

She sank to the bed, where just last night she'd given herself to Max. Hadn't she learned this lesson once before? The phone rang, but she ignored it. There was no one she wanted to talk to, no one she felt she could trust.

Maybe Sue was right. Maybe Kate should just go back to New York. Jeff would be home in a few days, and Nellie could handle things at the shop until he returned. Kate had an open-ended ticket for her return flight. Why drag it out any longer?

Between Tate's threats, her argument with Sue and her boss threatening that she'd lose her job if she wasn't at her desk Monday morning, going back to New York seemed like the only option. Some distance would give her a chance to think about her feelings for Max—without his irresistible backside around to distract her.

She rushed to the closet to grab her suitcase. The red pageant dress hung there like an accusation. Seeing it only confirmed Kate's decision. Ed Tate was right. Showing up at the reunion would only fuel the gossip. By now, half the town had probably heard all the lurid details of the way Tate had found them parked at Whiskey Overlook. They'd be shaking their heads, whispering behind her back, calling her names. Only this time they'd be right.

Kate had no intention of giving them the pleasure. By the time the reunion came, she'd be on a flight headed back to New York.

Her mother's cup rattled on the countertop. "Don't start with me," Kate yelled. She turned her back and began throwing clothes into the suitcase, determined to get out of Easy while there was still time.

* * * * *

Max pounded on Kate's door. He'd been calling all afternoon and there'd been no answer. She wasn't at the shop, so where could she be?

He jiggled the knob and the door inched open. "Kate? Are you okay?" He looked around then noticed the suitcase standing in the corner. "Kate?"

She stepped out of the kitchen and gave him a sheepish, almost guilty look. "I wasn't expecting to see you."

"Obviously." He jerked his chin at the suitcase. "What's this?"

Kate avoided his gaze. "You know I have to be back at work Monday."

Max took a slow, deep breath, trying not to jump to any conclusions. "Were you going to leave without telling me?"

"No," she stammered. "I…I was going to call."

"When? Once you were back in New York?"

At least she had the decency to look ashamed. He knew without her saying a word that she'd intended to do just that.

"I just need some time to think, Max."

He ran a hand through his hair, staring at Kate in disbelief. "I thought we were past the thinking stage, Kate." He gestured to the suitcase. "I thought we were past the running stage too."

He took a step closer, reaching out for her. "What about the reunion?"

She backed up and shook her head from side to side, as if she couldn't bear looking at him, couldn't bear for him to touch her. "I can't, Max."

He dropped his hands to his side. "Why?"

Kate turned away. "I've heard things. Things about Ed Tate and your sister. The pageant…"

"Oh, for Christ's sake." Max clutched his hands into fists. Anger hardened his voice. "That was ten years ago! No one even cares anymore, Kate."

She shook her head sadly. "It's not what you think, Max."

"Then what? What is it?" He could see her trembling, fighting for control. More than anything else he wanted to go to her—take her in his arms and comfort her. But her stiff posture warned him away. "Talk to me, Kate."

But she couldn't. She couldn't tell him what she'd overheard in Ed Tate's office. She'd seen the silent plea in Sue's eyes. As difficult as it was for Kate to know the truth, she knew it would be even harder on Max. He adored his sister—and Bobby. Kate didn't want to be the one to shatter his illusions.

Besides, Sue's threat still echoed in her mind.

What makes you think he'll believe you over me?

Who would Max believe? The sister who'd stood by him or the woman who'd left him behind? The trust they'd built over the last few weeks was a tenuous thing that, if nurtured, would grow strong and unbreakable over time. But they didn't have time, and Kate couldn't risk breaking that fragile thread by forcing Max to choose between her and his own flesh and blood.

The truth was, Kate wasn't sure who Max would believe, and she knew she couldn't risk being rejected again. Better to let Max believe the worst — that she was reverting to her old pattern of running away.

"I can't let it go. I can still feel the shame and humiliation and the frustration of not being able to defend myself."

"You could have defended yourself if you'd stayed and fought back. Don't you see Kate? It was running away that made you look guilty."

Max shook his head. "I should have listened to people who warned me not to get involved — that you'd just leave again."

Kate felt bitterness rise in her chest. "People like your sister?" She fairly spat the words out.

Max nodded. "Yeah. Like my sister."

There it was. She should just tell him. Get it all out in the open. Kate started to speak, but Max held up his hand and stopped her.

"Don't. Whatever you're going to say, don't do it. You haven't been here these last ten years. You don't know what Sue's been through."

Kate's shoulders sagged. "You're right. I haven't been here."

"And you don't intend to stay, do you?"

Kate looked away.

"Fine," he said. "I can't force you to stay. I'll be at the reunion tonight. If you decide it's time to stop running, you know where to find me. If not, well...if not, then go on back to New York and have a nice life."

He turned and walked out the door, never once looking back.

Chapter Twenty

Kate sat alone in the darkened room, her suitcase beside her, the airplane ticket in her lap. She'd been paralyzed with indecision since the moment Max walked out the door. Every instinct told her to run, but her heart kept her rooted to the spot.

She couldn't forget the look on Max's face when he'd realized she was leaving. He'd been devastated. Worse than that, he'd been disappointed. Kate knew she'd let him down...again. Still, he'd left her an opening — the reunion — putting the final decision in her hands. It was a choice she couldn't seem to make.

Kate caught her breath as the strains of Roy Orbison's "Only the Lonely" drifted in from the kitchen. A slow tear slid down her cheek. Her mother and Roy were both right. She was lonely. She'd been lonely for so long, even surrounded by thousands of people in a bustling city. What was waiting for her in New York other than a cramped cubicle during the day and an empty apartment at night?

Now she'd been given a second chance with Max — a chance to get back what had been stolen from them all those years ago. A chance to ease the loneliness once and for all.

All she had to do was let go of the bitterness.

Did it really matter what anyone else thought of her? She knew who she was, what she was. And so did Max. What else mattered?

Max's parting words echoed in her ears. *If you decide it's time to stop running, you know where to find me.*

Kate stood up. She knew what to do. It was time to let go of the past and embrace the future. She was tired of running. She was tired of being alone.

As if on cue, the telephone rang. Kate snatched it up, hoping to hear Max's voice on the other end. Instead she was surprised when Sue started talking, rushing through her monologue as if she was afraid she wouldn't be able to get it all out.

"Kate, just listen please? The things I said to you today were for Ed Tate's benefit. I didn't mean them. Maybe one time I did, but not anymore. Please don't leave."

"Sue, I've made up my mind…"

"No, don't make up your mind yet. Go to the reunion tonight. Everything will be clear then, I promise. Trust me, Kate. If you run away now, then Ed Tate wins."

Kate opened her mouth to speak, but it was too late. Sue had already hung up. If Kate hadn't already decided to go to the reunion, Sue's final words were enough to convince her. *If you run away now, then Ed Tate wins.*

She hung up the phone and walked to the kitchen. She slipped the airline ticket under her mother's cup. "Hang on to this for me, Mom. Let's hope I don't need it."

Then, knowing she was finally doing the right thing, Kate marched to the closet and pulled out the red dress. She tore the protective plastic off. The dress was as beautiful as the day her mother had made it.

Kate only hoped it still fit.

* * * * *

Max got dressed for the reunion, but his heart wasn't in it. If Sue wasn't so excited about tonight, he'd just stay home. Better yet, he'd drive out to the airport and stop Kate before she made the biggest mistake of her life. He'd get down on his knees and beg if he had to.

"She'll be there," Sue said, as if reading his mind.

Max turned, his eyes widening. "Wow. You look gorgeous, Sis."

She smiled, and it was the first genuine smile Max had seen on her face in a long time. It made her look younger, less battered by life. For a fleeting moment he remembered the carefree girl she'd been all those years ago, before life had beaten her down, before the reality of being a single mother with a special needs child had stolen the sparkle from her eyes.

Max held out his arm. "You'll be the most beautiful girl there." He tucked Sue's hand inside his elbow and walked her to the door. "Let's go knock 'em dead."

* * * * *

Kate stepped out of the car and stood with her shoulders straight and her head held high. The red dress fit perfectly, just as it had ten years ago. Now, however, instead of a reminder of her shame, she wore it as a symbol of pride.

She took a deep breath. Her heart pounded. She couldn't believe she was actually going through with this. If only she could convince her legs to carry her inside.

Suddenly, without warning, Max stepped out of the shadows. "I was hoping you'd make the right choice."

Kate gasped, flooded with emotions at the sight of him—from the tip of his snakeskin boots to the brim of his jet-black Stetson, and every mouthwatering inch of man in between. He was devastatingly handsome in his long black tuxedo coat with embroidered arrowheads. Her own personal Maverick.

He sauntered up the sidewalk and without even realizing she'd moved, Kate rushed to meet him.

"Hello darlin'," he drawled.

Kate melted instantly. If he hadn't wrapped an arm around her waist, she might have fallen to her knees.

He leaned close and brushed his cheek against hers, whispering softly into her ear. "You look gorgeous," he said. "You should wear red more often."

Kate's heart swelled with emotion. "I intend to."

His hand rested at her lower back, his thumb brushing slow, fiery trails over her skin. His touch sent shivers through her body, making it hard to breathe and impossible to think straight.

It wasn't until they were standing at the entrance and she saw the sign above the door welcoming the class of 1996 that fear set in.

Her step faltered and Max clutched her tighter. "Are you all right?" he asked.

"I...I can't do this."

"Yes you can," he assured her. "I'll be right here with you every step of the way. I won't leave your side."

She glanced up, blinking away the quick, hot sting of tears. "Promise?"

"I promise," he whispered. "For as long as you need me." He took her hand and placed it over his heart.

Kate realized she couldn't leave him. Not now. Not ever. But before she could plan a future, she first had to deal with her past.

She took a deep breath and hung onto him. "All right," she said, feeling like a condemned prisoner taking her first step toward the gallows. "I'm ready."

But she wasn't. Not really. And when they stepped through the doors and a hush fell over the room, she had all she could do not to run back outside and keep running until she reached the Atlantic Ocean.

Kate noted the looks of surprise as people she hadn't seen in ten years recognized her for the first time. The old paranoia surfaced as she imagined whispered conversations that all revolved around her.

"Head high," Max said in a voice low enough that only she could hear. His voice was calm and soothing, the same tone she'd heard him use to calm a frightened horse. "Easy darlin'. Slow and steady."

Max held her close as they made their way through the sea of curious stares. Kate straightened her spine, holding her head high and pretending a pride she didn't feel. It was all so familiar — the whispers, the sneers, the sliding looks of condemnation. Why had she ever agreed to this? Her hand trembled on Max's arm. He reached over and placed his hand over hers, giving it a reassuring squeeze as they made their way to their seats.

Max pulled out her chair and leaned close. "Breathe, darlin'," he said with a slow, steady smile.

Kate sat and gave him a brave smile in return, but even with her back to most of the room, she could feel all eyes on her. It wasn't her imagination. Nothing had changed.

And then, as hard as it was to believe, things got worse. Kate glanced at the dais and saw the honored guests seated onstage — the principal, the mayor, the sheriff, their class valedictorian — and there, at the end of the row, pointedly avoiding eye contact, was Sue Connors, Miss Easy County 1996.

The crown and sash Sue wore were like a slap in Kate's face. It was more than she could bear. A sob caught in her throat. She felt doubly betrayed. *Sue knew I was coming*, she thought. *Why hadn't she warned me?*

Seeing Sue wearing the crown and sash only reminded everyone of Kate's humiliation and the reason she'd left town in the first place. She sank deeper into her chair, trying to make herself invisible. She couldn't leave now. She would only call even more attention to herself. As hard as it was, she had to stay and play it out.

As the first speaker reached the microphone, Kate glanced at Max. His face was pulled into a tight, hard line. His eyes were narrowed into an angry glare. But he wasn't looking at Sue or anyone else on stage. Kate followed his gaze and nearly gasped when she saw Ed Tate leaning against the doorway, a smirk on his face. He looked smaller out of his uniform, but he still wore the air of a bully looking for a rumble. He wouldn't have to look far. Kate could feel Max coiling with tension beside her, his fists clenched tight at his side.

"I think I'm going to be sick," she whimpered.

Max turned to her, concern on his face. Then he smiled and pulled her close, covering her lips with his in a show that might have been more for everyone else's benefit than hers, but it gave her strength all the same. She wished they were alone so she could explore the kiss more deeply. She wished she were anywhere but here.

The speeches dragged on forever and each ripple of laughter felt aimed directly at her. And then, when Kate felt her nerves couldn't take much more, Sue stepped forward.

The room fell quiet, with only the rustling sound of Sue's taffeta skirt echoing over the speakers as she reached the podium. She glanced quickly at Max and Kate then cleared her throat and spoke into the microphone. "Ten years ago I had the honor and privilege of serving you as Miss Easy County. At the time I thought it was the most important thing in the whole world. But we were all younger then."

Max reached for Kate's hand, giving her strength for whatever was to come.

Onstage, Sue glanced around the room, taking in all the faces around her. "I've learned a lot since then, and some of those lessons haven't come easy." She looked pointedly at Max, who beamed proudly at his sister. Kate knew they were both thinking of Bobby and the trials they'd all gone through, the long hours and hard work they'd put in to make the ranch a place of healing.

"I've learned that a crown and a sash don't define the person you are. It's the love and respect of the people around you that really matters. Your friends, your family, your community."

She looked pointedly at Kate. "A lot has happened to us all in the ten years since we graduated. Each and every one of us has grown." She fell silent, her eyes cast downward as if searching for notes that weren't there. Then she looked up and the spotlight picked up a shimmer in her eyes. Her voice was no more than a hush, barely amplified by the microphone. "One thing I've learned is that ten years is too long for innocent people to suffer. Too long for wrongs to go unpunished."

Then she grinned. "But not as long as this speech, you're probably thinking." Nervous laughter rippled through the room.

"I'm sure you'd all like to get on with the festivities," she said. "And so, I'd like to start us off with the first dance." She turned and handed a tape to someone behind her, then stepped off the stage.

The spotlight followed Sue's progress across the room as the pre-recorded music began to play. Kate wasn't surprised to hear Roy Orbison's voice coming from the speakers. She felt a sense of destiny, of coming full circle. Even the song seemed somehow appropriate for what happened next, as Roy Orbison's honey tones began crooning "It's Over" through the speakers.

Across the dance floor, Sue stopped in front of Ed Tate and held out her arms. He gave her a nod of approval then shot Max a smug look of victory before leading Sue to the center of the dance floor.

"What the hell is she doing?" Max grumbled, staring at the couple in the spotlight.

Kate had no idea. Before she could even begin to guess, the music stuttered and stopped. The song was silenced and the sound of hissing echoed over the speakers as the tape continued to advance. Then, instead of music, the sound of Sue's anguished voice could be heard on the tape.

"They were all lies, weren't they? You made up those rumors about Kate Feathers and spread them around town, didn't you?"

An evil chuckle came over the loudspeakers, followed by Ed Tate's voice. "So what of it? I got nothin' to be afraid of." The menace in his voice was evident, even over the crackling hiss of the tape player. "You had your part in this too, and I'm not going down alone," he said.

In horrified shock, Kate heard Sue plead with him over the tape, claiming that he'd tricked her into believing his lies were the truth, arguing that she'd been trying to protect her brother. But Tate only laughed and continued threatening her.

The room was eerily still, the spotlight shining on Sue and Ed Tate, who were no longer dancing but glaring at each other like opponents at a wrestling match. Tate shook his head slowly as the tape continued playing out the horrible truth.

"All I'm saying is—if I go down, you're going with me. How would Max feel then? Do you think he'd want to keep you around his ranch, reminding him what a traitor you are? Then who'd take care of you and that little crippled kid of yours?"

His words were followed by a collective gasp and more shocked silence. Then all hell broke loose. Max growled and jerked to his feet, toppling his chair behind him as he rushed across the room. Everything seemed to take place in slow motion. Tate raised his hand. Sue stood staring at him, daring him to slap her in front of everyone. But Max reached them first, pushing Tate's hand aside and swinging his fist at the same time.

Tate went down hard and didn't come back up. Sue bowed her head, her body slumped. Kate was paralyzed in her seat. She couldn't move, couldn't go to Max. She had to know the rest, had to find out the truth as it played out on the tape recorder for everyone to hear.

Tate lay unconscious, spread-eagle on the dance floor. But his voice continued playing over the speakers, gloating that he'd lied about Kate all along and admitting that he'd purposely destroyed her reputation ten years ago and had no intention of stopping now.

Kate shook her head. Ed Tate had manipulated them all, including Sue and Max. But her vindication felt hollow. It all seemed so pointless. All those years lost, all the pain and regret. For what?

She glanced around, but people avoided her eyes, whether out of guilt or shame she couldn't tell. She couldn't find Max. He was hidden in a crowd that had formed where Ed Tate had fallen. Kate recognized the sheriff making his way through the crowd, his face flushed with anger. But where was Max?

Then the crowd parted and she saw Max with his arm around his sister. Her heart went out to Sue, who'd been used by a devious manipulator. She'd risked everything to finally put things right. She must have agonized over her decision to play Tate's confession on tonight of all nights, exposing him in front of everyone even at the risk of losing her standing in the community, as well as her brother's respect. And that was what finally spurred Kate forward.

Breathlessly she made her way across the room to Max and Sue's side. Sue tore herself from Max's protective embrace and turned to Kate. "I'm so sorry," she said, weeping bitterly. "Can you ever forgive me?"

Kate realized that despite everything she'd lost as a result of Sue's misguided revenge, there was room in her heart for forgiveness. "Yes," she said, wrapping her arms around the shattered woman. Now that she'd finally let go of the anger and resentment, there was room in her heart for a lot of things she hadn't allowed herself to feel before. Like forgiveness and understanding, and most of all, love.

Sue tore the sash from her dress. "Here," she said. "I wanted to give this to you tonight. It should have been yours all along."

Kate shook her head and refused to take it. "No. You were right when you said some things are more important." She turned to Max. "It wasn't the loss of the crown or the scholarship that nearly destroyed me," she said. "It was losing you. That's why I couldn't stay. I couldn't live here and see you every day and know I couldn't have you."

"And now?" he asked, barely breathing as he waited for her answer.

She stepped into his waiting arms. "Now I'd like to stay and find out where we can go from here. We've wasted ten years. Let's not waste another second more."

Max took the sash from his sister's hand, crumpled it and let it fall to the floor. "There's only one title you'll ever need from here on in, anyway. And that's Mrs. Max Connors."

All but forgotten, the tape began playing again, picking up Roy Orbison's song on the closing strains of "It's Over."

The final, thundering drumbeat matched the pounding of Kate's heart as Max pulled her into his arms, holding her possessively.

But despite Roy Orbison's heart-wrenching finale, Kate knew it wasn't over. Not really. In some ways, it was only just beginning.

Epilogue

ဆ

Kate never found out whether formal charges were filed against Ed Tate Jr. The fact that he'd left town in humiliation, stripped of his badge and his pride, was enough. Kate didn't know where he went and didn't care.

He'd left, and she'd stayed.

And here at the ranch, with the sunshine on her face and the whisper of a breeze feathering her hair, she wondered how she could have ever left in the first place.

Moving home, loving Max. It all seemed so easy now. Only her fears had made coming home hard. But now that she was here, she knew she'd never leave again.

She wouldn't be going back to New York. The city was wonderful, brimming with excitement, shimmering with colors. It was a bright, vibrant adrenaline rush. But it wasn't—had never been—home. Her roots had been nurtured in dryer soil, golden days and wide-open spaces.

She took a deep breath, drinking in the hot, dry and oh-so-sweet air of Arizona. She let it out with a soulful sigh, the word "home" settling around her like a well-worn robe.

So much had changed in the last six months. But one thing hadn't. Her heart still skipped madly whenever she watched Max work around the ranch—his long-legged gait, the rakish tilt of his Stetson. He was as gentle with the animals as he was with the kids who still came to the ranch for therapy. Max had even won Venus' trust with his quiet care. The once-frightened horse adored him and followed him around like a lovesick teenager.

She knew Max was there before she felt his arms come around her and had time for a contented smile before leaning back against his chest.

"Penny for your thoughts, darlin'."

"Mmmm…I was just thinking about how you've charmed Venus."

Max nuzzled her ear, murmuring softly. "Reckon I've got a way with women."

"Reckon so," she said, falling easily into the twang she'd never completely lost. "You have so much patience."

"And sometimes it pays off." His lips moved along her neck, leaving nibbles, kisses and seductive whispers in their wake. "Might take a few years—or ten—but the wait is well worth it."

Kate couldn't agree more. Like Nellie had said when she'd learned about Kate's engagement to Max, "Life is like a cup of tea. Sometimes you have to let it steep before you can appreciate the full flavor." Kate smiled. Who knew Nellie was the Plato of Earl Grey?

Kate turned into Max's embrace, resting her hand over his heart. The ring on her finger sparkled in the sunlight. After the reunion, Max had given her the tiny diamond engagement ring he'd been carrying around all these years waiting for her to come to her senses. It was perfect, symbolic. And like the ring, she'd come full circle.

Kate tipped her face and Max leaned forward, brushing her lips softly. She wrapped her arms around his neck, amazed as always at the way their bodies fit so perfectly together.

Max broke the kiss just as tenderly as it had begun. He brushed a wisp of hair from her forehead. "As much as I love kissing you, darlin'," he said, "I really need to get you home. You have a big day tomorrow."

A big day. Her wedding day.

The thought sent a shiver through her body and brought a dreamy smile to her face. She still couldn't believe it. She and

Max were getting married. Her mother had been right all along. The wedding gown waiting for her at home was proof of that.

She followed Max to the truck, waving goodbye to Bobby and Sue on the porch. Sue was still a little uncomfortable around her, ashamed of her actions and what it had cost. And sometimes Kate couldn't help feeling a tiny shiver of regret when she remembered the lies that had haunted her for the past ten years.

But that was behind them now. She was the one who'd run away instead of facing her problems. Kate had not only forgiven Sue but also come to admire her strength. Kate knew they'd work it out. They were family now. Sue and Bobby would be staying here at the ranch, living in the main house with Otis. Kate and Max would move into their own place, a bungalow Max had converted on the ranch property. Kate had already moved in most of her things, including the few belongings that she'd had shipped back from New York. But tonight she'd spend the eve of her wedding in her old bedroom. Max was traditional in that way.

They made the short drive in comfortable silence. When they reached her house, Max walked her to the doorway and held her close for a moment. "You've been quiet," he said. "Thinking about tomorrow?"

Kate nodded. "That's all I've been thinking of."

His grip tightened possessively. "You're not getting cold feet, are you? You're not thinking of running away again?"

The tone was casually light, but the smile on Max's face belied the serious question in his eyes.

Kate reached up and put a hand to his cheek, studying the face she loved and couldn't imagine living without. "Never," she said. "I've learned my lesson. No more running away. From now on I face my problems head-on."

"Oh, so now I'm a problem, huh?"

Smiling, Kate leaned forward and gave him one more kiss before sending him on his way.

"Sleep sweet, darlin'," he said with a sexy grin. "It's the last night you'll be sleeping alone. Tomorrow you'll be Mrs. Max Connors and I'll never have to let you go again."

"Mrs. Max Connors," she repeated. "Sounds perfect."

As Max turned to leave, Kate reached out and gave his bottom a playful squeeze. He turned and winked, chuckling on his way back to the truck. Kate stood in the doorway watching until he drove away, then turned and went inside.

The house was eerily quiet. It had been since the night of the reunion. Kate missed the ethereal sounds of singing, but the teacup had remained silent. Sometimes she wondered if it had all been in her imagination. Or maybe her mother's work here was done and her restless spirit had moved on.

Kate sighed and shook her head. No more looking at the past, she chided herself. From now on it was only the future that mattered. She reached out and fingered the cloud of white lace hanging from the doorway. Tomorrow was the beginning of a new life. "Mrs. Max Connors," she said out loud.

A sharp, shattering sound from the kitchen jolted Kate from her reverie. She jumped and ran to the kitchen, her heart pounding in her chest.

"Oh Sophie! What have you done?"

The cat jumped off the counter, mewling pitifully.

Kate knelt down and picked up the broken pieces of her mother's teacup. A sob caught in her throat as she cradled the cat in her lap. The cup was shattered beyond repair. Kate tried to tell herself it was just a teacup, that's all. But the sense of loss was deep and overwhelming. Her mother was truly gone now. She had to finally let her go. It was time to move on.

Sophie twisted out of her grasp and streaked across the room. Kate turned and caught a wisp of white. At first she thought it was her wedding gown hanging in the doorway. But then the form separated and took shape.

Kate gasped and got shakily to her feet, her voice trembling. "Mother?"

The image wavered, softened. Kate was sure her eyes were playing tricks on her. She blinked, but the image remained. It was Lillian, looking younger and more beautiful than Kate remembered.

Kate held her breath and stood rooted to the spot, afraid to move, afraid to shatter the moment. And then Lillian smiled, and Kate felt overwhelmed with a feeling of utter peace and contentment. No words were spoken, and yet Kate understood. Her mother was saying goodbye. Her work here was done.

Lillian's ghostly image nodded, as if understanding all the emotions churning through Kate's heart, as if hearing all the words that had gone unspoken. Then she lifted her hand to her lips and extended it in a kiss that felt more like a blessing than a goodbye.

The image shimmered through Kate's tears. In the distance, Kate heard the ghostly strains of Roy Orbison singing a soft and soothing farewell. As the sound faded away and her mother's image dissolved into mist, Kate was finally able to let go of her past completely. When she blinked again her mother was gone, and already Kate questioned whether she'd ever really been there to begin with.

But the sense of peace remained. "Goodbye," she whispered to the empty room. She closed her eyes and took a deep breath. Her past was finally behind her now, but her future had just begun.

Enjoy An Excerpt From:

HEAVEN AND LACE

Copyright © LINDA BLESER, 2006

ფ

The Copper Café was only ten minutes away and Ashley was early. Since the reporter thought they'd already met, it would look suspicious if she didn't recognize him, so she chose a secluded table across from the entrance where he'd be sure to spot her. Even though Lexi had described him, she couldn't trust her sister's powers of description where men were concerned. Lexi found them all incredibly handsome and sexy.

Her precautions were unnecessary. The moment he strode through the door she knew this was the man she was waiting for. He said something to the hostess then scanned the room. When his gaze swept over her he smiled, and she felt as if someone had flipped a switch and turned the lights a little brighter.

She caught her breath and smiled back, wondering why Lexi had let this one get away. He turned and thanked the hostess before making his way to the table, his movements confident and purposeful. Although he looked all business, she detected a boyish playfulness behind those sparkling amber eyes. One look in those eyes and she forgot all about Steve, her stopped-up toilet and her writer's block. Nothing else existed. Nothing but the copper glints in his eyes and the play of dimples when he smiled.

"I see you already ordered coffee," he said, setting his notebook on the table. "Do you mind if we order something to eat? I forgot to have dinner."

She laughed. "I thought I was the only one who forgot to eat when I was working."

He looked at her with what seemed like surprise, tilting his head and studying her in the candlelight. Ashley wondered if she'd given herself away already. What would Lexi have said? Probably something suggestive.

She blushed thinking of the possibilities and studied the menu, not trusting herself to get lost in those eyes again. "I'll have a salad," she said to fill the silence.

"That sounds good," he said, grinning. "Except I'll have mine with a burger on the side."

Ashley laughed again, her heart doing flip-flops when his grin broadened into a smile. She had to remind herself that this was an interview, not a date.

When the waitress refilled their coffee, they both reached for the sugar at the same time and their fingers brushed. She laughed nervously and pulled back, and Rick found himself enchanted by the delicate blush that sprang to her cheeks.

Was this the same Lace Kincaid he couldn't wait to escape from only hours ago? She seemed sweeter, more innocent somehow.

His notebook sat forgotten on the table while they ate. Although he'd been guarded at first, before long they were laughing and sharing more than coffee. Like the fact that they both adored "I Love Lucy" reruns and strawberry licorice, would rather own a dog than a cat, and preferred fishing to the opera.

"Speaking of fishing," he said. "I've got a little camp up on Saratoga Lake. It's just a two-bedroom, lakeside cabin that once belonged to my grandfather, but it comes complete with an array of reels and rods and a nice little fishing boat. Nothing fancy," he finished, feeling suddenly shy. What was he doing inviting Lace Kincaid fishing? He would have laughed at the idea this afternoon, but tonight it felt right. Perfect, in fact.

"I'd love that," she said, her face lighting up. "I'll bring the bait."

That smile was all the bait he needed. Her lips were full and sensuous. It was all he could do not to reach out and trace the gentle curve, imagining how they'd feel brushing against his. She looked away and he realized he'd been staring at her lips far too long.

The intimate little corner of the Copper Café began to feel like their own private haven as Ashley relaxed, surprised to realize how much she enjoyed his company. It was almost midnight before he turned the conversation around to her writing, and his insightful questions impressed her.

"You've read one of my books?" she asked.

Rick frowned slightly. "Well, to be honest, not until now. And only because I wanted to be prepared for this article."

Ashley waited, trying to read the expression on his face, but he didn't offer any further explanation. She wanted to ask which book he'd read and whether he liked it, but stopped herself. What if he hadn't? His opinion suddenly mattered to her. Did she want to know if he hated it? Especially now, when she was struggling with her own writing demons?

When he reached for the check, his fingers brushed against her wrist and Ashley felt a delicious tingle run through her. Her breath quickened and she held his gaze for what seemed an eternity.

He broke the connection first and cleared his throat. "Where shall I meet you tomorrow?"

Her heart fluttered. Tomorrow? She smiled and started to answer, then realized he wasn't meeting *her*. He was meeting Lace Kincaid, and Lexi would be playing that role for the rest of the week. Lexi would be sitting across from him, getting lost in his eyes, running her perfect fingernails across his hands. How long would it take her sister to seduce and win him? How long before Lexi had Rick Orlando wrapped around her little finger?

"I'll call and let you know," Ashley said. Something inside her wanted to fight for him, to win his heart before Lexi had a chance to charm him away.

Her shoulders slumped. That was silly. When had she ever been able to compete with her sister?

Never, she realized, reaching for her purse. And men like Rick Orlando didn't fall in love with plain, vanilla yogurt women in the real world.

Why an electronic book?

We live in the Information Age—an exciting time in the history of human civilization, in which technology rules supreme and continues to progress in leaps and bounds every minute of every day. For a multitude of reasons, more and more avid literary fans are opting to purchase e-books instead of paper books. The question from those not yet initiated into the world of electronic reading is simply: *Why?*

1. *Price.* An electronic title at Ellora's Cave Publishing and Cerridwen Press runs anywhere from 40% to 75% less than the cover price of the exact same title in paperback format. Why? Basic mathematics and cost. It is less expensive to publish an e-book (no paper and printing, no warehousing and shipping) than it is to publish a paperback, so the savings are passed along to the consumer.

2. *Space.* Running out of room in your house for your books? That is one worry you will never have with electronic books. For a low one-time cost, you can purchase a handheld device specifically designed for e-reading. Many e-readers have large, convenient screens for viewing. Better yet, hundreds of titles can be stored within your new library—on a single microchip. There are a variety of e-readers from different manufacturers. You can also read e-books on your PC or laptop computer. (Please note that Ellora's

Cave does not endorse any specific brands. You can check our websites at www.ellorascave.com or www.cerridwenpress.com for information we make available to new consumers.)

3. *Mobility.* Because your new e-library consists of only a microchip within a small, easily transportable e-reader, your entire cache of books can be taken with you wherever you go.

4. ***Personal Viewing Preferences.*** Are the words you are currently reading too small? Too large? Too... ANNOYING? Paperback books cannot be modified according to personal preferences, but e-books can.

5. ***Instant Gratification.*** Is it the middle of the night and all the bookstores near you are closed? Are you tired of waiting days, sometimes weeks, for bookstores to ship the novels you bought? Ellora's Cave Publishing sells instantaneous downloads twenty-four hours a day, seven days a week, every day of the year. Our webstore is never closed. Our e-book delivery system is 100% automated, meaning your order is filled as soon as you pay for it.

Those are a few of the top reasons why electronic books are replacing paperbacks for many avid readers.

As always, Ellora's Cave and Cerridwen Press welcome your questions and comments. We invite you to email us at Comments@ellorascave.com or write to us directly at Ellora's Cave Publishing Inc., 1056 Home Avenue, Akron, OH 44310-3502.

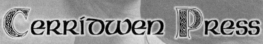

Cerridwen Press

Monthly Newsletter

News
Author Appearances
Book Signings
New Releases
Contests
Author Profiles
Feature Articles

Available online at
www.CerridwenPress.com

THE
☥ ELLORA'S CAVE ☥
LIBRARY

Stay up to date with Ellora's Cave Titles in
Print with our Quarterly Catalog.

TO RECIEVE A CATALOG,
SEND AN EMAIL WITH YOUR NAME
AND MAILING ADDRESS TO:

CATALOG@ELLORASCAVE.COM
OR SEND A LETTER OR POSTCARD
WITH YOUR MAILING ADDRESS TO:

CATALOG REQUEST
c/o ELLORA'S CAVE PUBLISHING, INC.
1056 HOME AVENUE
AKRON, OHIO 44310-3502

Cerridwen Press

Cerridwen, the Celtic goddess of wisdom, was the muse who brought inspiration to storytellers and those in the creative arts.

Cerridwen Press encompasses the best and most innovative stories in all genres of today's fiction.

Visit our website and discover the newest titles by talented authors who still get inspired—much like the ancient storytellers did...

once upon a time.

www.cerridwenpress.com